DON'T RUN AWAY

VANIA RHEAULT

*To the Fargo/Moorhead NaNoWriMo writing group.
Thanks for all the French Silk pie, French fries, and fabulous company!
I had a blast connecting with all of you.
(And a special shout-out to Jackie who showed me how to take out the extra spaces. I owe you one.)*

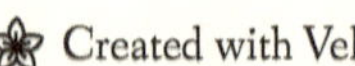 Created with Vellum

Her Frozen Memories
Her Frozen Promises

CHAPTER ONE

"Whoa! Here, let me get that for you."

Nikki Halstead sighed in relief. She didn't know what she was thinking taking the two large cardboard boxes full of books from her car.

The door swung open, but the boxes obscured her vision and she couldn't see who helped her. One of them slid toward her, and she held it steady with her cheek.

"Thanks," she told the male voice. "I appreciate it."

"No problem."

His voice was smooth and a little husky, and she shivered a bit as the words floated over her skin and shimmied down her spine. She imagined the voice whispering in her ear as he moved over her . . . Ugh. It'd been too long since she'd had sex. Alyssa was always on her case about going too long without, and Nikki finally conceded her friend may have a point. Too bad she was picky about the men she dated.

"I'm being really rude right now," the man said with a laugh, and suddenly Nikki was relieved of the weight.

She gasped in surprise but gratefully shook out her

arms. "Thank you. I don't know what I was thinking trying to carry them . . . both," she finished lamely, meeting the man's eyes. His light brown hair was sexily tousled, and she itched to run her fingers through the shiny strands. "Mr. Montgomery."

Nikki knew Dane Montgomery from various running events and from shopping in his store.

The store Dane hired her to manage.

Disappointed, she bit back a groan of frustration. She *was* picky and she would never, ever, sleep with her boss.

DANE MONTGOMERY KNEW great legs when he saw them, and the woman standing on the stoop of his apartment building owned a very fine pair. Her feet were clad in the newest running shoes, he noted, pleased, as his gaze traveled from her feet, along the smooth tanned skin of her slim calves, and slender yet muscular thighs. She wore cute little black running shorts that barely covered her ass, and her blonde hair hung in spirals from a ponytail centered at the back of her head.

Show me those baby blues.

He wasn't disappointed when he took the boxes from her, and she blinked at him in surprise. Her eyes were the bluest he'd seen in a long time, framed by long, black eyelashes. Her cheeks were pink from exertion, her lips glossed and sparkly.

"I think that's my dad." Dane laughed. "It's Dane. You know me?"

Her mouth quirked in a half smile. "You could say. I'm Nikki Halstead."

Well, shit. There went that. It was too bad because

there hadn't been a woman in a while who caught his attention the way Nikki had managed within the first five seconds of meeting her. He smothered his disappointment with a smile. "Nice to finally meet you. Let me take these for you. This floor or up?"

"Up. 205."

Figured.

"We're neighbors then, too. I live in 203. Are you moving in?" Silently, he groaned. *Nice and obvious.*

He carefully navigated the grey carpeted stairs; he didn't want to trip and make a fool of himself.

She led the way, and over the top of the cardboard boxes, he watched her hips sway. It explained the legs and the great ass. Couldn't find a better pair of legs than that of a long-distance runner.

"My friend Alyssa lives on this street. She knew I was looking on this side of town to be closer to your store, and she called me right away when she saw the 'for rent' sign outside last week. It all happened kind of fast, but I'm happy I snapped it up. I don't need the second bedroom, but I'm sure I'll manage to fill it up with something."

"No roommates?" Dane followed her to her door.

"Nah." Nikki bumped the wooden door open with her hip. "Alyssa spends the night sometimes. She might do that more now that I live closer. Plus, I didn't have a balcony before. It's worth the extra money I'm spending on rent. Put them down anywhere. I appreciate you hauling them up for me."

Dane squatted and set the boxes down in the middle of her living room.

Her apartment was the exact layout of his, except the opposite. The kitchen was to the right of the door, her bedrooms located to the left. Their bedrooms shared a thin wall; he hoped he wouldn't have to listen to her have sex with her boyfriend.

He pushed the unpleasant thought aside. "Looks like you've been moving in for a while."

A couch had already been brought up along with a mid-sized flat screen TV and stand. A matching love seat had been placed near the couch in a V-shape; they both sat in front of the television. She'd added a coffee table full of running and beauty magazines, and she'd kept the space near the French doors clear for easy access to the balcony.

"I'm surprised we haven't met before now while you've been moving in your things." He looked up from the boxes and smiled at her. "I like your shirt."

Nikki blushed. The logo of her Tower City Running Company T-shirt sprawled across her chest in elegant black script. "Yeah, well, it's the only place I buy my running gear, you'll see me in your stuff more often than not."

Dane pulled his eyes away from her and stood. Rubbing his hands together he said, "Great to hear. Ah, I guess I'll leave you to it then, unless you have more boxes in your car? I have a few more minutes to help you out."

"Only if you want to help me clean my old apartment," she teased, "there's nothing else. Thanks."

Dane reluctantly moved toward the door. He wanted to stay and talk to her, but he just met her for Christ's sake, and there would be time for that at the store.

He turned the doorknob to let himself out. "No thanks. I hate cleaning my own apartment. I'll see you on Monday, then." He frowned as an idea occurred to him. "Do you need more time? A few extra days to settle in?"

"No, that's okay," Nikki said, shaking her head, her hair brushing her shoulders. "We agreed on Monday morning and that's still fine with me. I'll see you then and thanks again. It was nice to meet you in person before I started. I've seen you around the marathon expos, and you know, at your store, but we've never been introduced."

Dane took her outstretched hand and nearly flinched at the contact. Heat traveled through his palm and up his arm.

He met her eyes. She wasn't as short as she seemed.

Nikki was the right height, and if he wanted to kiss her, he would only need to lean a little bit.

Her lips parted like she could read his mind.

Off limits.

He yanked his hand away. He'd hired Nikki to run his store, not warm his bed. Dane had a woman to do that anyway. There was no reason for him to damage what could be, *would be*, a perfectly professional relationship with the newly hired manager of his running shoe store because of an inexplicable attraction.

"See you Monday," he mumbled and shut the door behind him.

"Eyes like a Twix bar?'" Alyssa Barnes laughed. "Who sounds like the hokey romance writer now?"

"It's true, though," Nikki said, defending herself. "His eyes, they're like, light brown in the middle and dark brown around the edges."

"Don't you know him from before? Don't you know all the runners around here?" Alyssa took a sip of the pumpkin spice latte she'd brought them.

"I don't know every single runner in Tower City, Lyss," Nikki said crossly, then laughed when she caught Alyssa's smirk.

They were walking along a cemented sidewalk behind

Nikki's new home. The winding path twisted through a large city park dotted with man-made ponds, playgrounds, and acres of trees and flowers. The park had been the clincher for her when choosing the apartment. The trails were perfect for running, but today she was walking with Alyssa and sharing her story of meeting Dane the day before.

The air was turning cooler, the leaves changing to their glorious yellow and orange hues. Autumn was Nikki's favorite season, but October could still be warm in Minnesota and she enjoyed the afternoon sunlight warming her skin.

It was nice to take a break from unpacking; it had taken her hours to organize her kitchen. Luckily, Taylor Swift had kept her company.

"Yeah, I've seen him around, at the race starts and the expos when I volunteer at the booths in the spring. I think he's friends with Brett Sommers, the marathon director. But I've never *met* him, not in person. Not so . . . *close*. He smelled divine, like sweat and aftershave." She playfully growled in the back of her throat.

"You need to get laid."

"Says the woman who hasn't gotten any for as long as I have," Nikki replied dryly.

"I have my reasons."

"Yeah. We know what those are." Nikki shrugged. "But I haven't met anybody who's turned me on lately. The guy I met a couple weeks ago might've been okay, but he threw a tantrum when I had to move my stuff last weekend. I can't do high maintenance. He didn't even ask if I needed help."

"He was gorgeous, though," Alyssa said, grinning.

"Yeah, well, he thought so too. He can go be pretty somewhere else."

Alyssa sipped her latte. "I still don't understand how Dane didn't know it was you. You went to an interview, didn't you?"

"Over the phone. He said he liked my retail experience and my degree in Human Resources. He checked my references, and said he didn't want to waste time with a meet and greet interview if I was okay with it, and I was. I took the job over the phone the minute he offered it to me."

"So you're attracted to him. Find another guy to date."

Nikki nudged her friend's shoulder. Alyssa made it sound so easy, and maybe for Nikki, it was. She never lacked male companionship. But there was quantity and there was quality, and Nikki knew which one she'd prefer.

"My dad's trying to set me up with a friend's son. We'll see how it goes. What's been going on with you?"

She eyed the woman who'd been her friend since elementary school. She couldn't understand why Alyssa was having such a difficult time finding a decent guy. Alyssa was amazing, kind, smart, and self-sufficient. Men should have been beating down her door.

"Finished my last book, finally, and now I'm going to take a break for a while. I need to recharge. My publisher is giving me a few weeks then sending me on another God-awful book tour. After that, we'll see. I've been mulling around another plot idea."

"Aw. I hate it when you go out of town," Nikki said, kicking at a leaf blowing across the sidewalk.

Alyssa wrinkled her nose. "You'll be fine. You can't come with me every year."

"I know, but last year was so much fun! And I met that guy who wrote under a woman's name. He was so sweet. Too bad he lived so far away."

They were circling around a small pond, ducks floating

on the surface of the murky water. It wouldn't be much longer before it would turn cold outside, and they would need to fly south, and she and Alyssa would need to move their walks indoors.

"I barely saw you," Alyssa said, "and you were supposed to be keeping me company. Anyway, you'll find a guy to keep you occupied while I'm gone."

"We'll see. Maybe I'm trying too hard."

"No, you're not settling, and that's smart. I'll drop you off here. Thanks for the walk, Nik. And good luck on your first day tomorrow. I know you'll do great."

""Thanks. You'll have to spend the night sometime. I'll buy you a bed since I have two bedrooms now."

Alyssa shook her head and smiled. "Bye."

"Bye."

DANE TOOK A sip of his beer and watched Brett throw darts.

"Call Holly, get laid, and keep your hands off your manager," Brett said, pointing his beer bottle at Dane after missing the center of the dartboard . . . again.

"I know. I will," he said defensively. He hated being told what to do. His ex-wife had been a bossy bitch, and Brett's tone grated on his nerves, even if he was dishing up grade-A advice.

"Why the hell aren't you making it official with her anyway? Holly's great. She has her own life, and she leaves you alone. What more can you ask for?"

Dane scowled and took his turn. With his concentration off, he fumbled the dart, and it bounced off the side of the dartboard. "I'm not ready. Fuck." Poor throws all around tonight.

"If you can get all hot and bothered about your manager, you're ready. It's time to forget about what a witch Liz was to you. You know, the longer you stay single, the more satisfaction she feels. You can't let her do that to you, man."

"She's not keeping tabs on me," Dane said, but that was a big, fat lie. Liz knew he his every move; kept him under the heel of her boot for as long as she could.

Brett snorted. "The hell she's not. Every month you don't find someone is one more month she's fucked you over. Get over her already and move on."

Dane slid back into his chair and motioned to Ian for more beer. "I'm not moving on with Nikki. She's my employee."

"Are we still talking about her? I'm talking about Holly. Put a ring on it. She's not going to wait forever for your sorry ass."

"I don't see you dodging calls from your future mother-in-law about what color flowers are going to be on the tables at your wedding reception," Dane said. He was beginning to feel sorry he asked Brett out for a beer.

"We aren't talking about me."

Dane didn't bother to answer. Instead, he looked around the small bar he and Brett liked to frequent and nodded at Ian when the bartender set two more bottles on the high-top table.

Women rarely came by the place and for the most part, not many other people did either. Dane and Brett were friends with Ian, who ran the bar and bartended most evenings, and they were generally left alone on nights they stopped in.

Sitting at their regular corner table near the dartboard, he and Brett had spent hundreds of hours either plotting important life choices, consoling each other about God knew what, or simply growing up.

Dane had bought his store in this bar. He'd ended his marriage in this bar.

"You know, I really value our friendship, Brett."

Brett smirked. "You're drunk. Go home."

"No, I mean it. You were there for me at school, when I decided to buy the store, when I made the decision to file for divorce. I appreciate it."

Brett settled into a tall chair across from him and leaned back, spinning the top of his beer bottle on the sticky table-top. "You know what you can do to pay me back?"

"What?"

"Fucking train your manager and help me with this goddamn marathon. Jesus, there are days I don't know why I bother."

Dane laughed. "Because you enjoy the hell out of it, that's why. It took years for you to make a living off that race."

"It's a piss-poor living too, if you want to know the truth. I made more managing that chain of workout gyms."

"But you didn't have as much fun."

The bar was empty as usual.

The old jukebox played some kind of country music he didn't care for, but he didn't have quarters to change the selection. The huge room was dark, glowing neon beer signs decorating the walls. A wooden bowl of peanuts sat in the middle of the table littered with beer bottles, and Dane took one whole and popped it into his mouth. The salt of the shell mingled pleasantly with the taste of beer on his tongue.

He wondered what Nikki would think of this place.

"Come by the store tomorrow. You can meet Nikki and gripe about the race. You know, she's worked a lot of booths at your expos. After she gets trained in and comfortable maybe you can tap her to help you out, too."

"If she's as hot as you say she is, I'll tap her," Brett said and laughed when Dane glowered. "Get it under control. If things heat up and it goes to shit, do you know how fast she'd slap a sexual harassment lawsuit on your ass? She probably has the number memorized."

It was a sobering thought, Dane had to admit. He was tired of court.

"With that, I'm outta here," Dane told Brett, then spit the shell onto the floor. It was that kind of place.

"See you tomorrow, and hey."

Dane looked over his shoulder.

"You've helped me through some shit, too, so I get it. Thanks."

He waved and went home.

A BUNDLE OF nerves, Nikki was disgusted to find herself wide awake at five in the morning.

It was pitch black outside, the early summer sun gone, hiding in the autumn season.

There wasn't much more she hated than starting a new job. Even if it was her dream job. Her management position at Shine had been great. She'd worked with some terrific people, but when it came to making a difference, well, the store as a whole didn't do much. She tried to implement food drives and collect used clothes for the homeless in exchange for coupons, but she didn't have the support of top management, and her ideas fell to the wayside. It was frustrating to want to give back and be told no.

Taking the opportunity of the peaceful hour, she dressed for a run, hooking her exercise bra closed before slipping a T-shirt over her head.

She made a pot of coffee and sipped on a mug as she finished dressing. She hoped the fresh air would calm her nerves.

It's what made her like Dane's store. She'd be there to help with the food drive Dane held every November and bring what they collected to the Tower City food shelf.

In December, the store would collect old running shoes in exchange for a percentage off a new pair. The shoes they collected shoes would be shipped to a place that needed them. Last year they were sent to Haiti. And ever since he opened the store he worked with Brett and the marathon to provide needy kids in Tower City new shoes. For every runner's race registration, a child received a new pair. Last year the Tower City Running Company in affiliation with the Tower City Marathon gave away over ten thousand pairs of shoes to kids in Tower City. She had never been prouder to be a runner and to be part of such a great community.

Dane had done nothing but fabulous things since opening the store, and she wanted to be a part of that. She *would* be a part of that, starting at nine, but for now, she needed to run off her jitters.

She went to the bathroom one more time and then checked to be sure she had everything she needed for a comfortable run: shoes, running capris, running shirt, her favorite running jacket with the slits for her thumbs. The days were still warm but at six in the morning, it was cold and dark.

She adjusted her earbuds and selected a playlist on her phone. It would be fun to run the paths; a new route was always welcome. She'd enjoyed her walk with Alyssa yesterday, but it was slow going and she didn't see much.

Standing in the hallway, she fastened a lilac-colored GPS watch to her wrist. She was locking the door when she felt a touch to her shoulder, and she jumped, spinning around, gasping for breath. "You scared me," she yelled at Dane, and he winced. She pulled the earbuds from her ears. "Sorry," she whispered. "I already had my music playing. You scared me."

"Do you want to run with me?" he whispered back, teasing, a smile playing on his lips.

She studied him. He wore black running pants and a black jacket. Oh, he looked good. She tried to think of a way to decline, but her fingers and toes tingled, warmth spread through her belly, and her cheeks heated. Normally she didn't care to run with others because she liked listening to music, and she liked being alone with her thoughts. '

She wouldn't feel comfortable running with her boss. On the other hand, it was a good idea to be friendly with him, prove to herself she could control her feelings and not let them get the best of her. "I'm a little slow," she said, warning him. She loved to run, but she was more of a slow-and-steady-wins-the-race type of runner.

"Nikki, it's six in the morning. I think you'll be all right."

"Okay." She wound the earbuds' wire around her phone and tucked them into the inside pocket of her running jacket.

"Did you change your mind about the music?"

"It doesn't make any sense to listen to it when you're with someone. How would we talk?"

Dane grinned at her and led her down the stairs and outside. "You usually run this early in the morning?"

"No. This actually kind of sucks. The dark I don't mind, but I hate waking up so early. I tried to go back to sleep, but I couldn't."

She followed him out of the parking lot, over the grass that separated the apartment property from the park, and onto the cement sidewalk.

When he laughed, a shiver ran through her. Sexy.

"Do you walk for a minute or run right away?" she asked, unfamiliar with his habits. Every runner had his or her own way of going for a run. She liked walking for a minute, making sure all her gear felt good before starting out, but she knew of others who hit the ground running, literally, and didn't stop until their run was done.

"Let's walk for a minute."

Nikki walked alongside him, glad he chose the short warm-up. She needed it to stimulate her stiff muscles. It seemed as if her mind as well as her body disliked the early morning activity.

The stillness of the early morning cocooned them.

Traffic rumbled in the distance, but the sound didn't take away from the closeness of the moment.

Skittish about spending time with Dane outside of work, she broke the silence. "I prefer to run in the evening, but I'm a little nervous about starting today, and I thought a run would help me blow off some steam. I don't like starting new jobs." She met his eyes, but the darkness hid his expression.

Dane checked his GPS watch. "Let's go. How far were you running this morning?"

Nikki started jogging, conscientious not to start too fast too early to try to impress him. "I don't know. I feel all right.

Six miles? Seven? I was going to run until I wanted to head back. I went for a walk with Alyssa yesterday but I didn't see much of the paths. I'm not familiar with the mileage."

"I know a loop that's six. How's that?"

"Yeah, that's fine, if that's all you were going." She listened to their soft footfalls on the cement as they fell into an easy rhythm.

"You don't have to be nervous," Dane said.

Surprised he kept the thread of their conversation going, she said, "I'm that way with new jobs. I hate not knowing how to do things, and I'm worried about understanding how different brands of shoes fit and how to recommend them to our customers. I know what I like, and that's it."

"I'll teach you how we help customers decide, and there's a ton of reading material the manufacturers give us. You'll be an expert in no time. It's the same as different clothing brands. You're not a six everywhere, right? Eventually, you found out you're a four at one store but a ten somewhere else, and after you figured that out, you didn't shop there anymore."

Nikki laughed, and she snagged her toe on an uneven concrete slab.

Dane grabbed her upper arm and pulled her to his side. "Sorry. I shouldn't distract you while you're running a new route. Are you all right?"

Her eyes met his, her breath coming out in panicked little puffs as she tried to calm her racing heart.

His hand gripped her arm, and she felt the strength of his fingers through her running jacket. "Yeah. Thanks."

The sun was creeping over the horizon, and the black sky slowly turned purple, showcasing streaks of pink and orange. A light breeze cooled her sweat-dampened skin.

He looked concerned, a frown marring the smooth skin

between his eyebrows, and Nikki blinked at his kindness in his eyes. "It wouldn't be the first time I skinned my knees. Wouldn't be the last." She swallowed and pulled her arm from his grasp. "We should keep going. I'll be more careful. I know better than that."

Dane cleared his throat. "Just an accident. Come on."

As they ran, Nikki relaxed, and she stopped staring at the ground looking for every crack and crevasse that could trip her. She took in the trees, the little ponds, the playground equipment dotting the park. "This is beautiful. It's a nice change of pace."

"As long as you don't break your neck," Dane said. "Where did you run before?"

"Anywhere. Everywhere. My last apartment was near a park too, and a public golf course. It was nice, but I think this park has more mileage."

"There's a lot of trail. I run it almost every day, and I never get bored."

Nikki looked at him from the corner of her eye. "Why did you open your store? You haven't owned it long."

"Asked around about me before applying for your position?" he asked.

"A little, but I didn't need to, really. I've shopped at your store since it opened. It's a great place."

"I was tired of working in banking."

There was a hesitancy in his voice, and she wondered why he didn't want to talk about himself.

"I ran track in high school, been running most of my life. My parents were runners, are runners, and when I was a kid they encouraged me. I hated sitting behind a desk, and I did some research. I realized a store would fill a niche in the retail market here in the city." He paused to take a breath. "A friend of mine at the bank where I worked suggested I take a couple small business classes. You know, getting the loan, making the business work. I have a Bachelor's in business from the university, but these were, I don't know, more specialized. The same friend gave me the business loan because I trusted him with the interest rate, and here we are, I guess."

"That's brave."

She wasn't sure she'd have the guts to go out on her own like that. Her human resources classes taught her that there were too many things to worry about if she was her own boss, and following employment guidelines could be a nightmare. Now that she was manager of Dane's store, some of that would fall on her, but it wasn't the same as owning her own business.

"It's not bad. I sink most of my profits from the store into the loan. I didn't have a manager until I hired you; I didn't want to stretch the budget too tight. But Brett, Brett Sommers, you know the Tower City Marathon director, he's been bothering me to help him. He didn't give me much choice."

They fell quiet again and Nikki glanced at her watch, and with a tinge of disappointment, noted their six miles were almost over.

Dane was easy to talk to. The miles had been painless, drifting by quickly, and she was glad she accepted his offer. She wouldn't mind running with him again.

"I was lucky you wanted out of your office."

Nikki groaned, thinking of her time behind a desk, eight hours a day working at a computer. She agreed with him there. Sitting all day long had made her antsy and restless.

"Yeah, not one of my finer moments. We all make mistakes, right? It wasn't bad, and I don't regret the degree in human resources. I mean, as a store manager, I'll do a lot of what we learned in class, hiring, firing, blah blah, and with my degree I can ask for more, salary-wise."

She'd taken a hit accepting Dane's offer, but she'd known that going in. Working in her favorite store with other runners and making a difference in the community made up for what she lost in pay.

Dane grunted as they slowed nearing their building. "Yeah. The three free pairs of shoes you get a year must have tipped the scales in my favor."

Nikki flopped onto the grass wet with dew. "Hey, don't knock the shoes. The brand I like is expensive." She lifted a leg and waved her foot in the air.

They stretched without speaking, the early morning hour finally hitting her, and she sighed to herself. Her day was only beginning. No chance of a nap today.

Dane stood and held out a hand to help her to her feet.

She paused for a moment before taking it.

There was a sad look in his eyes, but she couldn't imagine what she'd said to make him feel that way. She curled her fingers around his, and he pulled her to her feet. Worry made the outer edges of his brown eyes crinkle. "Dane—" she started.

He turned away. "I would kill for a shower and some coffee, and I bet you would, too."

He dug his keys out of his pocket, unlocked the door to their building, and they trudged up the stairs together. "Listen," he said when they reached their apartments, "I would offer you a ride to the store but—"

"No, I understand. Sometimes I don't go home right after work. It's better if I take my own car."

"Okay. I'll see you later then."

"Yeah. I'll see you later."

Biting on her lower lip, Nikki waited until he stepped

into his apartment and shut his door with a soft click before stepping into her own to shower and dress for her first day at her new job.

———

BEHIND THE SALES counter, Nikki laughed with his only full-time employee while Dane sat at his desk in his tiny office calculating his employees' work hours for payday.

Eventually, he planned to teach Nikki how to do the paperwork for the store.

He needed to be able to be gone for days, even weeks, at a time, if necessary, and he'd show her how to do the ordering, the payroll, and the employee schedules. He wanted her to be able to completely run the store without his input. He had that much faith in her, that much trust. On a professional level. He wasn't ready to start a relationship, a true relationship, with anyone. He wasn't ready to trust a woman with his heart again.

When Nikki arrived at the store already knowing Margie, Dane had been surprised and pleased. They'd volunteered at a booth at Brett's running expo last June and had gotten to know each other during the four-hour block. They chatted like old friends, and Margie jumped in teaching her the basics. Margie gave Nikki a tour, taught her how to run the register, went over their return policy, and gave her the TCRC polo shirts she was required to wear as her uniform.

Nikki changed into one right away, and the black polo made her blue eyes pop against her pale skin. With her hair pulled into a high ponytail and running shoes on her feet, she looked as if she'd been working there for years.

He was ignoring payroll and eavesdropping on their

conversation about the quality of other area races when the little bell above the door chimed, and Margie call out, "Hey, Brett! Dane's in his office."

Dane leaned back in his chair, propping up on the two hind legs, as Brett introduced himself to Nikki.

He scowled when Brett took her hand and kissed her knuckles in an old-fashioned gesture that never failed to impress the ladies. It appeared to have the same effect on Nikki, and though he couldn't see her face, he heard her giggle and watched her wipe her palms on the back of her pants, drawing his gaze to her cute ass.

He fell forward, the legs of his chair slamming against the tile, and he glared at Brett when he flopped into the only extra chair in front of the desk.

"I don't know how you hired her without knowing what a babe she is," Brett said, shaking his head. "I think I recognize her from the expos, though."

"She already knew Margie. They're getting along pretty well." Dane tapped his pencil's eraser on his desk.

"You didn't meet her in a face-to-face interview?" Brett reached behind him into a mini-fridge and pulled out a can of sparkling water.

"No. I hired her over the phone after checking her references. I figured with her résumé she would find something quickly, and if I didn't hire her, someone else would. She looks great on paper, and her references couldn't say enough nice things about her."

"You could have looked her up on Facebook or something."

"You think I'm dumb, don't you? Give me one of those." Dane kicked his door shut to be on the safe side. He didn't want Nikki and Margie to eavesdrop the way he'd been. "I looked her up on Facebook, but her wallpaper is some inspirational quote and her profile picture is a mug of coffee."

"You couldn't see other pictures of her?"

"Her profile was locked down. Which is what I would've expected from a woman with an HR degree, anyway." He popped the can open and guzzled the lemon-flavored water.

"You're lucky you didn't end up with a dog. You could have been looking at a woofer all day."

Dane grinned. "And I keep wondering why you're still single. My mistake."

"I'm going to lunch. I told the office staff I'd bring back sandwiches, so I better get going. I wanted to meet Nikki though." Brett opened the door and whispered, "You're going to have a terrible time staying out of her pants."

Halfway between Dane's office and the store's door, he turned around and yelled, "Call Holly. I mean it." He nodded at Margie and Nikki. "Ladies, have a lovely day."

Dane sighed. He loved Brett. They were best friends, but sometimes he wanted to wring his neck. Not feeling it, even with a view of Nikki's ass, he grabbed his phone, wallet, and keys.

"Margie, you can keep showing Nikki stuff, right? I'm taking off for the day. I'm not into being here right now."

"No problem. I hope you're not getting sick. Better get your flu shot. 'Tis the season, you know."

"Right. Welcome to the Tower City Running Company, Nikki. I hope you like it here. We're happy to have you."

"Thanks. I'll see you tomorrow."

"Have a good day, guys," Dane said, and he escaped into the autumn afternoon.

"Who's Holly?" Nikki asked. She couldn't help herself. Not that she cared . . . exactly. During their run this morning they hadn't gotten too personal, and it wasn't her business if he had a girlfriend. In fact, maybe it would be better for her if he did.

Margie leaned against the counter, picked up a packet of GU, and started running it between her fingers. "Are you interested?" she asked, lifting an eyebrow.

"Just curious." Nikki blushed knowing the woman didn't buy it.

Margie was pretty, and she was a little jealous Margie had been working with Dane all this time. It wasn't warranted; Margie was married and if Nikki remembered correctly, had a couple kids. It didn't show, though. She was slim, a bit shorter than Nikki, and her light brown hair fell in waves down her back. Margie looked like she was about her age, too, but she was a more serious runner than Nikki, training for, and running, one or two marathons a year.

"If I wasn't married, I would go after him," Margie said, opening the GU and sucking from the foil packet. "Gross, what a horrible flavor." She spat into a tissue then wadded it into a ball and threw it into the garbage.

"The Gatorade chews taste better," she said.

"Yeah, they do. No, Holly is . . . most of the time I think she's Dane's booty call, but I've seen her in here to go to lunch with him. Maybe it's more? Maybe they go back and forth. They both seem to like the arrangement. She's been hanging around for a couple years now, but I don't think it's serious. At least, not on Dane's side."

"I'm not sure I could do that," Nikki said, straightening

a stack of running brochures on the counter near the register.

"You would if you were in love with him and waiting for more."

"I see what you're saying, but come on. Have some respect for yourself."

Margie laughed. "You mean, why buy the cow when the milk is free?"

"No. I like sex as much as the next girl, and if you want to be a booty call, go ahead. I mean, waiting for love. I think either it's there or it's not. Two years, maybe more? She's wasting time on a man who's not going to pan out. Even if it is Dane. She could be out dating, looking for someone who would treat her better."

Margie shrugged. "I could be wrong. I don't know her, or how he feels about her. Maybe she doesn't want anything more than what Dane is giving her. He's gotta be great in the sack, don't you think? Runners have that stamina."

"None of my business," Nikki said as the phone rang. Nope, she didn't need to think about how Dane would be in bed; she was certain he would be fantastic.

Because he would care.

"Tower City Running Company," Margie answered, smirking at Nikki, then paused. "Speaking." Margie frowned in worry and not a little bit of annoyance. "No, don't worry about it, Daniel. We'll figure something out. No, it's okay. Get better, huh?"

Margie hung up the phone.

"That was Daniel, one of our evening guys. He's calling in sick for tonight. Something's going on with him. This is starting to become a habit, and it puts the rest of us out. I can't stay. My husband's out of town for a couple days for his job, and I need to pick up my daughter from daycare."

"I'll stay. It's not a problem. Write down how I close and set the alarm. If I have an emergency, I'll call Dane and hope I don't interrupt anything." She squeezed Margie's shoulder. "I'll be okay. This is why Dane hired me. The manager always picks up the slack. I was the store manager at Shine for a long time, and trust me, I pulled doubles all the time; we were always short-staffed no matter how hard I tried to pad the schedule. We have enough time for you to write it all down and show me what to do before you go. You were a great teacher today, I'll be fine."

"Thanks, Nikki. I didn't understand why Dane wanted a manager because I thought we were doing fine, but I can see why now. I suppose he was tired of being the one to fill in—you know I'd be calling him if you weren't here." Margie pulled out a pad of legal paper and started a list in large, loopy writing.

"Why didn't you want the manager position? I'm assuming Dane offered it to you first before placing his ad."

"You're right, he did, but I'm too busy for this kind of bullshit." She pointed to the phone with her pen. "I have kids, a husband, I qualified for Boston, and I need to decide if I want to run that." Margie tapped the pen against her lips and added another item to the list. "I like this job, but I especially like being able to go home and not have to worry about what's going down while I'm not here. Personally, I work here for the free shoes." Margie winked. "I think that should do it."

"Where's the employee handbook? It should have the closing procedure in it."

"Employee handbook?" Margie asked blankly. "Ah, no. We don't have one."

Nikki frowned. "I better get on Dane because that's lawsuit heaven."

"Don't 'get on him' literally. I'm pretty sure he's taken, in some way, shape, or form. I better get going. My daycare provider gets crabby when I'm late."

"No problem. It was great seeing you again. I wish we would have connected online after the expo."

"I'll 'friend' you tonight if I have time to get on. Have a good night. Daniel's going to owe you big-time. Bye."

It felt strange to be alone in the store on her first day. She dusted racks and straightened clothing. She cleaned the counter and helped customers. Nikki relaxed when they didn't ask her for advice. She rang up sales without any incidents and was reading the manufacturer booklets she found under the counter when Dane came in a couple hours before close.

"Hey. What are you still doing here?"

"Daniel called in sick, and Margie couldn't stay. She had to pick up her daughter from daycare."

"You should have called me. I would have come in for you."

"Why? This is what you hired me to do. I worked a ton of doubles at Shine. It's no big deal. Margie wrote down how to close. I've closed stores before." She took his frown personally. "I know how to count out the register and fill out the deposit slips. The bank isn't far from here, which is probably why you do your business there. It will take ten seconds to make the deposit before I head home."

"That's not how I wanted your first day to go, though. And you went for a run this morning, you must be tired."

"I'll be fine." She took in his black pants and maroon dress shirt and tried to push away a prickle of jealousy. He had a date. "I'm glad I didn't call you. You look like you have somewhere to be anyway."

Dane cleared his throat. "Yeah, I needed to grab something out of my office."

"Margie told me you don't have an employee handbook. It's kind of dangerous not to have one. I know you don't have time to talk about it tonight, but we need to talk about me writing one up for you."

Dane sighed, and that sad look came into his eyes again.

"I can't afford to pay you extra for doing things like that. I told you I'm stretching my budget as it is to pay you what I am."

"'Things like that' *are* part of my job. It's no big deal. If you're worried about it, I won't work on it at home, okay? I'll do it here on my laptop between customers. It won't cost much to have a copy store print it and bind it with a spiral, and it might save you a thousand times the money in the long run."

He met her eyes. "I have something to tell you, and you probably won't like it."

Nikki squeaked in distress. "I've only been here a day. Are you already letting me go? Did I do something wrong?"

Dane dropped his keys with a clatter on the glass top of the counter and grabbed her hand. "God, no. Hiring you was the best choice I ever made. But—" Dane pulled back abruptly. "The day I offered you the position, I talked to your district manager at Shine, L something?"

"Lissette."

"Yeah. She was listed in your references, and I called her. The woman gave you such glowing reviews, and she even told me the Shine here in Tower City hasn't been the same since you left them to take that HR job. She let it slip she was going to call you since she found out you were looking at retail again and try to lure you into taking your old job back."

"So?" Nikki asked, confused. It didn't matter that Lissette wanted to hire her back. She'd applied for the manager at this store because she wanted it.

"I knew Shine could pay you double, maybe even triple, what I could, and Lissette confirmed it. It wasn't professional of her, and maybe it was a figure off the top of her head, but I think she was trying to scare me off. I loved your résumé, and your references were awesome, your HR degree was an extra bonus. I looked up your race times to make sure you hadn't lied to me about running, and I asked Brett to look your name up on the old volunteer rosters to confirm you'd really volunteered at the expos. I wanted you for my store. When Lissette told me she was going to try to hire you back, I called you right away and offered you the job."

"That's why you didn't want a face-to-face interview with me."

Dane rubbed his eyes. "Yeah. I didn't want to waste the time. I wanted to offer you the job while you still wanted it. So, if you want to take the job at Shine, I understand. I wasn't honest in the way I hired you."

"Lissette called me after I accepted your offer. I had coffee with her to hear what she had to say, but it was a professional courtesy at best. I wasn't interested. There were reasons why I left—I felt stifled there. Not . . . creatively. I could do what I wanted with the clothes, the displays, whatever. But," she lifted her eyes from the countertop, "I love what you do here. The food drives, the shoe donations. The big shoe giveaway for the kids during marathon week. I tried to get Shine involved in the community, and the top management, management above Lissette, didn't care about stuff like that. They cared about meeting sales goals, cutting costs. I get that. But there's more to life than making money. I took this job because I wanted to be associated with a store that makes a difference. It means a lot to me."

"Nikki—"

"Lissette told me how much they were willing to pay me, and I didn't care."

"You didn't care? How could you not care?" He pursed his lips and crossed his arms over his chest.

"I need to pay bills the same as everyone else, but as long as I can do that, I'm happy. I'm a runner, and this is my place." She hopped on the tips of her toes, making the curls of her ponytail bounce. "And I get free shoes."

"It's not enough."

"I appreciate what you're saying." She placed her hand on his arm, and her heart raced when the corded muscles tensed under her touch. "I like it here. I want to be here."

With you, she finished to herself. She pulled her hand away from his arm. No, no. Nope. She didn't take the job to be closer to Dane Montgomery. She barely knew the guy, and now she was thinking she was working here to be closer to him? That was setting herself up for a disaster down the road, and what a short road it was.

If things didn't work out between them she would lose her job, not to mention a nice apartment. Because God knew if they got together and broke up, she wouldn't be able to run the risk of bumping into him every day, in the hall-way, in the parking lot, grabbing their mail in the lobby, doing laundry. She would have to move, and she didn't want to.

Besides, he was taken. Margie said it herself, and she would know.

Nikki's place was behind the counter, not by his side.

She looked at him from across the sales counter. That's the way it had to be.

Dane didn't look convinced. "If you're sure."

"I'm sure. I'm a grown woman, and I know what I want. No one forced me to take this job. I wanted it or I wouldn't have applied for it. Now go do what you need to do. I'll be fine. And I promise I won't work on the handbook at home."

"All right," Dane said, picking up his keys from the counter. "I'll see you in the morning then. I was going to wait to teach you the closing procedure, but you're determined to jump in with both feet. And to think, this morning you were nervous."

"Goodnight, Dane," Nikki said and glared at him until he walked out the door.

She laughed when she realized he hadn't picked up whatever it was he'd come in for.

CHAPTER TWO

Dane didn't understand her. He mulled the whole thing over as he drove his truck to the piano bar where he was meeting Holly. He might've wanted to smack Brett in the face for the way he acted at the store today, but Brett was right—he couldn't get involved with Nikki. His skin still seared where she'd touched his arm to make her point.

Maybe Brett was right about the other things, too.

He and Holly had been doing this off and on thing for a long time, and it wasn't fair to her. He using her as an excuse not to look for a meaningful relationship. He had to decide if his relationship with Holly meant something to him or not.

He pulled into the bar's parking lot where Holly's vehicle already sat. He hated being late, but he'd needed that talk with Nikki. It still didn't feel right, but . . . who the hell was he to tell her where she should work? She chose his store, and he should be grateful for it.

Dane stepped inside the dim piano lounge and nodded at Holly who waved at him from a tall table along the black wall. Jazz drifted around him and his muscles loosened.

There was something about Nikki that put him on edge.

"Hey," he said, kissing Holly's cheek. "Sorry I'm late. I had to run to the store for a quick second, and there was a little crisis going on."

Holly tilted her head. "Nothing serious?"

Dane took a seat and nodded at the waiter who brought his beer. "Thanks for ordering for me."

"You're welcome. Things at the store okay now?"

"Yeah. One of the night guys called in, and my new manager is stuck working a double on her first day."

"And you feel bad? That's what you hired her for."

Dane studied Holly in the sparse light. Her red hair glinted in a sleek bob, her brown doe eyes sparkled, and her lips were pulled into a smile. She wore a green tank top threaded with gold and a black blazer hung on the back of her chair. He suspected she came straight from campus.

After Liz's brittleness, Holly's warm, easy-going demeanor appealed to him. Plus, her red hair had been an instant turn-on. Like Nikki's platinum-blonde hair. He seriously doubted he would ever date a brunette again.

"That's what she said," he said, then took a sip of his frosty beer.

"Then let her do her job. I'm glad she didn't talk you into staying. I've missed you. Midterms are crazy, and I'm sorry I haven't been able to get together until now."

"She didn't want me to stay. Told me to go, actually. She saw the way I was dressed and pretty much ordered me out of my own store." Dane frowned, resenting his plans.

No, that wasn't true. He'd taken Brett's advice, and he'd called Holly specifically to make tonight's date. Smoothing out his features, he shot Holly a thin smile.

His mind floated with her voice and the tinkling of piano keys. He wondered how Nikki was doing alone, how adorable she'd looked in her black running pants and TCRC polo, and how maybe it would be nice to be with her right now, alone in the store, listening to her laugh.

He accepted Holly's dinner invitation for later in the week with a slight nod of his head, and for the first time in a long while, he looked forward to going to work.

AFTER ANOTHER SUCCESSFUL day of teaching Nikki more about the store, Dane watched her through the huge front windows as she walked to a little silver car, slid in, and sat. He frowned in concern until he realized she must be checking her phone. He wondered who she was texting. A boyfriend? Probably setting up a date for this weekend.

"She's nice," Margie said, pulling on a thin coat.

"Yeah." Dane ran his thumb along the edge of the counter. He could feel Margie's eyes on him. "Why don't you get going? I'll stay until Christine gets here."

"Are you okay?" Margie asked. "You've been off the past couple days." She slung the strap of her purse over her shoulder and pulled her keys from her coat pocket.

"I'm fine. Getting used to the new dynamics of the store, I guess. It's been a while since we've had a new person working here. Have a good night, Margie."

"You, too." She paused, leaning against the doorjamb. "She's going to be fine, you know."

"Yeah."

Dane tried to shake off his negative temperament on his drive to Holly's house for dinner.

He didn't know what had gotten into him.

Nothing had changed, in fact, things were going better than ever.

Nikki was a dream manager, stepping up in ways he only hoped his manager would.

Brett wouldn't have to wait much longer for his help with marathon headaches.

Nikki gelled with the employees she met, was a quick learner, and never wasted time. Margie liked her, and that meant a lot to him. Margie had been his first hire when he opened the store, and he'd been disappointed when she'd turned down the management position.

Now he was glad; he wouldn't have met Nikki if Margie had taken the job.

"Hey, you," Holly said cheerfully when she answered the door. "Did you come straight from the store?"

"Yeah, sorry. I wasn't thinking. I didn't bring wine or dessert or anything."

"That's okay. Come in. I have fruit and cheese set out. Do you want a scotch? You look pale. Are you getting sick?"

Dane wiped his shoes on the mat inside her door and threw his jacket on a wooden decorative storage bench sitting in her foyer. "Yeah, sounds good. Margie told me I was acting off, too. The holidays are coming up. Maybe I'm dreading the family shit I go through every year."

He followed her into her little kitchen and sat at the breakfast nook on a backless stool. Dane took a sip of the scotch Holly poured him, relishing the burn down his throat. The alcohol soothed his frayed nerves.

"Tell me more about your new manager then," Holly asked. "I don't even know her name. Do you think she's going to work out?"

Dane's expression brightened. "She's great. I confessed how I hired her. That had really been bothering me, offering her the job after talking to the woman who threatened to bribe her away from me. All she did was laugh. I couldn't believe it. Her name is Nikki Halstead. I hadn't met her before hiring her, though Brett came into the store the other day and said she looked familiar. She's worked the expo for a couple years and already knew Margie, which was cool. She's willing to do extra too, like write an employee handbook. I told her I couldn't afford to pay her more, but she didn't care."

"She sounds like a keeper," Holly commented, stiffening, before collecting plates from the cupboard and silverware from the drawer.

"Definitely," Dane said. "I hope she stays at the store for a long time."

Holly set a little table positioned against the kitchen wall.

This was what a relationship should be about. Being able to talk with someone who wanted to know, who wanted to listen, without fear of being judged.

Like on his run with Nikki. That had been great—the sun rising, the cool autumn breeze blowing lightly around them, the peaceful quiet of the morning, and Nikki. Her willingness to fall into silence as they ran, the steady tread of their shoes on the sidewalk the only sound. And when they did talk, she cared about what he had to say.

That's what made him edgy around her.

Nikki could read him. She could read his moods on his face, and it made him uncomfortable. Like at the end of their run, she sensed something was bothering him, and the way she'd said his name . . .

"Dane."

Yeah, like that, but with a touch of sympathy, understanding, a need to know what was bothering him, a want to help. He'd run from her, unaccustomed to being an open book, unaccustomed to sharing.

"Dane."

Dane jerked in his chair, shooting his glass across the counter where it almost toppled over the edge of the breakfast nook. "What?"

"Dinner's ready," Holly murmured. "What were you thinking about?"

Being on a trail in a park at sunrise with another woman.

"Dreading the holidays, now that I brought them up," he said, scrambling guiltily.

"Well, Thanksgiving is still a ways off yet. Sit and eat before the food gets cold."

"It looks great, Holly. Thanks."

THEY SPOKE LITTLE during dinner, the way Dane preferred it. He liked being able to think about things, let the day bleed into the evening without noise scratching at his brain. It was one of the things he liked best about Holly. She could leave him alone without bitching about something.

Liz could never keep her mouth shut; if she wasn't yelling at him, she was bitching about all the things she wanted, all the places she wanted to go, all the things he couldn't afford to buy them.

He gritted his teeth, remembering the hate in her eyes as she'd scream.

Viciously, he stabbed a bite of chicken, threw back another lowball glass of scotch. The first time he'd slept with Holly, he'd been prepared for the endless chatter afterward, but it hadn't come. She'd tucked herself into his side, and she'd let him be, as if knowing he needed the peace and quiet.

He took a deep breath and tried to give Holly a reassuring smile.

This whole evening had been a big mistake.

In silence, he helped her with the dishes, loading what they could into her dishwasher, doing the others by hand. There was a feeling of anticipation in the air, and despite his reservations, he flowed with the mood of the evening, and he nuzzled Holly's neck as she dried her hands on a towel.

"It's been a while," he murmured, smoothing her hair.

"It has," she said, her eyes wide.

"What?" Dane asked, pulling her close, slipping his hand under her shirt. "Did you think I wouldn't stay?"

"You seemed . . . I don't know," Holly said brushing her hand over his cheek. "Distracted, during dinner. Moody. Actually, I was thinking you'd prefer to be alone tonight. It's okay if you want to go."

Dane gazed into her green eyes as he cupped her breast in his palm. He knew where he wanted to be, and he couldn't; he'd need to take the next best thing. "No, I want to stay, if you want me to."

"Yeah, let's go into the bedroom."

Holly led Dane into her room where he immediately pulled her shirt over her head and unclasped her bra. He kissed her, pushing his tongue into her mouth, yanking her closer, his cock stiffening against her belly.

This was a bad idea, he thought as Holly undressed him, but he was hard and he would look like a fool if he backed out now. He didn't know why he was even there; he could barely remember agreeing to Holly's dinner invitation.

"Turn over for me," Dane said, pushing her onto the mattress, not giving her a choice. He didn't want foreplay. Usually, he got her off first; she loved it when he played between her legs, loved watching his fingers moving in and out of her.

But tonight his heart wasn't in it, and he took her from behind, gripping her hips, only going through the motions.

He wanted to get this over with, wanted to leave. Thinking about Nikki, her shining blonde hair, bright blue eyes, and soft skin, he imagined what it would feel like to be inside her instead. To feel her warmth wrapped around him.

Picturing Nikki naked made him come, and he pulled out, dripping onto the carpet in his haste to get away.

"What's going on?" Holly asked, tears glittering in her eyes. She crossed her arms over her breasts as she watched him dress.

"I shouldn't be here. I need to go."

Dane pulled on his clothes, his eyes on the floor. With his heart pounding, and Holly sniffling behind him, he let himself out of her house and into the cool evening without a word of goodbye.

Idling at a stop sign, he banged on the steering wheel. What in the hell had come over him?

Everyone kept telling him he was acting differently lately, and he felt out of sorts. He shouldn't have accepted Holly's dinner invitation feeling like this. And he sure as hell should never have ignored the alarm bells going off inside his head when he decided to make love to her. Because he hadn't wanted to look her in the eye, he'd turned her over to take her. How stupid, selfish. Scotch rolled in his stomach, he ran his fingers through his hair.

Groaning, he tried to concentrate on the traffic. That hadn't been making love. He'd screwed her and ran.

That's all tonight had been about, but their relationship had always been more than friends with benefits. He genuinely liked her, admired her. They *were* friends, or they used to be. He wasn't sure what they were anymore, especially after tonight. There must have been something about her he liked, but he'd never craved her, not the way a man should crave the woman he desired.

He parked his truck in his parking space. It wasn't late, and the October night was mild. Maybe he needed a long, hard run. It would clear his head. He was putting his key into his lock when sobbing came from Nikki's apartment, spilling into the hallway.

Panic and scotch drove Dane to pound on her door. His heart hammered as he waited for her to answer. "Nikki, open the door," he yelled, needing her to open it *right now*. He was about to bang on it again when it swung open and Nikki stood there in a pair of pink and white striped boxers and matching pink tank top. Her hair spilled around her shoulders in a riot of curls and Dane gaped at her, breathless. He'd never seen her with her hair down before.

Her nipples hardened under his gaze, and her cheeks flushed as he stared. "What is it?"

Dane stepped into her entryway and grasped her shoulders. "You were crying. Are you all right?" he asked.

Nikki's nostrils flared, and she wrenched her shoulders from his grasp, taking a step back. "You need to go home."

"But the crying—"

The woman still wept, and he looked over Nikki's shoulder in the direction of the sound.

"I'm watching a movie."

Dane stepped into the quiet hallway. "I'm sorry," he

mumbled.

"Dane." Nikki hurried after him and grabbed his wrist. "Are you okay? Do you need to . . . talk?"

He backed away from her, pulling from her grasp. "No. I . . . I thought . . . I'm glad you're okay." He turned to his keys hanging in the deadbolt. "I'm sorry."

"Goodnight."

"Night."

Dane breathed a sigh of relief when he stepped into his apartment. God, he was stupid. What did he think he was going to do for her? She could've been having a fight with her boyfriend, or her parents. She could have gotten bad news, and he wouldn't have been able to help her anyway.

Forgetting the run he'd planned to take, he stripped and stood under the spray of his shower as hot as he could stand it.

Nikki never mentioned Dane's late-night visit, and she was relieved when he didn't approach her about it, even to apologize.

He stayed locked in his office during the day while she learned the store's operating procedures from Margie.

She brought in her laptop and began typing out the policies as she learned them. Later she would shape them into a professional handbook, but for now, she started a list.

Friday night she closed the store while Dane did paperwork in his office. She emptied the register, reported the credit card sales, and wiped the counter down with glass spray. After her closing duties were finished, she grabbed the dress she brought with her from their small break room.

Using the store's only fitting room, she changed into the

black lace dress and black stiletto heels. Her legs still glowed with traces of her summer tan, and she was glad to skip wearing stockings for one more night. She twisted her usual ponytail into a bun at the back of her head and slipped in a few pins to hold it in place. After freshening her makeup, she was ready.

She did one last quick check in the mirror and smiled in approval. The dress had been a steal, marked down at a store in the mall. It boasted a conservative neckline with black lace sleeves, scalloped lace edges running down her shoulder blades. The dress exposed her back—she couldn't wear a bra—and she wore a backless bodysuit with cups for support.

Nikki hoped it wasn't wasted.

She knocked on Dane's office door.

He pulled it open and looked her up and down smiling. "Hot date?"

Nikki grimaced. "Not really. I'm doing my dad a favor and going out with his friend's son. He's in town for a convention and didn't have anything to do tonight. I'm ready to go. Are you ready, or did you want to lock up?"

Dane shook his head. "You go on. I'll lock up and run to the bank."

"Okay. I'll see you Monday." Nikki turned to go and heard Dane's low whistle. She took it for what it was and saucily looked over her shoulder. "Like?"

"I would have to be dead not to like it. Have fun."

"Doubtful, but I'll try. Hey, at least he's a doctor. Maybe we'll hit it off, and he'll keep me in the lifestyle to which I'd like to become accustomed."

She laughed, but her heart dropped to her feet when the smile slipped from Dane's face, and she rushed to the door to get away.

"It was a total waste," Nikki grumbled to Alyssa on their walk the next afternoon.

"Was he ugly?" Alyssa asked, trying to push stray strands of hair into her elastic while holding onto her coffee.

Nikki took the warm paper cup, and Alyssa fixed her hair that had blown loose in the wind. "No. He was okay looking, if you could get past his ears. They stuck out a little. But he's a podiatrist. A foot doctor? And after he found out I run and worked in a running shoe store, all he could tell me was how bad running was for the bones in my feet. I thought I was supposed to worry about my knees. I don't think I could have listened to that for the rest of my life."

"Well, he paid for dinner, I'm assuming, so there's that. Where'd you eat?"

"Glass House," Nikki said, naming the most expensive, trendiest restaurant in Tower City.

"It wasn't a waste, then. Their desserts are to die for. So, how's it going with Dane? He saw you last night, didn't he? You didn't waste time going back to your apartment to change."

"No, I changed at the store. He thought I looked pretty, not that it matters, but I don't know, he seems, sad, some-how. I can't put my finger on it."

"And . . ." Alyssa encouraged, then sipped her coffee.

"He did something strange a couple nights ago."

Alyssa frowned. "Strange good, or strange bad? Are you in trouble here?"

"I don't think so. I left work Wednesday and it was fine, I came home, ate dinner, started watching a movie." She paused for a moment, tried to match words with her feel-ings. "I was watching *Ever After,* and I was at the part where the prince is supposed to marry that one woman, but she doesn't want to marry him and she's crying hysterically?"

Alyssa nodded and waved a hand for her to hurry up. She knew the part—*Ever After* was one of their favorite movies.

"Out of nowhere there's a pounding on my door, and it was Dane. He's gripping my shoulders, and he's like, are you all right? Why are you crying?"

"That doesn't sound weird, it sounds sweet. He cares about you. You know, that *is* romantic. I might use it for one of my books. It sounds made up."

"It wasn't sweet. It was . . . I don't want to say creepy because it wasn't. But . . . I think he'd come from his girlfriend's house. He smelled like alcohol and sex. That was the weird part. And he had this look in his eyes, I can't even describe it. Like . . . maybe they had broken up? Or they'd been fighting, maybe. But then why would he smell like sex?"

"Are you sure that's what it was? Maybe he went for a run." Alyssa bent down to pick up a rock, and she threw it as far as she could. It plinked into the pond water.

"Maybe," she said doubtfully. "But whatever it was, it was pretty strong." Nikki wrinkled her nose.

"What did you tell him?"

"I told him I was watching a movie, and he should go home. He muttered an apology and went to his apartment." Nikki kicked at some leaves. "I feel bad for him though. He looked lost."

"They probably had a fight." Alyssa added drolly, "Every couple does, I've heard."

"Sometimes it's better to be single. At least no one's bitching at you."

"Speaking of single, when are you picking up your cat from your parents' place?"

"What does that have to do with being single?" She stuck her tongue out at Alyssa. "I"m not a crazy cat lady. And I'm not sure. Pretty soon. I'm done unpacking, and my dad will want an update on the date thing. Maybe Monday or Tuesday. Dane doesn't have a set schedule for me right now. I've been working days and nights to learn both routines."

"No weekends?"

"Not yet. I'll have to closer to Christmas, I suppose. Though, I don't see the store getting too terribly busy. I know we'll run sales, but it's not the best place to find gifts."

"You'll get some traffic, though."

"Yeah. But it won't be like working at the mall, that's for sure. When are you going on your tour?"

"There was an issue with dates, and my publisher had to postpone it until January. My parents are bugging me to fly to Florida for Christmas, but it's the last thing I want to do."

"Let's do Thanksgiving together. My parents are going on that cruise, remember? It'll be fun."

"Sounds perfect. I might start a new book for the hell of it. You know I'm bored when I'm not writing. And hey, I don't have anything else to do."

"You can't use my scene after making fun of it."

"I didn't make fun of it. I said it was romantic, so I can't make any promises."

She blew out a breath. "I'll talk to you later," she said as they approached the parking lot attached to her building. After giving Alyssa a hug, she took her empty coffee cup to throw in the garbage.

"Hey, Nik?"

Nikki met Alyssa's eyes and was surprised to find a wealth of compassion in them. "Yeah?"

"If he's hurting, give him a break, will you?"

She froze. "I haven't done anything to him."

"I know, but . . . look, don't get mad okay? You like him, I mean, deny it, but I know you *like him*, like him, and if you're trying to keep things professional, you might come off as callous, or bitchy. Ease up, and maybe he'll talk to you. He has a girlfriend, and they might be going through a rough patch. That doesn't mean you can't be his friend, even if he is your boss."

Nikki bit her lip, knowing Alyssa was right. She did like Dane, and she'd been trying to keep her distance because he was her boss and he wasn't available.

"Okay. I hear what you're saying. If he needs someone, I'll try. But I can't get close to him if he's taken. That's asking for a broken heart."

"I know; it's tough. Hang in there."

She'd only known the man for a week, but what she knew of him she liked. There was no point in lying to herself.

She wished he would ask her to go for another run. Maybe if she suggested it, she could encourage him to confide in her. It seemed while he was running he opened up more.

But he had Brett too, and she doubted Brett was his only friend.

On the other hand, she could take Alyssa's advice to heart and give friendship a chance. If she could keep her feelings to herself, she could at least strengthen their working relationship. All he'd done since beating on her door was hide in his office.

It was worth a try, and Alyssa was usually right. If she told Nikki she was acting like a bitch, she probably was.

She trotted up the stairs to her apartment and took stock of her cooking ingredients. Before long she had lasagna baking in the oven, and a red she was especially proud of waiting on her kitchen counter.

After she tidied her living room, she stepped onto her balcony. If she leaned over the railing enough . . . yeah, his truck was parked in his parking space. Inside, she grabbed her phone and sent Dane a text. *Dinner?*

Her mouth twitched when he came back with, *I planned to eat some, yes.*

Do you want to eat it here? She typed back.

She laughed when she read, *That's too far. I have to walk you know.*

You run marathons. I think you can handle it.

Dane wouldn't stop teasing her. *Is it better than cereal?*

Nikki shook her head and typed, *It is if you like lasagna.*

When he didn't reply, she thought maybe he didn't want to take her up on the invitation and didn't know how to tell her without hurting her feelings. She was debating on what to do when there was a knock on her door. She grinned, relieved.

"Hey," she said when she opened the door. "For a second I didn't think you were going to come."

"I had to change. I was sitting alone on a Saturday night, and I didn't look fit for company."

"You didn't have to do that. Come in. It hasn't changed much since you brought in the books. I don't have much furniture since it's usually only me, but make yourself comfortable. I have some wine to go with dinner, but I have beer, too."

Dane took a seat at her kitchen table. "You're home

alone on a Saturday night, too. Don't you have a boyfriend?"

She blinked at the forward question. "No. I don't think guys want to put up with me—I must be too high maintenance. At least, that's the vibe I get. My relationships don't last long."

Nikki held the bottle of wine in one hand and a bottle of beer in the other.

Dane nodded to the beer. "I don't buy it. What happened to the guy last night? The doctor?"

Nikki rummaged in her junk drawer for her bottle opener. She popped the top off his beer and handed it to him, hoping he didn't mind the bottle because she didn't own any pilsner glasses. She grabbed the corkscrew and handed him the wine bottle.

"What do you do when you're alone?" he asked, amused.

"Struggle."

He laughed and opened her wine. "Here."

She smiled at him. "Thanks."

"So, the doctor?"

Nikki poured her wine into a coffee mug printed with Will Run For Wine, and she sat at the table across from him.

It was late in the day, and his five o'clock shadow was going strong. She itched to rub her palms over his jaw.

He wore a TCRC t-shirt and black warm-up pants. She suspected that was what he usually wore no matter what day or time it was.

She looked similar, still wearing the clothes she wore to walk with Alyssa: running capris and a baby blue t-shirt. Her feet were bare, and her hair was pulled away from her face in a ponytail that was starting to sag. They were a pair, for sure.

She leaned over and said with a straight face, "Did you know running hurts your feet?"

"If you wear crappy shoes, yeah. What does that have to do with anything?" He took a pull of his beer.

"The doctor last night. After I told him I did a lot of running, that's all he talked about. I don't think he was too impressed when I said I would only think about his advice to stop. He was nice, I guess, but it was obvious our interests didn't match. Besides, he lives in Ohio. Who wants to live in Cleveland?"

The oven buzzed, and Nikki jumped up to take the lasagna out.

"Do you need any help?" Dane asked.

"Now he asks," she said. "Putting the lasagna together is the hardest part. No, it's okay. While the lasagna sets I'll put breadsticks into the oven to heat up."

After dinner Dane offered to help her clean up, but she declined. He sat at the table as she washed the dishes and reflected on their pleasant meal.

He hadn't mentioned Holly, and she hadn't pried.

They talked about the store and about her parents' cruise over Thanksgiving week.

He didn't talk about his parents or spending the holiday with them, and she wondered why. She needed to thank Alyssa. The woman knew more about Dane than Nikki did, and Alyssa hadn't even met him yet.

Nikki put away the lasagna dish and rested her head against the cabinet door. Nikki definitely needed to thank her—Dane could turn into a good colleague and friend.

She wasn't sure what they would do for the rest of the night. She didn't want to kick him out, but they didn't know each other well enough to spend an evening together without it feeling awkward.

Lowering to her haunches, she put away the glass dish she used to bake the lasagna and wracked her brain for something they could do to end the evening on a positive note.

DANE LEANED AGAINST the kitchen sink and watched Nikki place a clear dish in the cabinet.

He didn't want to eat and run, but it would be awkward to try and stay. And yeah, he wanted to stay. Going back to his empty apartment held little appeal. Being with Nikki, he could let his guard down and breathe.

Until recently, spending time with Holly had felt nice too, but this was different.

This was *more*.

Dane liked listening to her voice; he appreciated the bits of information she shared about her parents and what she used to do before she took the position at his store. She made him feel good, and he must be feeling damned low now because the thought of going back to his apartment lodged a stupid lump in his throat.

She caught his eye from her crouched position on the floor. "I'm sorry I don't have dessert. I try not to keep stuff like that around."

He shuffled his feet and looked away. "It's no problem. Listen, I should—"

"Would you like to stay and watch a movie?"

He feigned nonchalance when he was thankful for the invitation. "What did you have in mind? Some chick flick, I suppose?" he said to cover his relief.

Nikki laughed and led him from the kitchen into the

living room. "We can share the couch," she told him, avoiding the awkwardness of where to sit.

He would have taken the loveseat, it looked like a comfortable, a smaller version of the pink, cream, and green floral pattern of her feminine sofa, but sitting close to Nikki sounded better.

"When Alyssa spends the night, we have to play a game to decide what to watch. She's the one who likes the chick flicks, but I'm more of a horror girl, and there's not a lot of opportunity to mesh the two. We use this website called Flix Roulette. The only rule is we have to watch the first movie that comes up, no ifs ands or buts about it." Nikki brought up the website with the remote and moved the pointer. "You want to click it? Then if a horrible movie comes up you can't blame me."

"This is the weirdest thing I've ever heard." Dane clicked the 'spin' box shaded in red.

"Oooh, ouch. *The Lair of the White Worm*. Don't tell me you've seen it?"

"No, I can't say I have, but look, it has Hugh Grant in it. That must mean it's an excellent flick. You and Alyssa do this a lot?" he asked leaning into the sofa.

"We've found some decent movies this way. Before this gem starts I'm going to make some coffee. Want some?"

"Yeah, sure. Can I do anything?"

"Nope, it will only take a minute."

Dane rested his feet on the coffee table. He didn't notice it when he dropped her books off, but the table wasn't a table at all, but an old packing crate. A wooden box just waiting for people to prop their feet onto it, settle in, and relax. If he had something like this at his place, he would be full of junk, and maybe hers was too, but he resisted the urge to look.

Conversation with Nikki was easy, and he was even pleased with the movie. He wasn't against chick flicks at all, and he would have sat through one to be near her, but the roulette game was a surprise. It told him she was open to new things; she didn't need to have her own way. That was important to him because Liz . . . no, he didn't want to think about her now.

As the scent of coffee wafted through the air and he waited for Nikki to come back, a wave of shame hit him. He would have to apologize Holly for the way he'd treated her.

In the kitchen, Nikki stood near the coffee maker waiting for it to drip enough to fill their mugs, and his heart thudded heavily beneath his ribs.

He never, ever, would treat her that way. If she ever let him into her life, he would treat every moment with her as if it were his last.

Dane didn't want to admit thinking about Nikki was what made him act out at Holly's, and he regretted being there feeling the way he had that night. He should have gone home. No, scratch that. He shouldn't have gone in the first place. It was too late for regrets, but he could at least apologize. In person.

Nikki interrupted his thoughts. "Black, right?"

"Yeah. Thanks."

She handed him the mug, and his fingers brushed hers. Her touch made goosebumps cover his skin. "I don't have coasters. The table top is fine, you can see it's pretty beat up —I picked it up at a flea market. Or use a magazine. Whatever. I'm pretty easy-going."

Dane doubted that. He hadn't met a woman who was truly as easy-going as she claimed, except for Holly, but he hadn't given her any rights to complain about what he did.

He took a sip of coffee then put his plain black mug

onto the table. He pulled a pink throw from the back of the couch onto his lap and caught a whiff of sugar. Holding the fleece up to his nose, he inhaled. "Why does this smell like cake?"

Nikki took a seat next to him. "It's body spray. One of my exes hated it. 'Why do you gotta smell like a goddamn bakery every goddamn day?'" she mimicked in a deep male voice.

"He said that to you?" Dane couldn't believe a man would talk to her that way.

Nikki stared at the TV, hiding her expression. "It doesn't matter."

It obviously did matter, and when he touched her shoulder, he was stabbed with remorse when her eyes flattened to mask her feelings.

She pulled her ponytail elastic out of her hair and leaned against the cushions. "I'm ready when you are. I can't wait to be wowed by this intelligent piece of cinema."

Dane poked her in the side, making her giggle. "Wait until next time. We'll see what *you* get." He shut his mouth. Who said there would be a next time?

Nikki didn't seem to think anything of it. "My spins are awesome. You'll see."

She clicked 'watch on Netflix' then pulled a full-sized bed pillow into her lap.

Dane rested his arm against the back of the couch, and Nikki eased into his side. He bit back a sigh of contentment and leaned against the cushions to watch one of the dumbest movies he'd ever heard of.

"That was horrible," Dane laughed two hours later, clicking off the app and the TV. When Nikki didn't respond, he looked down, prepared for her to be angry they wasted time on such a terrible movie. So much for easy-going. "Nikki . . ."

She was sleeping.

He took the pillow from her lap and placed it against the arm of the couch. Pulling her against him, he brought her legs up onto the seat cushions. Dane spooned with her, one arm underneath the pillow, the other resting over her stomach.

He lay awake for a long time, listening to her breathe.

STIFF AND SORE, Nikki stretched and ran her tongue over her teeth—her mouth tasted like old coffee. She must have fallen asleep on the couch again. A heavy arm was wrapped around her waist, her butt pushed up against . . . oh, she was lying with Dane on her couch.

Dane mumbled and pulled her closer.

She'd fallen asleep toward the end of that crazy movie they watched last night. She covered his hand that rested on her stomach. What would it feel like to wake up with Dane like this every morning?

She imagined they were a couple. They would make lazy Sunday morning love, then she would fix them break-fast to eat in bed. They would make love again and then maybe go for a run. In the evening, they would meet up with friends for dinner or stay in and watch movies before a busy Monday morning.

She imagined she could wipe away the unhappiness haunting his eyes.

Yeah, right. He probably had a million texts from Holly, wondering where he was.

She gently rolled onto her back trying not to disturb

him, but when she flicked a glance his way, he was already awake. "Hey," she whispered.

His eyes were beautiful. Like black coffee, with the right amount of cream.

No, what she told Alyssa was more accurate. Deep dark chocolate with a gooey caramel center.

Her body was pressed against him, and her legs were tangled with his at the end of the couch.

A smile crept over Dane's mouth, and it took her breath away. "Hey."

His hair stood up in messy spikes, and his eyebrows were dark slashes above his eyes which were framed with long black lashes. Her pillow had creased his cheek, and she resisted the urge to run a finger along the pink line.

She wanted to trace over the stubble along his jaw, continue down his throat and over his hard chest. He was handsome, and staring at him made her heart patter.

But it was more.

It was the look in his eyes, millions of emotions hiding in their dark depths. With a sinking feeling, she wondered how dangerous it would be to get involved with this man. His hand still rested on her stomach, his other arm under her head.

"I'm sorry I fell asleep on you last night."

"You missed a great ending."

She fought a smile. "I'll have to trust you on that."

"What? I don't get to make you watch it again?"

"There are no do-overs," she said, and her breath hitched when a look of want moved across his face.

Dane lifted his hand from her stomach to her cheek. "I want to kiss you," he whispered, moving the pad of his thumb over her cheekbone.

She swallowed, debated letting him give her what she

wanted. No point in denying it. "I don't think it would be a good idea. You're my boss."

"Just once, but if you don't want me to, I'll get up right now and leave you alone."

She couldn't bring herself to tell him no, and Dane lifted onto his elbow and lowered his head. Softly, back and forth, his lips grazed hers, and she moaned, moving into the kiss.

Giving into her desire, Nikki raised her hand to his jaw, relishing the sharp stubble beneath her fingertips.

Dane shifted his head and probed her lips with his tongue asking her to open for him.

Nikki parted her lips and pressed her body closer as his mouth explored hers.

She wanted closer, God help her, she wanted closer, and she succumbed to the need and pulled him nearer, wrapping her arms around his neck.

He rolled on top of her, not breaking the kiss, and Nikki felt him hard and thick against her. As he burrowed into her, she tilted her hips inviting him even closer. She wanted him to pull her running capris down. Not all the way, but enough to . . .

All the warnings she'd told herself came rushing back. He was kissing her when he had a girlfriend. He was her boss. She was *this close* to losing her dream job, her apartment.

Nikki tore her mouth from his. "We shouldn't."

He broke the kiss and studied her for just a moment before pulling away. She sat up, and he stood, putting a much needed distance between them.

She was torn between being relieved and disappointed; want had soaked her panties all the way through.

She tried to smooth her curls.

"Don't." Dane stilled her hands. "You're beautiful. Don't."

Nikki dropped her hands and looked down at her lap. "I'm sorry. You probably know I wanted . . . but we can't. You're my boss, and you're seeing someone. It wouldn't be right."

"I understand. It's okay," he said, deep lines appearing between his brows.

Nikki trembled as he brushed her hair away from her face.

"Thanks for dinner last night, and the movie. Nikki," he paused, pulling his hand away but returned to feather her jaw with his fingertips. "I don't want us to be uncomfortable around each other. It would be nice if we were friends. I shouldn't have kissed you. I'm sorry."

"I wanted you to," she admitted, taking his hand. "But my job . . ." *And your girlfriend,* she finished to herself because she didn't want to sound like she was harping at him. "Don't be sorry now, but I'm afraid if we got carried away, we would be later."

"Yeah, I get it. How about a run later? I enjoyed the one we went on last weekend."

She squeezed his hand, relieved he wasn't giving her a difficult time. "I would like that very much."

"Okay. I'll text you a time."

"Okay." Nikki wanted to fall into his arms, wanted to push her lips to his, but she followed him to the door instead and locked it after he stepped into the hall.

She'd done the right thing—stopping had been the right thing to do. It didn't make a difference the look he gave her when she told him making love would be a mistake almost broke her heart.

CHAPTER THREE

D**ANE STOPPED AT** the florist's and bought a bouquet of Holly's favorite flowers—long-stemmed pink roses. It wouldn't make up for treating her the way he had the other day, but he didn't think anything could.

He'd been a prick, and maybe he had been for the past two years, but dammit, if she'd been unhappy with their arrangement she should have said something. All this time, he'd been upfront about what he wanted from her and what he was willing to give her, and she could have walked away anytime.

Cradling the bouquet against his chest, he rang her doorbell and prayed she would open the door. He hadn't called to find out if she was going to be home, and he'd been relieved to see her car sitting in the driveway when he arrived at her house.

Dane tensed as he heard her walk down the hallway and his palms were sweating by the time she answered the door.

They stared at each other for a moment in tense silence.

"Well, I have to say I'm a bit surprised," Holly said. "I

thought maybe a text? Or an email? Maybe a card? Oh, but I don't suppose they have a card that says 'I'm sorry for the quick fuck before I ran away like a coward.'"

Dane grimaced, but clutched the flowers, taking the brunt of her anger.

Holly scowled. "Come in, I guess. We can't leave things the way they are."

"I would appreciate it."

Leading him to the living room, she scoffed. "I don't think I care much about what you want right now."

"Listen, Holly, I'll let you spew all day. I know I deserve it."

She laughed, but the sound was bitter and angry. "That's the thing though. You don't. I knew what I was getting into, and I liked it. Well, maybe I didn't like it, but I didn't mind it." She sighed. "Let me take these and put them in water. They're lovely. Thank you."

Dane sat on the couch as she found a clear vase and filled it with water. Sprinkling in the green packet of vitamins the florist added to the bouquet, she didn't seem to be hurting. She looked good dressed in black slacks and a russet-colored sweater. Her hair was pulled back into a sleek ponytail.

"Can I get you anything? I have coffee made."

"That would be fine, thanks."

She brought him a mug, and blowing out a breath, sat down opposite him in a floral wing-backed chair. "This is my fault as much as yours."

Dane ducked his head, embarrassed. "Are you talking about the past couple years? Because nothing about the other night was your fault."

"Dane," she murmured, then looked away. "It was last week at the piano bar I knew things had changed between us. I didn't want to see it. I should have called everything off that night, let you go then, but I didn't want to lose you. I didn't want to admit I already had. I shouldn't have invited you to dinner, and I certainly shouldn't have encouraged what we did after. But I thought . . . maybe the intimacy would bring you back."

"I don't know what's wrong with me." Dane didn't want to bring his feelings for Nikki into it.

Holly moved to the couch and sat next to him. She rested her hand on his shoulder and used her other hand to make him look at her. "Stop beating yourself up about that. I let myself get attached to you. You never gave me any promises. I'm the one to blame. But we are done, aren't we?"

Dane nodded, forcing himself to meet her eyes. "And the shitty part is, I don't even understand why. I've never had a problem with us. Things were perfect."

She laughed, and the strain on her face fell away. "Things were good," she agreed. "Until you met Nikki."

"She's only my manager." That's all she would ever be to him.

"That's what you might want her to be, but she means more to you, or you want her to be more, and I'm happy for you. Even while I was crying after you left, I was hoping she'll be everything you need her to be. Liz hurt you, irreparably, I think, sometimes. I hope Nikki can prove me wrong and heal that hurt."

Knowing she deserved complete honesty, Dane said, "I don't know if anybody can."

Holly ran her fingers through his hair. "If she's the right woman, she will. But you have to give her a chance. Don't block her out. Not like you've done with me. It didn't matter how hard I tried, or for how long, we were never going to get past where we were. You never let me in."

Dane blew out a breath. He'd deliberately kept her at arm's length. "I don't have to worry about that. She doesn't want more. She wants to keep it professional, and I need to respect that. Nikki's a terrific manager, and I don't want her to quit. I've put my blood, sweat, and tears into that place, and I need a break, even if it's only to help Brett with the race. I need her."

"Have you told her how you feel?"

It should have felt strange talking to Holly about another woman, but somehow, it didn't. "She invited me for dinner, and we watched a movie afterward. We fell asleep on her couch, and I kissed her this morning."

"Did she kiss you back?"

He took a sip of coffee and closed his eyes at the memory. "Yeah."

Holly pressed a kiss to his cheek. "Then the rest will come. Where does she live? Close to the store?"

"Down the hall." Dane cleared his throat.

"Oh, Dane."

"What?" he asked defensively, not caring for her tone implying he was an idiot. He already felt bad enough as it was. "I didn't ask her to move into my building. It's only a coincidence. I hadn't even met her before she moved in. I helped her with a couple boxes, and I had no idea who she was. You know I didn't do a face-to-face with her."

"I know, but take it slow. She has a lot to lose if it doesn't work out between you."

"Nothing's going to happen."

"Silly. Something already has. Now, do you want to stay for lunch? I can make sandwiches, and I have some potato salad from that deli you like."

"No, thanks. I'm going running with Nikki later. She

thinks you and I were still together when I kissed her this morning, and I need to explain what's going on."

Holly rolled her eyes. "She *is* perfect for you, isn't she?"

"I don't know. I've known her for a week. That's not a lot of time to know anything, to do anything."

"Well, it was enough time for her to destroy what we had."

"I'm sorry I hurt you. For all of it. But it wouldn't feel right, staying together now. Even if you were happy with the little I could offer you." Dane stood and moved toward her door. He didn't want to stay any longer. He'd apologized, and she accepted. It made him feel better to know she was going to be all right.

Impatiently, he fingered his truck's keys in his jacket pocket.

"It's okay. I hope you find the peace and happiness you're looking for. You deserve it. And if you need to talk, need advice or anything, call me. We're still friends."

He kissed her cheek. "I might take you up on that. Bye, Holly. Thanks."

In his truck, Dane sighed in relief, flexing his fingers on the steering wheel. He was fucking glad that was over.

NIKKI WAS CLEANING her apartment and doing laundry when she remembered the store meeting scheduled for that night. The thought of meeting the rest of the employees in a formal setting made her nervous. Dane didn't employ a large staff, but she hadn't met them all yet, and she wanted to make a good impression.

She needed to find someone to date to make herself stop thinking about Dane.

The only problem was, she didn't have anything on the horizon. Caught up with moving and learning her new job, she hadn't gone out in a while, bar-hopping with her friends.

While the store held a running group on Thursday mornings, the time held little appeal. The run was too early for her, but it would be a way to meet new people, and as the store manager, she probably wouldn't be able to avoid the group runs forever.

She needed to do something to keep her thoughts away from Dane; vacuuming her living room floor didn't help.

There was no point in denying she wanted him. If he wasn't her boss, she would have been all over him this morning, even more than she had been, she admitted with a rueful quirk to her lips.

That, and if he didn't already have a girlfriend.

She wasn't too happy with him. What did he think he was doing kissing her while he was seeing someone? Well, kind of seeing someone.

Maybe it was part of their agreement. Margie said Dane and Holly weren't really a couple. It seemed odd to Nikki though, and if he thought he was going to get the same agreement from her, he could think again. She wasn't into that. She wanted her man for keeps.

She wanted to fall in love, get married, have kids, the whole thing.

The man she married would love her blindly, passionately. Forever.

Her cell phone chimed with a text, and she looked over from folding her laundry.

Run?

She answered Dane's text. *What time?*

In a few minutes. I need to change. Dinner after?

Can't, she replied. *Store meeting tonight?*

Shit. I knew I hired you for a reason :)

Nikki smiled, relieved it seemed like they were going to get along despite their kiss and the abrupt way he left her apartment that morning. It was too bad he was everything she was looking for in a man.

She was tying her shoes in her small hallway when Dane knocked on her door.

"I completely blew off the meeting tonight," he said by way of greeting. "Luckily I already ordered the food otherwise I'd be scrambling. After tonight you can organize these."

"You always order food?" Nikki slipped her apartment key into the slim side pocket alongside the thigh of her running capris.

"Pretty much have to," he said, holding the building door open for her. "It's the only way I can get everyone to give up an hour on a Sunday night without a lot of bitching."

"But it's only once a month though, you said, right?"

"Sometimes we skip a month if there's nothing going on. Tonight, we'll get you introduced, talk about the holidays, what's expected to keep the store running smoothly, yada, yada. It won't take long. Sometimes there'll be an issue we need to discuss, but everyone is comfortable talking with me, and these meetings go pretty fast. I hired a good group of people."

They were quiet as they started their run, the mild autumn Minnesota weather treating them to another sunny late afternoon.

Nikki was becoming familiar with the trails, and she jumped over the concrete slab she'd tripped over the first time she ran with Dane. She'd felt it then, the attraction.

She'd felt it the first day she met him, when he took the boxes from her, and she'd looked into his eyes.

"Nikki?"

"Yeah?" She was already getting to know him, and she knew he was going to talk about their kiss.

"About this morning, I want you to know when I kissed you, Holly and I weren't technically together anymore. I don't want you to think I was cheating on her. I don't know what Margie told you—"

"She said you weren't really a couple, but this isn't any of my business."

"I made it your business when I kissed you this morning. Listen, we had a fight earlier this week—"

"Wednesday, you mean, the night you came to my apartment?" Something had been going on with him then.

"Yeah. We fought, and we both knew it was over but it was something we weren't ready to admit. I talked to her this afternoon. I wanted to be sure we parted on good terms, but we're done."

"I'm sorry to hear that."

"I'm not. She deserves better than what I was giving her. Whatever Margie told you was probably the truth. We weren't together, not in a committed relationship. I think we were using each other to be with someone. Or I was using her to be with someone. I honestly don't know what she was doing with me."

Nikki knew what Holly was doing. She was hoping for a future, she was hoping for a ring, a loving father for her children. Invested her time, her attention, in the man, hoping one day it would pay off.

It didn't.

Nikki didn't blame her, really. When she looked at Dane, she saw in him what Holly saw too. The kindness, the gentleness. The vulnerability hidden beneath the rough exterior.

For a few minutes she focused on the run, breathing in the crisp air, the steady rhythm of her heart, and tried to gather her thoughts.

"I don't know if a relationship would work between us, and I'm sorry if I was somehow involved in your breakup. I mean, if you weren't my boss, I admit there would be something there, but you know working together makes it difficult." Nikki's skin prickled with discomfort. She hated talking about things like this.

"Yeah."

"I want us to be friends, I want us to have a comfortable, professional working relationship. Last night was fun, and it would be great to do that again . . . maybe without the kissing part."

"Okay. I'll take it easy, all right?"

He sounded reluctant, but Nikki admired him for listening and being willing to do what she asked.

"How about letting me take you to the meeting tonight? It doesn't make any sense to take two vehicles."

If he was okay with being friends, she would meet him halfway. "That sounds good."

THE MEETING WENT well. Dane had done a great job hiring his staff. They all seemed to admire and respect him, and they enjoyed working at the store. A few of them had even seemed familiar from the huge running expo where she volunteered every spring.

Nikki met Daniel who apologized profusely for always calling in sick. He'd seemed a bit nervous, but she was his new boss now, so to speak, and some people tensed up naturally when meeting authority figures.

She kicked off her shoes and hung her running jacket in the closet.

Daniel seemed like a good kid, and hopefully, she could help him stay on track and keep better attendance in regard to his shifts.

Maybe they could implement a perfect attendance policy for the holidays. For every week an employee worked their scheduled shifts, that employee would be entered into a drawing. At the end of December, they could draw a name for something, like a gift card to Grill, the steakhouse near the running store. It was something to think about because it was always difficult to encourage your employees to work during the holidays. There were always better things to do, like parties and family gatherings.

Nikki was proud to be part of the running community in Tower City, and meeting everyone tonight made her even surer she'd made the right choice accepting Dane's job offer.

Amused, she shook her head at his concern he'd stolen her away from Shine. It was sweet.

In her bedroom, she changed out of her work clothes and into pajamas.

In the quiet, Dane's TV filtered through her wall.

Nikki gave in to the temptation to listen, and she pushed her ear to the wall between her bed and night table. She couldn't make out what program he was watching, but on the other side of the wall, there was some shuffling and the mattress springs squeaked. He must have jumped onto his bed.

Appalled, she jerked away. For God's sake.

She needed to find a guy and get Dane out of her mind. Her ringing cellphone saved her from more analysis of her high-schoolish behavior, and she glared at her ex's name glowing on her screen.

"Hello?"

"I wasn't sure you would answer," Eric said.

She sat on the edge of the bed, freeing her hair from her ponytail, being careful not to press her cheek onto her phone's screen and accidentally hang up on him. "I wasn't sure if you dialed my number deliberately."

"I did. I've been thinking about you a lot lately, and I think I made a mistake."

She didn't know what to say. Six months ago he'd dumped her to date someone else, and she'd missed him. They'd gotten along well, and she'd been disappointed they hadn't been able to explore what could have been.

"Alexa didn't work out?"

"It didn't take long to realize she wasn't you. I don't know. Could we like, grab a drink or something, sometime? If anything, to catch up?" Eric cleared his throat.

He sounded unsure, and that wasn't like him. Eric was usually a confident, take-charge kind of guy. He had charisma to spare, and she loved it. "All right."

Eric released a breath, and a swooshing sound came through her phone's speaker. "That's great. Say when and where and I'll pick you up?"

"I've made some changes since we've last talked. I have a new job. I won't be free until Friday night."

"No problem. How about I text you on Thursday, and we can make plans then, okay? I, ah, appreciate the chance, Nik."

"Yeah, that sounds good. I'll look for your text on Thursday."

Huh. This might be exactly what she was looking for. A

relationship she could invest time in, someone to take her mind off Dane.

She lay in bed, relieved. She liked Dane. Too much. If things worked out between her and Eric, Dane would no longer be a temptation, and her position at the store would be safe.

BY THE MIDDLE of the week, Dane was struggling. He hadn't realized what a void Holly filled in his life until she was gone. Talking on the phone, silly texts, stopping by her house for a meal and sex after working at the store. She took up hours of his time that were now a black nothing. He paced restlessly around his kitchen.

A burst of laughter came from Nikki's apartment, and he scowled in jealousy. Someone was having fun. He was knocking on her door before he could even think about what he was doing. Fuck. What if she had a guy at her place? He'd look stupid. Desperately, he ran through a list of bogus excuses about the store he could use if she wasn't alone.

He winced when Nikki opened the door dressed in fleece lounging pants and a skimpy little tank top.

"Hey. What's up?"

"Nothing," he muttered, backing away from the door in embarrassment. "Forget it."

"Who's at the door, Nik?" a female voice hollered.

Leaning backward toward the kitchen Nikki said, "Dane." Bringing her eyes back to him she asked, "Alyssa's here. Do you want to meet her?"

He didn't feel like meeting anyone, but he said, "Yeah, sure." Why didn't he think? What had he been hoping for? Dinner and another movie? She'd made it clear there wasn't going to be anything between them. He had to stop knocking on her door because he was lonely and wanted an excuse to see her.

Nikki led him into the kitchen where a black-haired woman sat at the table, a full glass of wine and a bowl of chips in front of her. Politely making introductions Nikki said, "Dane, this is Alyssa Barnes. Alyssa, Dane Montgomery. Alyssa's a writer and my best friend. She lives in the apartment lofts down the street. Alyssa already knows who you are—I've told her about working at the store."

Alyssa stood and held out her hand. Dane shook it as he studied her. Her green eyes were gorgeous. She carried some extra pounds, well, a lot, but nothing a few months of running wouldn't take care of. But Nikki said Alyssa didn't run—they went on walks together. Too bad.

"It's nice to meet you," Alyssa said. "I've heard a lot about you."

"All good, I hope," Dane said, though he doubted it.

"Sure. Nikki doesn't talk shit about anybody."

"Most of the time," Nikki said, grabbing a bottle of wine and a wine glass. "Sit down and join us. You just crashed Whine and Wine Wednesday."

Dane sat across from Alyssa. "What's that?"

Alyssa crunched a chip. "It's where we drown our sorrows. Only, Nikki has her shit together for a change and doesn't have anything to bitch about."

"I've dominated my share of Wednesdays," she said as she topped off hers and Alyssa's wine glasses and filled a glass for Dane, emptying the bottle.

"Go ahead," Alyssa encouraged him.

"Go ahead and do what?" He stared at her from across the table. She wore similar lounging pants to Nikki's, but a huge grey sweatshirt with the neckline cut out drooped over a bare shoulder. She wasn't wearing a bra.

"Whine. Start small," Alyssa suggested. "It helps."

He didn't know what the hell to talk about. He took a chip to buy some time, and out of nowhere, a small white kitten jumped onto his lap. "Holy shit," he yelped as its claws dug into his thigh.

"Don't scare Princess Snowflake," Nikki said, pulling the cat from his legs and placing the kitten in her own lap. "You're not allergic, are you?"

Dane shook his head. "No, but I didn't know you had a cat."

"She was at my mom and dad's while I moved because I didn't want her to get hurt or be in the way. I adopted her from the shelter a couple months before I moved into this place."

Dane watched her hold the cat over her face, making kissy noises. It was adorable and purely Nikki. He imagined Nikki cuddling with the cat at night, or watching a movie with the cat napping in her lap.

He wanted to be in that picture.

Fuck.

He should never have broken things off with Holly. No, that was shitty. He couldn't keep using someone because he was lonely and bored. Maybe he'd done that subconsciously for the past two years, but to do it now, while he had feelings for Nikki, would be unfathomable.

He had enough reasons to feel like an asshole.

"Look at him scowl," Alyssa said, lifting her glass in a toast. "Someone needs to whine. Come on."

Anything he had to complain about was too big to talk about here.

If he brought up his non-existent relationship with his

parents, then he would have to explain they'd sided with Liz in the divorce and didn't talk to him anymore.

That would lead to Liz and what happened there, and quite honestly, he wasn't sure if he would ever explain to Nikki what destroyed his marriage. He was ashamed he'd been taken for a ride when he'd loved his wife very much. He'd tried to honor his vows and make her a good husband. He'd tried to please her, and nothing he did had been enough.

No, he didn't want to go into that here. He could drink a bottle of wine, and it still wouldn't be enough to lubricate him into speaking about it.

"What if you don't have anything to complain about?"

"There's always something. My something is Nikki's trying to get me to go to some kind of singles mixer before Thanksgiving. You know what kinds of people go to those?"

"Single?" Nikki laughed and plopped Princess Snowflake onto the floor.

"Desperate," Alyssa said, then took a deep swallow of wine.

"Pfffft. Right. Where the hell else are you supposed to meet people?"

"Cosmo says to meet them at the grocery store, at the juice bar, that kind of thing. The gym."

"Yeah, that works. Come on. If you met a guy at the grocery store it would be melon jokes for the rest of your life. You should write a book about finding love online and set up a profile for research."

"I don't want to meet a man."

Dane's eyes moved back and forth between the two women.

"One day you'll get lonely," Nikki told her, squeezing

her hand. Nikki worried about her friend, and Dane liked her even more. He was in a hell of a lot of trouble.

"Look, here's my Whine for Whine and Wine Wednesday—every man I meet eventually tells me I'm fat, and he doesn't want to be with me unless I lose a few pounds. I'm done trying."

"They're idiots," Nikki snapped. "You're fine."

Alyssa glared at Dane. "I'm not even going to ask you what you think."

"That would be . . ." Dane swallowed. "I don't think I would say the right thing anyway."

Alyssa burst out laughing. "Probably not. You're definitely between a rock and a hard place here."

"Thanks for admitting it." Dane grinned, deciding he liked Alyssa. She told it like it was.

"Besides, you don't need to go to a mixer now that Eric called you."

"He's an ex," Nikki explained when she caught his puzzled gaze. "He broke up with me to date someone else, and he called the other day wanting to meet up. He said it didn't work out, and he regretted calling off our relationship."

"It's a good thing," Alyssa said, patting Nikki's arm. "You were pretty bummed when he broke up with you, and now you get a second chance."

"Yeah," Nikki murmured.

Princess Snowflake jumped onto Dane's lap again. He ran his hand along her soft fur as she walked around in tiny circles on his thighs, pushing her paws into his running pants, finally settling down, resting her head on his stomach.

"If you're going to crash Whine and Wine, you have to at least share one thing," Alyssa said, shifting her attention back to him and kicking his shin under the table.

Dane grimaced. She wasn't going to let him get out of it. It was his fault for knocking on Nikki's door. He turned to Nikki for support, but she was staring into her wine glass and wouldn't meet his eyes.

"I hate the holidays because I end up spending them alone, or playing drinking games with Brett."

Humiliated, he picked up his wine and chugged the remainder. He didn't know how in the hell Alyssa managed to get him to admit that.

"Brett doesn't have family in the area?" Nikki asked, reaching over to pet her cat.

Dane fought the urge to jerk away. Her hand was too close to his cock, and he imagined how it would feel if she stroked him the way she was caressing her kitten.

Standing to pour more wine from a new bottle, Alyssa asked, "Who's Brett?"

"Are you trying to get me drunk?" Dane asked, grateful for the distraction as she filled his glass.

"You give good Whine." Alyssa patted his shoulder.

"Brett is the Tower City Marathon director and a friend of mine. He was a late-in-life baby, and his parents hadn't expected to have children. His mom was like, almost fifty when she found out she was pregnant. They weren't close while he was growing up. He always felt like an accident, and they treated him like one. Now they live in a senior living community and prefer to spend the holidays with their friends."

It was a lot easier to talk about Brett's problems than his own.

"That's too bad," Nikki said, finally looking at him.

"You two should spend Thanksgiving with Nik and me. My parents live in Florida, and I'm not visiting them this year. Nikki's parents are going on a cruise and won't be here. The four of us could cook and watch the parade. No one should have to be alone during the holidays."

"I'll ask him. I appreciate it. It sounds a lot better than spending it with Jack."

"Who's that?" Nikki frowned.

Dane chuckled. "Jack Daniel's. Booze."

"Oh! Bring him along if you like. Though Alyssa and I prefer wine. And we'll have lots of coffee, of course."

"I better get going. I'm sorry I crashed your party, but it was fun."

"It was nice meeting you," Alyssa said.

"You too." Dane stood up.

Nikki followed him to the door.

"Hey, are you all right?" Dane asked, staring into her eyes. Not wanting Alyssa to see them, he leaned against the door, out of Alyssa's sight.

Nikki shook her head and stepped into his embrace.

She shuddered as he put his arms around her. He was surprised by her display of affection; he thought holding her on her couch was the last time he'd get to do this. "It will be okay."

"I don't know what I'm doing," she said, resting her cheek against his shoulder.

Nikki had to make her own choices. He couldn't pressure her into a relationship; he could lose her forever if he rushed, pushing her into something she wasn't ready for.

But he loved holding her like this, breathing in the scent of . . . she smelled like pumpkin tonight. His chin rested on the top of her head. "Pumpkins," he murmured.

"For fall."

When she looked up at him, Dane fell into her eyes and drowned in their blue depths. Pain and hesitancy, mixed with a little confusion, shadowed her expression, and he smoothed the worry from the corners of her eyes, lightly running his fingertips over her skin.

"It will be okay. I promise." He pressed a kiss to her forehead. "Have fun with Alyssa. She's been drinking a lot, I hope she's staying here."

Nikki nodded.

"Good. Goodnight, Nik. I'll see you tomorrow."

"Okay. Bye."

Unable to stop touching her, Dane rubbed his thumb along her cheekbone. "Bye."

Princess Snowflake mewed pitifully by the door as it closed behind him.

Huh. There was something there, and maybe, if he was patient enough, she would stop fighting it and give him a chance.

A thought chilled him. Unless she picked up where she left off with that jerk, Eric.

Then they were finished before they could even start.

* * *

"I know, baby," Nikki said to the kitten, bending down to pick her up after the door closed behind Dane. "I know how you feel." Childishly, she stomped into the kitchen. "Why did you have to mention Eric to Dane?"

"Why not?" Alyssa narrowed her eyes. "You're not dating Dane and don't want to. Why not mention another guy? There's nothing between you, is there? You weren't *kissing*, were you?"

"No! He kissed my forehead when he said goodbye, that's all."

"He wants more, Nik. He looked hurt when I mentioned Eric."

"I can't. I want it, but I can't. What if things didn't work out? I don't have the best track record going for me, you know that. What if things went horribly wrong, and we broke up? How could I go to work every day? How could I live here? He lives right next door for Christ's sake. Most of my life depends on my relationship with him now—it's ridiculous. I don't know how I got so tangled up with him, but I would be a fool to mess with that. It's better to leave things how they are."

"But what if you took a chance, Nik? What if it *did* work out? What if he fell in love with you and wanted to marry you? What if he wanted to give you the kids you want? What if he's The One? You're going to throw that away?"

"What if he ruins my life?"

"And what if . . . he doesn't?"

NIKKI LOVED WORKING at the store. She knew all the policies and procedures, and she learned how to recommend shoes for their customers as Dane said she would. During the slow times, she continued to work on the employee handbook.

Brett came in often, and he and Dane would sit for hours locked in Dane's office.

One sunny morning an older gentleman came into the empty store.

"Morning," she said, typing a new policy into her laptop. "If there's anything I can help you with let me know."

She always took a mild approach to helping customers. Sometimes they wanted to browse the clothing and running aids such as belts and water bottles, or they came in for anti-chafing sticks and energy gels. If they needed shoes they told her right away as all their stock was stored in back and customers needed her to retrieve their sizes.

"I actually need a new pair of shoes, and I was wondering if you could teach me how to run."

"Teach you?" Nikki quickly tapped a few keys to save the progress on the handbook.

He shuffled toward her, his faded blue eyes twinkling. He wore loose-fitting running pants, a t-shirt, and an unzipped windbreaker.

"My doctor said if I want to keep running I need to fix my posture. I have back and neck pain when I run. He recommended someone watch me and tell me what I'm doing wrong. Do you think you could help me, young lady?"

"Of course. Let's set you up with new shoes first. Are the ones you've been running in working for you?"

She watched the man walk, analyzed his gate, and recommended a pair of shoes from a different brand than what he'd been wearing previously.

He tried them on, walked the length of the store, and told her they were comfortable.

"Perfect. I'll meet you in the parking lot," she said, then after a quick knock on Dane's door, peeked her head into his office. "I'll be outside for a second."

Nikki left Dane's door open so he could listen for customers, and sprinted outside to help her customer. This was the part of her job she liked best, and she hoped Dane didn't mind.

"Ooookay," Dane agreed, and shrugging, he turned his attention back to Brett.

"What's she doing?" Brett asked, the bell tinkling as Nikki left the store.

Curiosity getting the better of him, Dane said, "I don't know, let's go see."

Through the front window, they watched Nikki standing with an older man. She gestured for him to run in an empty section of the parking lot.

Dane leaned against the glass and smiled when she shook her head. She looked adorable in her running pants and a TCRC polo shirt. Today she had her hair up in a ponytail but wore a TCRC baseball cap, her hair threaded through the hole in the back. She straightened the man's back with one hand between his shoulder blades and the other pressed against his chest, and she gestured to him to look ahead while he ran, not at the ground.

Brett whistled.

"What?" Dane asked, not taking his eyes off her. She was running now, showing him proper posture. She looked ahead, her back straight, her elbows bent, loose by her sides. She had a terrific gate for a runner.

"You finally did it, man. I didn't think you would after the way Liz screwed you over."

"What?"

"You're in love with her. I can't believe it."

Dane squinted against the sunlight.

Nikki studied the man as he ran with the suggested adjustments. She nodded and high-fived him when he was done. She spoke with him for a few more moments then waved goodbye.

"No, I'm not," Dane said, annoyed. He liked spending

time with her, he wanted to sleep with her, there was no denying that, but no one, *no one,* said anything about love.

Brett slapped his shoulder as Nikki opened the door of the store. "Yeah, you are. See you later, Coach Nikki," Brett said with a wink as he stepped onto the sidewalk.

"Brett's done working with you already?" Nikki asked, taking her place behind the counter.

"Yeah, for now, I guess. What were you doing out there?"

"Oh, he needed help with his posture. I recommended he join a gym and do some cross-training to strengthen his back and abdominal muscles. Running was hurting him, and his doctor told him to get some help. I could see why. When he ran, he was twisting himself into a pretzel."

"That was nice of you to help him. You could have sent him on his way."

"Nah. I wouldn't do that. He bought shoes, and he's going to join the running group. You know," she said, "the store doesn't have a Facebook page or a Twitter account, only the website."

"I haven't had time," he snapped. "I've been too busy trying to make the store turn a profit, and I was forced to set up the website for online sales. Social media hasn't exactly been a priority."

"I wasn't criticizing you. I was asking permission to do it myself. I can use the store's email address to create the accounts, and you can moderate the activity whenever you want. It will help with sales, too, get the store's name out there more. And the runners who are in the running group could chat on the page like they do on Brett's marathon Facebook page."

"Whatever you think."

"I didn't mean to make you mad." Nikki pulled at the end of her ponytail.

"It wasn't you."

It was Brett and his stupid ideas.

He wasn't in love with her. Damn Brett for putting that in his head.

He hid in his office for the rest of the day.

NIKKI FINISHED HER shift, and at five, when the evening person came in, she handed over the counter and changed for her date with Eric. She regretted now saying she would go.

She remembered how it felt being held in Dane's arms the night he crashed Whine and Wine Wednesday.

It'd felt good, and he seemed to understand her confusion.

He stayed away from her, respecting her decision to keep their relationship professional. She was the one who'd stepped into his arms, and she'd been relieved when he hugged her to him.

Nikki wanted that.

She wished she had a crystal ball that could tell her a relationship with Dane would work out if she took the leap.

"I'm heading out in a minute," she told Dane, leaning into his office.

Pushing his chair away from his desk, he said, "You clean up nice, I have to admit."

His smile seemed forced, and she felt horrible she told Eric he could pick her up at the store. "I, ah, prefer my running gear, to be honest. Anyway, have a great weekend."

Through the window in Dane's office, she caught sight of Eric's Mercedes. "There's my ride."

"Nice car," Dane muttered. "I suppose he's going to take you somewhere fancy to try to get back onto your good side."

"Glass House," she said, staring at the floor, too embarrassed to meet his eyes.

She hadn't intended to make Dane jealous or to rub in his face how much money Eric made, but what else would he think when Eric drove his Mercedes to pick her up and take her to the most expensive restaurant in Tower City?

"I better not keep him waiting. Night."

She was an insensitive jerk, and she wanted the ground to swallow her whole.

Pushing back tears, she fled.

As the door thumped closed behind her, Nikki shakily drew in a deep breath of autumn air, and she took just a second to calm her nerves as Eric climbed out of the car.

"Hey," he said, opening the passenger door for her. "It's nice to see you again. You look fantastic." He kissed her cheek, his breath feathering over her skin.

"Thanks. It's good to see you too."

Settling in her seat, the smooth leather molding to her body, Nikki sighed, conscious Dane was watching them through his office window.

With guilt weighing on her, she smiled at Eric as he eased behind the steering wheel, wishing the night were already over.

DANE WATCHED NIKKI's date open her door. He kissed her cheek before she slipped inside, but her head was turned and he couldn't see her smile at him. As Dane was sure she did.

There was no way he could compete. He gathered up his things to leave for the day. Glass House, a Mercedes. What did the guy do for a living? Real estate like Liz's new husband? Developing? There was money to be made there; Tower City grew by the thousands every year.

There was nothing he could do about it, except tonight he was getting good and drunk.

Eric pulled out her chair in the restaurant's dining room decorated in understated colors of black, grey, and a greyish-blue. A shiny lacquer covered their black table, and it glinted in the soft light appearing almost silver as it rained down from the gleaming fixtures.

First, they'd stopped for drinks at Rhapsody, an upscale bar not far from Glass House. They were early for a Friday night and had been able to avoid the line, Eric would've been able to get them past the bouncer anyway. A fifty here, a hundred there, money didn't matter to him because he had so much of it, but that wasn't why she'd dated him before, and it wasn't why she'd decided to give him another chance.

She studied him over the candle flame centered on their table in a perfect glass house, the fire making the sides of the house glimmer, a small open chimney allowing the heat to escape.

Eric's black hair curled over the collar of his dress shirt, the front swept back from his forehead. His eyes were a sparkling hazel, crinkling in the corners when he smiled. His nose was strong, the perfect size for his face. Eric's teeth were flawless—his parents spent thousands of dollars on his smile. While they'd been dating, he'd mentioned it a time or two.

With their occupations and social circles, they shared few things in common, and she wondered, not for the first time, what he saw in her.

She'd met him working her HR job for the Tower City Public Utilities office. He'd come in for a meeting and talked with her until it was time for his appointment. After he'd called her, she realized he'd taken one of her business cards from her desk when she'd turned away to answer her phone.

"I think you're even more gorgeous than the last time I saw you," he complimented her, smoothing his tie. "Champagne?"

Nikki raised her eyebrows. "Are we celebrating?"

Eric raised a hand, and the waiter hurried over. "Maybe. A bottle of your best, please."

Nikki relaxed as they ordered, and she listened to him say all the right things. She was surprised at all the details he remembered about her life, and as they ate, she answered his questions.

"You can't make much money working there," Eric said, frowning, after ordering them coffees and a slice of choco-late cake to share. "I'm sure you took a pay cut leaving the utility company."

"I did. And Shine wanted me back, too. Dane tipped them off I was returning to retail when he called my district manager as a reference. Lissette offered me an obscene amount of money to straighten out the store. They've lost a couple managers since I left, and the place is a mess. The shopping center isn't happy."

Eric frowned. His olive colored dress shirt made the

green of his eyes more pronounced, and they snapped with distaste. "But now you live next door to Dane and work in his store? I don't understand." He took a sip of coffee.

Faintly, Nikki smiled, relieved the decision of whether or not to keep dating Eric was taken out of her hands.

All those months ago he'd realized what she had not—they were not a good match.

To Eric, success was measured in money and status, not happiness. Alexa hadn't worked out for him, but he would soon find another woman like her. A woman who wanted to wear the designer clothes, who wanted to hostess the parties Eric was required to throw for his company. His wife would be perfectly made up, bear him the perfect children, who would be raised by the perfect nanny, who would supervise the cleaning staff that would clean their perfect house.

That wasn't her.

She was Flix Roulette on the couch with popcorn . . . and Dane. In her perfect little apartment with her perfect little kitten, secure in her perfect little job in her perfect little world.

"I lost you. Where did you go?" Eric sighed and pushed the dessert plate closer to her. "You've met someone, haven't you?"

Nikki opened her mouth to deny it.

"No, don't bother, Nik. I can see it on your face. You were gone. You were thinking about him." He chuckled. "Snooze you lose, right?"

"I might have met someone." She took another bite of cake. "But he doesn't have anything to do with us. You knew before I did we weren't going to work out. This is all really nice," she said, lifting her arms to encompass the restaurant, "but it isn't me."

"I didn't appreciate that about you when I had it. If we

were together, you would ground me. You would keep me sane. You would make sure I knew what was important and wouldn't let me get carried away."

Nikki covered his hand with hers. "After a while, you would hate that, hate *me*, for holding you back. You like it here."

He flipped his hand over and laced their fingers. "Yeah. I do. Are you finished? I'll drive you back to your car."

"It was nice to catch up with you," she said as they drove the busy streets to Dane's store. "I'm glad you called, even if it didn't work out."

He pulled into the Tower City Running Company parking lot and idled next to her car. "Me too," Eric said, the orange glow of the lights drifting through his windshield. He placed his lips against hers. "Nothing?"

Nikki laughed and patted his cheek. "Nothing. Sorry, Eric."

He groaned. "I guess I'll live. Be careful driving home and thanks for meeting me. Goodnight."

"Goodnight, and thanks for the meal. It was lovely."

Nikki slid out of his car. She didn't notice Eric drive away as she leaned against her vehicle to search in her purse for her keys.

The October breeze chilled her bare legs, and her shoes were killing her. She shouldn't even be wearing the dumb things, but she loved how they made her legs look.

She sighed. It was late, she was tired, and she wanted to go home.

A loud crash from inside the store startled her, and she jerked her head toward the noise, almost dropping her purse in surprise. Sucking in a deep breath, she grabbed for her phone to call 911. Someone was stealing from Dane, from his store, and she couldn't let that happen.

Wait.

Maybe it was Dane checking on something. She approached the building, her heels clicking against the pavement. She tried to look through the tinted windows, but she couldn't see anything. The track lights they kept on for security were dark.

She was about to use her key to open the front door, but it was already cracked open.

"Dane?" she called, her thumb hovering over the connect button for 911. "Dane?"

A figure behind the counter was bent over the register.

"Hey, what are you doing here?" In the dark, one of her heels caught on the long rug laying in front of the door, and she stumbled.

A tall man dressed in black stepped from the register. He held a fistful of cash, and his features were hidden by a mask over his mouth and a stocking cap sitting low on his forehead. Only his black beady eyes were visible, and they pinned her to the floor as he strode toward her.

"Who are you? What are you doing in here?" Nikki didn't think to be afraid. Tower City was a low crime city, and she'd never felt scared living there. Not even on her runs in the dark. "I'm calling the cops."

A loud crash came from the backroom, and when she turned that way, the thief backhanded her.

The right side of her face exploded in pain, and she crumpled to the floor, her head spinning, stars dancing behind her eyes.

Her thumb pressed 'connect' before she lost consciousness.

CHAPTER FOUR

Dane trembled with rage. After he answered the call from the officers who first arrived at the store, he jumped into his car and drove like hell.

They said a woman who claimed to be his store manager was being treated in an ambulance in the parking lot, and could he see her home? She'd interrupted a burglary in progress, and two others were being detained.

Nikki sitting in an ambulance meant she was hurt. If she had interrupted someone stealing from the store the bastard would have done anything to keep from getting caught.

He prayed like hell she was okay. He would die before she was hurt protecting his store. His stupid store. It wasn't worth her life.

Thank God he hadn't gotten drunk like he'd planned. Instead, he'd tired himself out with a fifteen-mile run, took a long shower, and was in bed, lights out, before midnight.

It wasn't the greatest way to spend a Friday night, but since he'd broken up with Holly, it was his usual. He didn't want to think about Nikki and what she was doing with Mr. Rolex.

Bright blue and red lights from the police cruisers swirled in the parking lot when he pulled in. He wanted to go straight to the ambulance but was waylaid by a detective who wanted to speak with him.

"Dane Montgomery?" the plainclothes detective asked after he stepped out of his truck.

"Yeah. Nikki, my manager—"

"She's being looked over," the detective interrupted him. "I would appreciate it if you would try to identify the two thieves who were caught in your store by Miss Halstead."

Dane bit back a growl of frustration. "Yeah, sure."

"Also, I'll need you to go to the station afterward to take your statement."

"Whatever you need . . . Detective?" Dane asked, unsure.

"Detective Walker, I apologize," the detective said, flashing a badge he didn't bother to look at. The cop led him to a police car with the lights still flashing and the engine running. A uniform sat in the front waiting to leave.

People from surrounding apartment buildings and businesses still open at that hour, mainly bars and restaurants that served cocktails, were gathered in the parking lot to watch the commotion. News crews filmed the scene. Uncomfortable and aware several people were watching him, he shuffled behind the detective.

Detective Walker opened the rear car door and allowed him to peer inside.

"Daniel?" Dane asked in disbelief, glaring at his part-time sales associate and a man sitting next to him. Both young men had their hands cuffed behind their backs.

"What the hell, man?" He scrubbed his face. "Did you hurt Nikki?"

"No! I would never hurt—" Daniel yelled.

Detective Walker slammed the door. "You know those punks then?"

Dane nodded. "I know Daniel Ortiz. He works for me. Worked for me." Daniel wouldn't be going anywhere near his store, not ever again. "I don't know the other guy. What do I have to do now?"

The detective wrote something inside a small spiral notebook. His hair was going grey, and he wore a blue shirt with a blue and grey striped tie. He didn't wear a jacket to ward off the chill, only a grey suit coat, and a forgotten pair of Wayfarer sunglasses on the top of his head.

"The young woman who stopped . . ." the detective consulted his notebook, ". . . William Ortiz, took a nifty little knock to the side of her face. We can confirm she works for you?" Detective Walker met Dane's eyes and Dane nodded.

"We'll have guys in your place to dust for prints, and you'll need to take the inventory, though we don't think anything was moved off the property. The cash Mr. Ortiz took from your register has been confiscated and bagged for evidence. You'll get it back eventually, after those punks are booked and charged. The young woman is a bit shaken. We've already spoken with her, and I've taken her statement. We may need to speak with her again, but for now, we can have an officer accompany her home."

"I'll do it and make sure she's not left alone, then I'll go to the station. I'll cooperate, Detective Walker," Dane said, holding out his hand for a handshake, "but I want to make sure for myself Nikki gets home safely."

Detective Walker looked Dane in the eye. He didn't hide how he felt about her, and the detective nodded, his eyes narrowed, obviously understanding she was more to Dane than only an employee.

"I would appreciate it. Miss Halstead is in the ambulance with an ice pack. The EMT said she wouldn't need any more medical care other than some OTC pain meds and another ice pack."

"I'll take care of her. Will I ask for you at the station?"

"Yeah, please. I'll be driving straight there. You know," Detective Walker said, "we only caught them because Miss Halstead had the presence of mind to dial 911, and an off-duty officer who was eating a late dinner with his wife in the restaurant across the parking lot heard the call. You were lucky." He chuckled. "Though I'll never understand what they thought they were going to do with a hundred pairs of running shoes. It takes all kinds."

Dane ignored the detective's mumbling.

An officer stepped out of his line of sight.

Nikki sat in the back of an ambulance, her legs hanging off the edge. Black stilettos were strapped to her feet; a shiny black purse sat next to her on the ambulance floor. The hem of her black dress rode up her thighs, and a light blue dress coat slid off her shoulder. She held a disposable ice pack to her face, and her head hung low, as if she were crying. Her hair had been pinned into a messy knot on the top of her head, but now the pins were falling out and her curls were escaping down her neck. Earrings glinted in the lights from the cop cars still parked in the lot.

Nikki looked exactly like the elegant ladies Liz had always aspired to be. Money couldn't buy class. Liz could chase the gleam all she wanted, but she would never match Nikki's shine.

She looked up and spotted him. "Dane!" she cried and struggled to stand.

A female EMT stopped her from trying to jump off the back of the ambulance.

Dane hurried across the remainder of the parking lot and enveloped her in his arms. "You stupid little girl," he murmured into her hair, one hand rubbing her back, the other hand on the back of her head, pushing her face into his chest. "You stupid little girl. Don't you know what it would do to me if anything happened to you? You stupid, stupid, little girl." Dane choked, and he was forced to stop talking.

Nikki pulled back, and Dane suppressed a groan. The right side of her face was beginning to darken into a deep purple bruise.

Noticing his dismay, the EMT reassured him, "Her cheekbone isn't broken. The swelling would be a lot worse if it were. The jerk didn't hit her that hard—she was lucky. She could have had a concussion or a broken jaw. She'll need some pain reliever, but that's all. You can bring her home. She said she was here to pick up her car, but I don't advise her driving. She's still pretty shaken up."

"I'll take her home, thank you." Dane nodded at the woman, wishing she would go away.

Nikki frantically searched his eyes. "I'm sorry," she sobbed, her hands fluttering at her sides in agitation. "I'm sorry. I didn't know. I thought you were doing something and I went inside to see if you needed help. I couldn't see— he'd turned the track lighting off. By the time I realized it wasn't you, he'd already spotted me. I called the police—"

"Shh, shh," Dane whispered, cradling her against his chest. "I'm not mad at you. Shh. I was so goddamned worried when I got the call. I didn't know what was going on. The officer who called me wouldn't tell me anything over the phone. It scared the shit out of me."

Nikki wiped her eyes. "You're not mad at me?"

"No, baby. This wasn't your fault. I'm damned glad you're okay." He framed her face in his palms and looked into her eyes. "Really, if something happened to you, I don't know what I'd do." He kissed the top of her head. "You wanna blow this popsicle stand?"

Nikki offered him a watery smile. "Yeah."

"I'll drive you home, okay? We'll pick up your car later." Dane put one arm under her knees and lifted her gently into his arms. "It's okay, I've got you."

Nikki tucked her head under his chin, and he sighed.

<hr />

DANE HELPED NIKKI change into pajamas, gave her some ibuprofen, and settled her into bed. He smoothed her hair from her forehead and kissed her bruised cheek. "Try to get some rest."

Reluctant to leave her by herself to go to the police station, he went into the kitchen and grabbed Nikki's purse. He found her phone and brought it to life, thankful it wasn't password protected. He didn't remember Alyssa's last name, but he searched Nikki's recent calls. Eric's number at the top of the list made him feel like shit, but he tried to ignore it and he pressed Alyssa's picture hoping she would answer.

A woman picked up right before voicemail answered the line. "Hello? Nikki? Why are you calling so late? Is everything okay?"

"Hey, Alyssa, it's Dane. Listen, things aren't okay. Nikki interrupted a burglary at the store, and she's a little roughed up. I have to go to the station and give them my statement and do some paperwork or something. I don't want her alone."

"You don't have to say anymore. I'll be right there."

The line went dead.

It wasn't ten minutes later when Dane opened the door for Alyssa. "Thanks for coming. I didn't want her by herself. She's sleeping right now, but—"

"It's no problem. What happened?" Alyssa took off her coat and hung it in the coat closet already at home in Nikki's apartment. She wore pajamas and hadn't taken the time to bring a purse.

"I'm not sure. Her date picked her up at the store, and I think she was grabbing her car."

Dane ran his fingers through his hair.

"We talked for a minute before I brought her home, and she told me she heard something and the security lights were off. She thought it was me and wanted to see what I was doing in the store so." He rolled his shoulders. "Some asshole was robbing the register when she caught him. He hit her to get away, but she was still able to call 911. One of my employees was cleaning out my stockroom."

Alyssa hissed in sympathy. "I'm sorry."

"All I care about is that Nikki's going to be okay. The EMT said she'll be fine, she'll only need more painkiller once the stuff she's taken wears off. Her cheek looks bad. I don't care how many pairs of shoes . . . Those bastards." He checked the time on his phone. "I need to get to the station. I want those bastards to pay for what they did."

"I'll stay with her tonight, don't worry about it."

His eyes went flat. Of course he wouldn't be coming back. He'd go home, to his own apartment, after he was finished at the station. He nodded, not meeting her eyes. "Yeah. I'll go home after I'm done then."

Alyssa sighed. "I didn't mean it like that. I meant, take all the time you need." She reached out to smooth his arm, but he pulled away and opened the door.

Dane shook his head. "No, it's fine. She doesn't want me here. Goodnight, Alyssa, thanks for staying with her."

NIKKI SAT UP, gasping. She dreamt she was on the floor of the store, the cold tile beneath her cheek, loud voices buzzing around her head. The stretcher. Someone checking her heartbeat. A woman asking if Nikki could hear her.

"It's okay. I'm right here."

"Alyssa." Nikki breathed a sigh of relief. "How did you know?"

Alyssa pushed Nikki down onto the pillow. To pass the time she'd been reading one of Nikki's books in the dim light of the bedside lamp. "Dane called me to sit with you. He had to talk to the police, and he didn't want you alone."

Nikki rolled over onto her side and met Alyssa's eyes. "He's not coming back, is he?"

"No. He thinks you don't want him here."

Tears leaked from her eyes, and she buried her face into her pillow. Her brain was fuzzy from lack of sleep, and even with the extra painkiller Dane gave her before she fell asleep, her cheek throbbed. "Why would he think that?"

"How was your date with Eric?"

"Oh."

"Yeah, oh. How *was* your date with Eric? I take it with all this concern for Dane you didn't get back together with him?"

"We wouldn't last. Not for the long haul. He knew that when he broke up with me. He wanted to give it another try, but I didn't see the point. He's champagne and caviar. I'm Clif Bars and Gatorade."

Alyssa rubbed her shoulder. "I don't know what you're looking for, but you've got a good guy hanging around and I think he could be what you want, what you need."

"You think so?"

Setting the book on the bedside table, Alyssa nodded. "Yeah, I do. He looked like shit when I got here. He was worried about you."

"No. He was worried about his store."

"Are you deliberately being obtuse? Did that asshole knock all the sense out of your head? Keep this up and you'll lose him. Of course Dane was worried about you. He called me to sit with you because he didn't want you to be alone. A jerk wouldn't have cared and would've left without a second thought. Stop being a bitch now and give him some credit. He's in love with you. Get your shit together and either reciprocate or cut him loose and break your own fucking heart."

Alyssa's blunt words made her wince.

Dane's face, etched with worry when he rescued her from the ambulance, came back to her. He said didn't know what he would do if something happened to her. Alyssa was right—Dane did care about her. She was scared to take the chance, but he would eventually give up and she couldn't let him do that.

In light of what happened, Dane being her boss seemed like a small thing now. All it took was a fist to the face to see it.

"I'm sorry." Alyssa sighed. "That was uncalled for. Especially this late, and after what you've been through. You should try to get some more sleep. Dane wanted to sit with you, but he's at the police station now and probably will be for most of the night, then he'll need to get some sleep, too."

Wrapping the blanket closer around her shoulders, Nikki burrowed her head into the pillow. "You're right. I'll help him with the store tomorrow. I'll see him tomorrow."

Alyssa shut off the light. "And the day after that, and the day after that, if you want it."

IT WAS A hell of a night.

Dane called two of his employees and left them messages saying they wouldn't need to work their weekend shifts. Being closed would cut into his revenue, but there was nothing he could do. He needed to order a new register, take inventory. He needed to call the security company and ask them to look over the system and to change the security codes.

After he was through at the station, he drove back to the store. Even at that hour, the roads were busy and he forced himself to focus on the traffic. The last thing he needed was to rear end someone because he wasn't paying attention. He tried not to picture Nikki lying on the floor, and he angrily clutched his truck's steering wheel.

In his office, he used the printer to make a sign, and he taped it to the front door to let customers know the store would be closed indefinitely due to unforeseen circumstances.

He was setting the alarm, praying it would do its job, when his cell phone rang. Hoping it wasn't Alyssa calling about Nikki, he grabbed it quickly. He almost didn't answer when he saw Brett's name, but if Brett heard the news, he'd be worried.

"Hey."

"You sound like shit, but I was watching TV and saw what happened, so I guess you have an excuse. Are you all right? The store wasn't open, was it? Was anyone hurt?"

"No, the store was closed. The thief was one of my employees, hoping to clean out the back. He brought a buddy who decided to pry into my register. Nikki was picking up her car from the parking lot and thought it was me. She got a little roughed up when she went in to check to see if I needed help, but she managed to call 911. Without her, the cops said they would have gotten away."

Brett groaned. "That's fucked up. Is she going to be all right? Are you with her now? Should I let you go?"

"No. I'm at the store. I'm going to have to contact the insurance company, take inventory, and call the security alarm people to come out here. I don't know when I'll be able to reopen. Nikki's got a friend with her. I was about to head home."

"Well, let me know if you need anything."

"Will do."

Dane didn't sleep much. He lay in the dark and rubbed his eyes. He was falling for a woman who had no interest in him whatsoever, and he let go of a sure thing in Holly for Nikki.

It was only the loneliness talking; he would never purposely use someone. But thanks to Holly, he'd forgotten what it felt like to be alone. Maybe it was a good thing to be alone for a while. Put his head on straight.

Dane propped himself on his elbows. A muffled sound, almost like a mewling, filtered through the wall and he unashamedly put his ear to the cool surface.

Nikki was crying. There was another voice, a low

murmuring sound, and Dane figured it was Alyssa, calming her down.

It would make sense for Nikki to have nightmares. He wondered if she'd call Mr. Rolex to spend the day with her tomorrow. She'd seemed okay when he put her to bed, but being assaulted would stay with her for a while, and she wouldn't want to be alone.

He wouldn't blame her if she was too scared to go to work, or if she wanted to avoid working at night because she wouldn't want to be at the store after dark. Maybe she would even quit.

Dane hoped she wouldn't sue him.

That would be perfect.

Her crying faded, and he hoped Alyssa had been able to help her fall back asleep.

He wished like hell he could be there with her, that she wanted him there with her.

Dane gave up on sleep. He kept listening for her to wake, and he heard her two more times throughout the early morning.

Finally he rolled out of bed and was brewing coffee when a knock sounded on his door. Alyssa stood in the hallway wearing her coat and holding her car keys.

"Nikki's dozing," she said, then bit her lip.

"What?" Dane tensed, his fingers gripping his mug.

"It's not my place, but . . . thank you for not calling Eric last night. She didn't get back together with him. I know it's not any of my business, but Nikki has a lot of integrity, you know? Personal ethics. She likes you, but she doesn't want to. She thinks it will complicate things. You're her boss, and well, she's not like that."

"You don't have to say anymore, but I can't stop talking to her. She hasn't been at the store for long. As soon as she's more comfortable, I can be there less, but I'm still teaching her how to run the place."

"You think I'm not on your side, but I am. I wasn't warning you to stay away from her. I was telling you because that's the only thing standing in your way. She likes you, and if you have the patience, you can wear her down. I shouldn't even be telling you this because it's none of my business," she repeated, taking a step back. "I have to go. I didn't get any sleep."

"I heard her crying a of couple times."

"Yeah, she did. Can you stay with her today? She wants you to."

"I was hoping."

"Okay. I'll tell you one more thing, then I'll never interfere again. She wants it all: the ring, the house, the dog, the kids. Maybe not in that order, but it's what she's always wanted. If you don't, let her find someone who does, okay? Bye."

"Bye, and thanks." Not wanting to waste any time, he didn't wait for Alyssa to disappear down the hall before letting himself inside Nikki's apartment.

Princess Snowflake mewed at his feet, and he picked her up. She began to purr against his chest. He checked on Nikki and found her tossing and turning. Going with his instincts, he crawled between the sheets next to her, plopping the kitten on her pillow. The cat settled in, and her purring filled the room.

Dane wrapped his arms around her, fitting his body close to hers, and she calmed in his arms. The faint morning light snuck through the cheap blinds covering the windows and highlighted her purple and puffy cheek. After brushing a light kiss across her temple, he fell asleep.

Nikki turned onto her side and snuggled into the body holding her. "Hmmm," she breathed. "Dane." She knew his scent, and she was happy he was here in her . . . bed. She opened her eyes and pulled away.

In his sleep, he tightened his hold on her, and she allowed him to pull her toward his chest again. The cotton of his University of Minnesota Tower City sweatshirt was worn from several washings, and Nikki rested her bruised cheek against the soft material, inhaling the aroma of baby powder fabric softener.

She didn't remember when Alyssa left and Dane had taken her place. To have such wonderful friends made her a lucky woman. But Dane wanted more than friends, and Alyssa's advice finally sank in.

She would lose this man if she didn't get her shit together. Eventually, he would move on, and she would hate herself forever if she let that happen.

She was ready to trust him, to try to be more. They could date, spend time together outside the store and get to know each other better.

He kept secrets he hadn't shared with her, such as why he didn't celebrate the holidays with his parents, or why he had let himself get lost in a relationship with Holly when it hadn't meant anything.

She wanted to know if those were the things that put the sadness in his eyes. She wanted more Flix Roulette, more dinners, more mornings like this, after nights . . . She wanted Sunday brunch, game night with friends. She wanted those things with Dane.

But first, they needed to put the store back together again.

"Dane," she whispered, shaking his shoulder.

He nuzzled her hair. "Hmm?" he mumbled, his lips finding her temple, kissing her lightly.

"The store."

"Closed, baby. Go back to sleep."

"But . . ."

"Nothing we can do. Come here."

Nikki shivered when Dane reached beneath her pajama tank top and splayed his hand over her stomach. He didn't try to go any higher, and she was torn between being relieved and disappointed. She wanted him, and if he touched her, he would know, too. But he was a gentleman, and she'd been assaulted last night. He would never try to take advantage of her.

She let out a shuddery sigh.

His eyes cracked open. "You're not going back to sleep, are you?"

"No." She was still tired, but now she'd decided to take a chance on Dane, she didn't want to waste another minute, even if it was sleeping in his arms.

He rubbed her back, and she wiggled closer into his hard chest, their legs tangling beneath her sheets. "I heard you crying last night. Are you okay?"

Her heart melted at his concern, and she brushed his lips with hers. "I'm better now that you're here."

Dane rested his forehead against hers. "I didn't want to leave, so I did the next best thing. I'm sorry I couldn't be here."

"Thank you for calling Alyssa. I'm sorry about the store."

"I'm sorry you were hurt, baby. Listen, last night I was thinking, if you want to quit, or if you're not going to be comfortable working nights—"

"I'll never quit."

"I hoped you wouldn't, but goddamn, last night. Seeing you sitting in that ambulance, I couldn't breathe. I could barely think. Do you want to get out of here today? The weather is gorgeous, well, it's supposed to be. Let's get out of town for a while."

"Where?"

Dane pressed a kiss to her lips and Nikki closed her eyes in pleasure. "How about you let me worry about that." He ran a finger down her cheek. "Why don't you take a shower, get cleaned up. I'll go back to my apartment and pack what we need. Put on your running gear, okay?"

"I don't think I'm up for a run."

"I know. But you'll be more comfortable where we're going, okay?"

Nikki told herself to trust him. "Okay."

She suppressed a groan when he pulled away from her and rolled out of bed. She took a few minutes to breathe in his scent from the pillow. Princess Snowflake played with her hair, wrapping her claws around her curls.

Giggling, she pulled her hair free as the scent of coffee filled her bedroom.

Oh. She could love a man who made her coffee.

PACKING A LUNCH for Nikki and himself in a cooler he kept for days like this, Dane almost didn't hear his phone ringing. He'd left it in the bedroom on his dresser when he changed into fresh clothes.

He needed a shower but didn't want to leave Nikki alone for too long. Not wanting to miss the call, he dashed down the hallway and grabbed his phone. It could be the detective on the case, calling with news. He needed to reopen his store as quickly as possible.

"Hello?"

Through their thin wall, he heard water rush through the pipes as Nikki turned her shower on. He didn't know how long she'd be, and he wanted to be waiting for her when she finished.

"Dane. I'm sorry about your store. Is Nikki okay?"

Holly's voice came through his phone, and Dane gritted his teeth in frustration. He didn't want to be on the phone with her now.

"Thanks. She's okay. It could have been a lot worse, you know, when you walk into something like that. How did you find out so fast?" Dane wedged his phone between his cheek and shoulder and went back to making sandwiches.

"It made the front page of the Tower City Journal."

"Really? I haven't seen the paper yet. There were news crews there last night, too," Dane said, sliding the sandwiches into plastic bags. He dropped them into the cooler with a half bag of ice. When he bent to dig for chips in his cabinet, the phone bobbled, and he almost missed it when Holly asked, "Do you know who did it? The paper didn't say."

Straightening the phone, he shoved a bag of Doritos into the cooler on top of the sandwiches. He hoped Nikki's cheek didn't hurt her too much. Soup probably would have been a better option, but he didn't have time to do anything about it now.

"An employee of mine and one of his buddies. He'd been acting off lately, and I think it's because he was planning this and probably felt guilty as hell."

"That sucks," Holly murmured.

"I knew he was struggling financially, you know? Being

in school and working at the same time is hard, we've been there."

"No excuse, though. I'm glad Nikki will be okay."

"Yeah, thanks," Dane said, the phone slipping again. On impulse, he added two bananas in case Nikki needed something soft to chew.

"Well, I wanted to say I'm sorry. I know you must have a million things to do."

"I'm spending the day with Nikki. She's pretty shaken up. Thanks for calling."

Dane didn't give her a chance to say goodbye. He disconnected, slammed the lid closed on the cooler, and went to wait in Nikki's apartment for her to finish getting ready. He didn't want her alone for a second longer than she needed to be.

THEIR HANDS RESTING on the seat's blue fabric between them in his truck, Dane's fingers laced with Nikki's. She looked better after a shower, coffee, and a light breakfast. Her eyes were clear, and she wore makeup that completely covered her bruise. She looked as if last night never happened.

It had been tough to make himself roll out of her bed, but it was just as well—he hadn't expected Holly to call, and he didn't want to speak to her in front of Nikki. It was sweet of her, but he hoped she wouldn't make it a habit. No, he would rather have stayed in bed, cuddled with Nikki all morning, but he was eager to spend the day with her outside the city.

Alyssa had talked with Nikki, but he hadn't been prepared for the drastic change in her. He hoped her kissing him, her wanting to spend the day with him, meant she was considering a relationship.

"Where are we going?"

"Nope. I said it was a surprise." Dane's cooler slid around the bed of his old truck.

It wasn't a Mercedes, and he wondered what happened last night. When Eric picked her up at the store, Nikki seemed happy and boy, had she dressed for the lucky bastard. She'd looked spectacular last night.

He caught a glimpse of her out of the corner of his eye. She looked beautiful now, too, dressed like he asked in running capris, a Tower City Marathon running t-shirt, and a running jacket tied around her waist. She wore her TCRC baseball cap, her ponytail threaded through the back.

But she cut Eric loose, and he wanted to know why.

Eric had everything he thought Nikki wanted, what *all* women wanted. The money, the status, the clothes, the car. He probably lived in a penthouse downtown or a mini-mansion in one of the new developments outside the city.

Doubt began to creep in. What was she doing with him in his piece of shit truck, looking forward to his surprise?

He scoffed.

Yeah, his surprise.

He didn't have any money to take her anywhere. He couldn't take her on shopping sprees at her favorite stores, wouldn't be taking her to Glass House tonight for dinner. Wouldn't be surprising her with expensive lingerie before a night of hot sex in the most luxurious hotel Tower City had to offer. Wouldn't be giving her diamonds with her mimosa at a trendy brunch the next day.

He felt stupid, but it was too late to back out. They were almost there, and Nikki would want an explanation if he turned the truck around. Then he would feel like even more of an idiot than he already did.

He held in a sigh and turned onto the road that would take them to Eagle Pass State Park.

Miles and miles of running trails snaked around the park. There were bridges over the Eagle Pass River, a campground with a shelter in case they needed to use the facilities, and quiet.

He drove past the cabin office where visitors paid for a parking pass. He paid for a yearly pass, and the orange sticker was already stuck to the inside of his windshield. He ran there often, and Nikki did too, but she'd been busy moving and learning how to manage the store, and he took the chance she hadn't been to the park for a while.

Apparently, no one else thought to visit today, but that suited Dane just fine, and he parked in the empty parking lot.

Her silence told him all he needed to know as she stared out the passenger side window at the trees dotting the edge of the lot. They were starting to lose their leaves and all shades of orange, yellow, gold, and brown fluttered over the ground.

The sun blazed from the canvas of a blue sky, white clouds floating lazily by. It was a warm October day, and Dane had brought her to the middle of nowhere.

"Nikki, I'm sorry—"

"How did you know?" Nikki interrupted him, turning on the truck bench, tears in her eyes. "How did you know I needed to come out here?"

Dane released his seatbelt and moved closer to her. Gently, he framed her face in his palms. "Because after last night, I needed it, too."

She sniffled. "Thank you."

"You don't need to thank me. And we have all day. I brought lunch."

Nikki turned her head and kissed the center of his palm. "Let's go!"

THEY WALKED THE trails for hours, admiring the changing colors of the trees, rambling through miles of prairie and woods. At one point, they lost their direction and it was over three hours before they made their way back to Dane's truck for the cooler.

Neither of them complained.

The tranquility calmed her, and she breathed in a huge lungful of air. The wind blew gently, the sun shone brightly, and she was with Dane.

She couldn't have asked for a better day.

They both used the shelter restrooms before Dane laid out a blanket near the river.

Nikki spread out on top of it, taking off her cap and pulling the elastic out of her hair. She relaxed even more with the sound of the river moving swiftly along the rocks, the birds singing in the trees. Closing her eyes, she was grateful she could feel peace after last night.

Dane pushed a cold bottle of water into her hand.

She sighed in contentment; they hadn't run into another soul all morning. Despite the burglary, she was happier than she'd been in a long time. Somehow Dane had known she needed this and made it happen.

She'd been caught up in life, wasting time at Shine, going to school, working the HR job she eventually grew to hate.

Dane's presence in her life had given her back her

spark. She hadn't realized what she was missing, but now, because he'd taken a chance on her, she felt complete.

She didn't know how to express her gratitude or how to tell him how much she appreciated how thoughtful he was.

"Not hungry?" Dane asked, running his fingers over her bare arm.

Meeting his gaze, she shivered. They were alone, and though he hadn't made a move while they shared her bed, she worried about how much he wanted from her. She wasn't sure if she was ready for more, but she wanted him to kiss her.

They had a lot to talk about, too, but she didn't want to ruin the perfect day with a serious conversation. They had plenty of time to explore their relationship.

"Maybe. What do you have?"

"I brought some fruit, chips, I made sandwiches . . ." He trailed off. "Not your gourmet fare."

"It sounds perfect. This has been a lovely day. Thank you."

Dane moved the cooler, the melting ice clinking against the insides as he pushed it out of his way. He lay on his side, his head propped in his hand, and he huffed out an embarrassed laugh. "You know, you're the only woman I know besides Margie who would appreciate a day like this."

"You didn't bring Holly out here?" Nikki asked. They'd been together for a long time.

Dane snorted. "Are you kidding? She would have been bored to tears in two seconds flat. She's a city girl all the way."

It made Nikki feel better he hadn't brought Holly to the park. She wanted something that belonged to only them.

"What about you?" Dane asked, playing with her hair.

"I've never dated anyone who would want to come out

here. You're the first runner I've" —she rushed on, not ready to classify their relationship— "which is strange, you know? Running is such a large part of my life, you'd think it would be natural to date someone who's into it as much as I am."

"Same for me," Dane said. "Holly never cared I ran all the time, but then we didn't have the kind of relationship where she could call me on it even if it bothered her."

"I don't think I could do that. Have such a loose connection with someone." Nikki closed her eyes and tried to block out his words. She wasn't ready to talk about this.

"Hey," Dane said, turning her head to make her look at him.

Nikki snapped her eyes open.

"I'm not going to apologize for what I had with her. She gave me something I needed, and I took it. Maybe that makes me a jerk, but she let me. She could have walked anytime, and I would have understood. She was hoping it would turn into more, I realize that now, but I broke things off the minute I realized I had feelings for you."

He paused, drew in a breath.

"Well, to be honest, she saw it a lot faster than I did, and it didn't take her by surprise when I called it off. She took it as well as to be expected, but cutting ties with someone is always difficult, no matter what kind of relationship you have."

"I wasn't asking you for an explanation," she murmured, but he hadn't given her one.

"Well, I'm asking you for one," he said, keeping her head still, not allowing her look away. "I want to know what happened between you and Eric last night."

With her thumb, she wiped at the condensation on her water bottle. "We dated for a while. I thought it was going well, but . . . he owns his own software company, and I don't travel in those circles. When you're that rich, I guess there's pressure to date your own kind, and he broke it off with me to date the daughter of one of his clients. It didn't work out between them, and he wanted us to try again."

She snuggled into Dane's chest and stared over his shoulder, too embarrassed to meet his eyes while she talked about her relationship with another man.

When he rested his hand on her stomach, she blew out a breath.

"During dinner last night, he caught me daydreaming, and I was thinking about you. He asked me if I met someone, and I told him yes." She smiled as his grip on her shirt tightened. "He told me he wanted me to ground him, to remind him of the important things in life. I might have done that for a while, but he's always lived in that world. He would have grown to resent me for not fitting in. In all the months we dated, we never played Flix Roulette." She lifted her hand to his cheek. "Will you kiss me?"

"Yeah," he whispered before touching her lips with his. "I'm glad you told him no, but you're wrong. You would fit into that world just fine."

"Too bad for him I don't want to be there," she murmured against his lips.

"But it's good for me." Dane tightened his hold on her. "Sleepy, baby?"

"Yeah."

"Take a nap, sweetheart. We have all day."

DANE COULDN'T KEEP the smile off his face.

Yesterday had turned into one of his best days, ever, even with all the doubts he felt on their drive to the park.

After eating lunch, they stayed until sunset, walking the trails, following the river. They found rocks spanning bank to bank, and Nikki hopped along them, crossing the shallow river on the large flat stones. She stopped to wave at him, and he took her picture.

He immediately made it his wallpaper for his phone.

She was gorgeous standing there, the sun setting, the leaves changing in the background, the river flowing around her.

As he placed shoes on the stockroom shelves, he asked himself if that was when he'd fallen in love with her.

It didn't matter.

Dane watched her stock boxes of running shoes on the shelves by brand and size. It didn't matter when, only that he did.

What he would do about it was something else.

He didn't have the money for a wife. Nikki wanted the whole package, and he couldn't afford to give it to her, not now. If they got married, if she wanted kids right away, he wasn't sure how they would manage. Forget buying a house. It would make more sense for him to run the store himself again while she worked somewhere else. She had the skills to work anywhere for a hell of a lot more than he was paying her.

"Thanksgiving's getting closer. Have you talked to Brett about spending the holiday with us?" Nikki asked, moving on to another brand to re-shelve.

She'd wanted to help him clean up the mess in the store, and he hadn't the heart to turn her down. He'd been worried about how she would feel going back to where she'd been attacked, but she hadn't said anything about it. She'd only expressed her concern and disappointment Daniel could have been a part of something so terrible.

"I'll ask him one of these days. I haven't seen him for a while."

She gave him a pouty face over her shoulder. "Because of me?"

"Partly. My store did just get robbed. Life happens."

"You don't have to stop seeing your friends because of me, and you could let me do this." She waved her hand around the stockroom. "It's part of my job—you don't have to help."

"He understands. And one of these days he'll do the same to me, when he meets someone. But if it makes you feel better, I'll see what he's doing tonight. Will you be all right? We haven't been apart in a whole . . ." he checked his phone for the time, ". . . thirty-six hours."

He laughed because spending time with her was what he wanted more than anything else in the world, and she was feeling sorry about it.

"You're teasing me because I spun such a great movie last night. I told you my spins are awesome." Nikki wound her arms around his waist and tilted her head to smile at him.

Dane lowered his mouth to hers and tenderly kissed her lips. He laced his hands through her hair and his mouth traveled from her lips down her jaw to her throat. He nuzzled the tender spot beneath her ear, and he chuckled when her breath hitched.

It had hurt to spend the night with her and not make love to her. She wasn't ready, but it had been difficult not to spread her legs and burrow between them, finding her welcoming heat.

He needed her to want it as badly as he did, and he didn't want her to regret anything she did with him. Their new relationship may not survive if he rushed her.

She still had doubts about being involved with him, and he had to prove to her they were all unfounded; he would never hurt her.

"I don't think *The Love Boat: A Valentine Voyage* is anything to brag about." His heart warmed when she giggled.

He would wait for her as long as he needed to.

"It looks like the store is put back together," Nikki said, stepping from his arms.

"We should be able to open soon."

"Okay. Then I'm going to go home and get some laundry done. I need to change Princess Snowflake's litter and run my dishwasher." She frowned, the skin between her eyebrows puckering.

"Hey. We both have stuff to do, and you're making me go out tonight. Don't feel bad for wanting some space," he said, pulling her back into his arms. "We've spent a lot of time together lately, and I know you want to take it slow. It's okay." He rubbed her back.

"Wait." She grabbed her purse from the floor and pulled out her keyring. She detached a small silver key and pressed it into his hand, wrapping his fingers around the metal. She pressed a kiss to the tops of his fingers. "This is my spare. I haven't given to Alyssa yet, but I want you to have it instead. If you want to come over after you go out with Brett, you can. Or not. It's up to you."

"You don't have to do this," he murmured. "I'm fine with the way things are. You need time, and I understand that. We haven't had the standard 'date and let's go out to get to know each other better' start to our relationship."

Nikki nodded. "Fine," she said, with a twinkle in her eye. "I'll take it back, then." She made a grab for his hand.

"Oh, no you don't," he said, dodging her. He turned,

advancing on her instead, and she shrieked, running across the stockroom.

"Come here," he growled, and he grabbed her around the waist, lifting her off her feet. He chomped playfully at her neck, and he was rewarded with a mouthful of hair. Listening to her laugh made him feel like the happiest man in the world.

He didn't think life could get any better.

***

GRINNING, DANE HUNG up the store's landline phone. This weekend was going to be fantastic.

Nikki stood at the counter typing into her laptop. Every day she worked on his handbook, and he appreciated her effort. He treasured everything she'd done for him in the short time she'd been working at the store, and this was his way of telling her thank you. He dropped a brochure in front of her.

She scanned the front. "Oh, that would be amazing. Are you going?"

"Yep," Dane said, not able to keep a straight face.

"You're lucky. You'll have a great time."

"So will you."

"But how can you afford . . .?"

"It's all comped, don't worry about it," he said, smoothing her curls. "I know the woman handling the retreat. She's trading us the fee for the exposure. She wants us to write about our experience on the TCRC blog, our new Facebook page, and she wants us to tweet about the activities in real time while we do them."

"That would be wonderful," Nikki murmured, leafing through the glossy pages, looking at pictures of happy people running, eating alfresco on a beautiful patio decorated with gorgeous flowers and candles flickering in the setting sun, and listening to guest speakers. "I've never been to one of these, but don't you want to take someone else? Brett . . . or . . . Holly?"

He pulled her into his arms, and she stiffened. He huffed in frustration. "We're the only ones here."

"But someone could come in any second," she said, stepping from his embrace.

"Come here, then." He pulled on her arm and forced her into his office. Leaving the door ajar, he pressed her against the wall and crushed his mouth to hers.

With a soft whimper, she wrapped her arms around his neck and gave in to his kiss, letting him nudge her mouth open and slip his tongue inside.

He grabbed her ass and pulled her closer, his erection wedged between them, pressing into her belly.

He wanted her, God, he wanted her.

He didn't make a habit of one-night stands.

In the two years he'd been with Holly, he'd been faithful to her, however fucked up that had been, and he'd never, ever cheated on Liz, even though she'd accused him of it to cover her own guilt. His vows had meant the world to him, and Liz had thrown them away.

In that time during the divorce but before dating Holly, he hadn't been with anyone, too raw to put himself out there, even for meaningless sex. Especially for meaningless sex.

Being with Nikki was different; it was right. He loved her, was starting a relationship with her, and he wanted to show her that love, that commitment.

But this wasn't the time or the place.

She fiercely guarded her position, and because of the

robbery, she already had one reason to feel uncomfortable; he didn't want to give her another one.

Reluctantly, he took a step away but still held her in his arms. "Holly and I are over, and I want to go with you. Will you go on the retreat with me?" He ran a thumb over her lips. "Please?"

Nikki sighed and didn't say anything about his impatience or his aggressive kiss. He wanted to do everything right with her, and he'd come close to losing control. He kept saying he would give her time, and he had to make good on his promise.

"Who will run the store?"

"The same people who run the store every weekend. Margie will know we're gone, and she'll be available if anyone needs help. It won't make a difference we're out of town."

Dane paused to nibble on Nikki's lips.

"Marta Braddock is the director for the retreat and an old friend of mine. I asked her for separate rooms."

"That's not going to cause any trouble?"

"No. She wants us there, and she wants to make sure we're comfortable. We'll have a good time, and I want you to meet her."

"If you're sure," Nikki said, not sounding convinced.

"I am. Running and wine country. Nothing will go wrong. Stop worrying and enjoy the chance to get out of Minnesota for a while."

After that, she relented, and Dane made himself relax. He wanted her to have fun and not worry about a thing while they were gone. They were starting something special, and he didn't want to do anything to jeopardize their relationship.

It was why, even though she'd given him her key, he

hadn't used it. It had been nice catching up with Brett the other night, and he was glad Nikki had suggested it. But after the bar, he texted her to make sure she was all right and to let her know he was going home.

He didn't want to use the fact they lived next door to each other to spend more time with her than he normally would. They both needed space or they'd get burnt out, and that was the last thing he wanted.

He wanted Nikki for the rest of his life, and because of it, he had to remember he could be patient. Their relationship was a marathon, not a sprint. Take it slow, take it easy, and the rest would come.

"I don't want to mess this up," Nikki pleaded, her eyes filling with tears.

Dane ran a hand down her bruised cheek. She wore makeup again today, but the bruise was fading. "You can't. I know we've been moving fast, but there's no time limit. Take all the space you need as long as I know . . . I'm not sharing you with other men."

<hr>

NIKKI DANCED THROUGH her bedroom wearing her pajamas.

They were leaving the next morning, and she was thrilled. She hadn't flown for a long time, and the whole idea of traveling to California and sharing the retreat with Dane filled her with anticipation and excitement.

Her phone rang, and she glanced at the display. She almost didn't pick it up when she saw Eric's name on the screen, but he'd been such a good sport about their dinner he didn't deserved it.

"Nikki, I saw the news about the store. Are you all

right? I made a couple calls to the police station, but no one would tell me anything."

"Hi. Yeah, I'm okay." Nikki sat on the edge of her bed, and Princess Snowflake played with the hem of her pajama bottoms.

"I'm sorry I didn't stay to make sure you made it home safely. What was I thinking leaving you in the parking lot alone?" Eric said, disgust clear in his voice.

"It wasn't your fault. I was the dumb one who went into the store instead of calling the cops. But I thought it was Dane, and I didn't want the police to come if they didn't need to."

"Still, I'm glad you're okay. Did they catch who did it? Maybe you shouldn't work there anymore. Nothing like that happened at Shine, not with the mall security they have patrolling the building. You should give them a call, sweetheart."

Nikki frowned. It didn't matter he called her sweetheart, it was an endearment lots of people used casually, but she didn't like him suggesting she leave the store. "I couldn't. I love working there, and I wouldn't leave because of something like that. How are you? Working late?"

Chuckling, he said, "I am, as usual. You need a break, a vacation," he suggested. "I do, too. We could . . . go somewhere together. As friends . . . or . . . maybe more." He took a breath. "Sometime."

"Well, actually, I'm going to a running retreat over the weekend. I've never been to one before, and it should be a lot of fun." She paused and swallowed. They'd already done this once, and she hated having to tell him again. "Eric, I don't think it would work between us. I know you feel bad about leaving me in the parking lot, but it was my fault I went in there. You don't need to take responsibility for it, or think you need to pay me back somehow."

Eric's sigh carried through the phone, and Nikki's heart skittered. She didn't want him thinking he could have another chance.

"That sounds like something you'd definitely enjoy, Nik. I hope you have a great time."

"I hope so, too. Thanks for checking up on me. It's late, and I need to get some sleep—we fly out early in the morning," she said, hoping he would take the hint she was traveling with someone.

"Right. Goodnight."

"Goodnight. Go home and get some rest."

Uneasy, Nikki disconnected the call and plugged her phone in to charge on her nightstand. It was nice of Eric to check in with her after he found out she'd been hurt, and it was like him to take the blame for something that wasn't his fault.

But she hoped he wouldn't call her again.

Not even as friends.

CHAPTER FIVE

Filled with expectation, Nikki bounced on the bench in Dane's truck. They were on their way to the airport and she couldn't contain her glee.

She went over their itinerary: departing Tower City at one in the afternoon, a short layover in Dallas, then arriving by five, California time. The airport shuttle would drive them to the retreat where they would settle into their rooms and attend the welcome dinner later that evening.

Her excitement made Dane laugh, and she couldn't keep the grin off her face as he parked in long-term parking and helped her with her luggage.

They both packed all their belongings into carry-ons and each brought an additional bag they would stow beneath the seats.

Nikki giggled, thinking of his surprise she hadn't needed a full suitcase.

She'd studied the brochure and noted she only needed one nice dress for the second night at the retreat when a fancy banquet was held featuring the two keynote speakers.

Otherwise, all she'd need was her running gear. After

they arrived, she would need to make a quick stop at the resort's souvenir shop for toiletries because they weren't allowed on the plane.

While Dane checked them in, Nikki waited patiently, her eyes darting around the busy airport.

She shivered.

She'd dressed for California weather in a sundress, thin cardigan, and sandals, wanting to look pretty for Dane while they traveled, but she realized now she should have worn her regular running clothes. She would have been just as comfortable but a lot warmer. She made a mental note to wear warmer clothes on the way back; November had brought the bitter temperatures Minnesota was known for, even if snow hadn't fallen yet.

Yesterday afternoon, Alyssa had stopped by Nikki's apartment before the trip, and she'd asked Alyssa to check on Princess Snowflake.

"Go and have a fun time," Alyssa said, petting the kitten while Nikki packed.

"I plan to." Nikki beamed as she added running shorts to her carry-on. "Dane said he booked us two rooms, but honestly, I think we would have been okay with one. He's sweet though, not assuming I would want to share so soon."

"You guys haven't done it yet? What's going on?" Alyssa asked, exasperated.

Nikki sat down on the bed, a running shirt balled in her hands. "I don't know. I kind of feel like, Dane is special, and I don't want to fall into bed with him too quickly. Besides, we haven't known each other long, and we've had a lot going on. I want to. I kind of thought we would the night he stayed at my place after he took me to the park, but we only cuddled."

"Jesus, how many guys would share your bed and not

make a move on you? I hope when he asks you to marry him you say yes. You're never going to find another guy like him."

Nikki scoffed in amusement. "We've known each other a couple weeks. Now we're married?"

"I think it will happen. Wait and see."

Dane's hand on her arm snapped her back to the present. He was done checking them in and held a thick stack of papers containing their boarding passes.

"We better get through security. We're running a little behind."

Once they reached their terminal, Nikki realized Dane needn't have worried. They made it with plenty of time to spare, but since they were traveling first class, they were allowed to board not long after finding the gate.

He scanned the seat numbers. "Do you want the window?"

"I'm not five," she said, giving Dane room to stow her carry-on in the luggage rack above their seats.

"Oh no?" He grabbed her around the waist and tickled her. "You act like it when your favorite protein bars don't come in the shipment on time."

Nikki shrieked, eliciting several glares thrown their way by other passengers boarding the plane. He pulled her into their seats, and Nikki landed in his lap, laughing, tears welling in her eyes.

A stewardess stopped by their seats, an indulgent smile on her red-painted mouth. "Well, I don't have to ask where our newlyweds are. We were instructed to serve you a bottle of champagne, and we will as soon as we reach altitude, okay?"

"Oh, but we're not—" Nikki started, only to be interrupted by an older man clearing his throat with irritation.

"We're the newlyweds, ma'am," he grumbled across the aisle, correcting the stewardess with a sharp frown. His new wife looked as unhappy, scowling at Nikki and Dane.

The stewardess winked. "I am *so* sorry, sir," she apologized. "We'll be sure to serve you your celebratory bottle of champagne as soon as we are cleared to move about the cabin. Congratulations, you two. You look absolutely thrilled."

The stewardess rolled her eyes, and Nikki tucked her face into Dane's shoulder and laughed.

Taking advantage of Nikki in his lap, he tilted her head and kissed her, cradling her in his arms. "You look pretty," he said, his hand brushing her collarbone near the strap of her sundress. "I love it when your hair is down. You're beautiful."

Nikki brushed his smooth jaw with her fingers. *Thank you,* she wanted to say, *I love you.* But she kissed him instead. She wanted to tell him how she felt, wanted to tell him how happy he made her, but there wasn't any reason to rush, and she wanted a sign from him that he felt the same way before she confessed.

When he asked her to stop dating other men, she'd been confused and hurt, but it reminded her how little they knew each other.

He had every right to ask, and it helped them grow closer knowing they could be open about small issues in their relationship.

Settling in her seat she pushed down guilt bouncing around in her heart. Maybe she should tell him Eric called her last night, but it seemed an innocent enough phone call.

Well, maybe not that innocent.

Eric *had* suggested they go on a trip together, but he had

to have known how crazy that was, and she hadn't even acknowledged his offer.

She hoped he was only making sure she was okay after the robbery, and she didn't want to start her vacation with Dane on a bad note by bringing up her ex.

Shoving Eric out of her mind, Nikki looked around the first-class cabin. The flight attendant hadn't pushed the cockpit's door closed, and she spoke to the pilot, leaning over his shoulder. "I can't believe all this is for free."

"We were lucky you set up those accounts. I went to school with Marta but after graduation, she moved back home. She was surprised I opened a store because she knew L—" Dane stopped.

"She knew who?" Nikki asked.

"Uh, she knew I had gone into banking after graduation. When you created our Facebook page for the store and listed me as the owner, she spotted it. She's kept up with news about Tower City's running community."

"She runs too? She's not just the retreat coordinator?" Nikki's skin prickled. Dane was keeping something from her.

"Yeah. We all ran track at school. I'm glad she found a way to combine her business degree with running." He paused. "I always kind of thought she would end up with Brett. They dated while they were in school, but then she moved back to California."

"Why was she in Minnesota anyway? If I lived in California, I don't think I would leave."

"The University of Minnesota, Tower City, gave her a full ride to run track on their team, and she'd heard awesome things about our coach. She wasn't completely alone up here. I think she still has an aunt and uncle who live up north."

"How come Brett isn't dating anyone? Is he still hung up on Marta?" Nikki buckled her seatbelt and let him steer the conversation away from him and the store.

The stewardesses were checking the baggage holds above the seats preparing for takeoff, and Nikki smiled at one who walked by them.

Dane pulled out the latest issue of Runner's World from his duffel bag. "No, I don't think so. As far as I know they're still friends, but that's all. He doesn't want kids. He was miserable growing up, and he says he doesn't want the responsibility of making a child happy. After the second or third date, he'll tell a woman he won't ever want a family, and they don't last long after they know that."

"That's sad," Nikki murmured, pulling a book out of her bag.

"You want kids?"

"When I find a woman who doesn't, I'll send her Brett's way."

Dane looked out the window.

"Hey, are you okay?" Their conversation had turned serious, and she was happy she hadn't brought up Eric. Their relationship didn't need more complications.

"Yeah." He kissed her forehead. "Have you flown before? Are you okay with takeoff and everything?"

"I get a little queasy, but after we level off I'm okay. I try to read through it."

"What are you reading anyway?" Dane took the book with the red cover from her hands. On the front, a couple was locked in a steamy embrace.

"It's a romance."

"Do they have sex in these books?" Dane teased, flipping through it.

"Of course they do," Nikki said, swiping the book from

his hands. She whispered over the flight attendant's safety speech. "It's what couples do when they fall in love."

"People who don't love each other have sex, too," he pointed out, opening the front cover of his magazine.

"This is a romance. They always end up together at the end."

Dane snorted. "That's not real life."

Nikki put a hand to his cheek and made him look at her. She didn't notice as the plane taxied down the runway. "It can be, for some people."

And there was the pain again, she thought, staring into his golden-brown eyes. Right there, right in the center of his beautiful irises, the crinkles around the corners framing the hurt. She wanted to make his pain go away, but she couldn't if he wouldn't confide in her.

Baby steps, she told herself. They were both new at this.

Dane pressed a kiss to the center of her palm. "You think we have a happily ever after coming to us?"

"I think we have a fantastic shot." And oh, she wanted the chance.

Nikki leaned her head against Dane's shoulder and began to drift off. Last night she couldn't shut her brain off, imagining the fun they'd have this weekend, and she'd barely slept. Settling in for the flight, the sleepless night caught up with her.

She didn't mind when Dane grabbed her book and began to read.

Dane finished the book as the plane circled over the airport preparing to land, and he was disgusted to find that yes, indeed they were together, forever. The guy had been a prick through the entire book, and only her love made him see what an asshole he was and change for the better. What a load of bullshit. And the woman was the same, a selfish bitch who realized if she didn't straighten out he was going to leave her ass.

Yeah, that had worked with Liz.

Nikki teased him for reading her book. She bought another at a bookstore during their layover in Dallas, and she said he could read it on the flight home. It was the last thing he was going to do.

The book's unbelievable happy ending put Dane in a foul mood, and being separated from Nikki on the shuttle to the resort from the airport didn't help.

Instead, he was sitting next to a woman who had flown in from South Dakota, and she was trying to involve him in a conversation about winter running. No, he didn't run outside when it was twenty below Fahrenheit. Yes, he used a treadmill. Yes, he owned one. No, he didn't like it. The woman didn't seem to mind his bad attitude, and when the shuttle hit a hole in the road, she was jostled closer to him. She didn't seem to mind that, either.

Dane glared at the driver, though the driver was too enamored of Nikki, who was riding shotgun, to feel the animosity pouring from him, seated in the far back.

Nikki spoke to the driver, but he couldn't make out what she was saying. The driver laughed, occasionally taking a peek at Nikki's legs showcased quite nicely in her baby blue sundress and white sandals.

The drive from the airport took over an hour, and he sat cramped on the last bench, staring out the window, trying to ignore the annoyingly chipper woman. He wished they would have rented their own vehicle, but it made sense to use the shuttle because they wouldn't be driving anywhere else while they were at the retreat.

Last one out of the van, he had to catch up with Nikki in the parking lot when they reached the hotel. She waited for him, typing on her phone, their bags at her feet.

She beamed. "I'm tweeting about our drive here. Remember to take pictures for the blog and our Facebook page. Are you tired? You look crabby."

"I'm fine," he muttered. "Let's check in."

He stood in line, and he watched Nikki wander around the lobby taking in the huge fireplace, the little tables with knickknacks, and flip through some of the brochures sitting on a wide glass coffee table. He frowned when a man approached her and started talking to her, putting a hand on her arm. She nodded at something he said and tilted her head Dane's way. Good. She was telling him she was taken.

"Sir?" The front desk agent cleared her throat. "Can I have your name please?"

Dane told her his and Nikki's names, and he sighed when she handed him only one key card. "We were supposed to have two rooms."

"I'm sorry, sir," she apologized. "We have you booked for only one king bed suite."

"I set up these reservations with Marta Braddock. We should have two rooms."

"I'm sorry sir," she said again, her smile strained. The line behind Dane snaked around the lobby, and she was the only agent working the desk. "We have you booked for one room, and the resort is full. The suite is equipped with a couch? Perhaps that will suffice for the weekend?"

Dane groaned in frustration. Nikki agreed to go because they wouldn't be sharing a room. She'd be difficult, like Liz. She would insist he find another room, or find someplace in town to sleep. He'd miss most of the activities commuting back and forth to a different hotel. There went his relaxing weekend.

Dane slid the keycard from the desk and found Nikki, now speaking to the woman who'd tried, and failed, to claim his attention in the shuttle.

"This is Stephanie," Nikki introduced them. "She's from South Dakota."

"We've spoken." A bubbly brunette wearing running clothes, Stephanie held out her hand. "But I didn't catch your name?"

"Dane," he muttered, taking her hand briefly before dropping it in disinterest.

Stephanie, looking between Dane and Nikki, sensed his tension and moved on to introduce herself to someone else.

Dane took Nikki by the elbow and steered her toward the elevators. "Our reservations got screwed up, and we only have one room. I'm sorry."

He jabbed at the button to close the doors before anyone could join them.

She leaned into him and covered his mouth with hers, giving him a tender kiss. "Hmmm," she sighed. "That's okay."

Dane growled and tried to push her away. "What do you mean, that's okay?"

Wrapping her arms around his neck she said, "It's fine. It's not like we haven't slept in the same bed before. What's wrong? It's more than the rooms." She ran a finger lightly over his frown lines on his forehead, and he turned his head to avoid her touch.

He ignored the hurt mewling sound she made as she stepped away.

The elevator doors opened, and Dane strode ahead of

her through a white stone corridor, windows open on either end to catch the late afternoon breeze.

Their suite was magnificent with white marble flooring, gold rugs scattered about. The sliding doors were covered in a white gauzy material and opened onto a stone balcony. Through the open doors, the deep blue of the pool sparkled in the sun. A four-poster king-sized bed covered in a gold bedspread was positioned against one wall, two matching nightstands on either side. A hot tub sat in one corner and a door opened into a large bathroom.

He turned away from the elegant room and asked Nikki, "Are you sure this is okay? I could check with Marta . . ."

"It's fine. We'll be going down for drinks and the meet and greet in a little while. Do you want to lie down for a bit? I slept on the plane, but you didn't. Why don't you rest? I'm going back downstairs to find some coffee. Do you want me to bring you back some?"

Dane grabbed her upper arm, his fingers digging into her skin. "I don't understand you."

"What did I do?"

His grip tightened, and Nikki winced. "Why aren't you angry? Why aren't you yelling at me? Blaming me for the mistake? Telling me if this trip would have been paid for, this wouldn't have happened?"

Gently, she placed her hand on his. "Dane, I'm not her. Whoever it is you're thinking about now, I'm not her. Please, let me go."

If Liz were here instead of Nikki, she would have been screaming, blaming him for the mistake and ranting about his idiocy in taking something for free, because he was too stupid to earn decent money to pay for it himself.

With his head hanging in shame, he would have sat and

waited out the tantrum all the while thinking he wasn't a good enough husband to make his wife happy. And God, all he wanted to do was make Liz happy because he loved her so much.

He hadn't been enough, and she'd found someone who was.

Dane wasn't enough for Nikki, either, for this beautiful woman who, right now, was looking at him with her heart in her eyes, who only wanted him to nap because he hadn't slept on the plane. He owed her an explanation, and he would give it to her this weekend. Then she would know it, too.

"I'm sorry." When he let go of her arm, Dane cringed; a band of red marred her creamy skin. He'd vowed never to hurt her, to never treat her the way he'd treated Holly, but he already put his hands on her.

She brushed a kiss on his cheek before stepping into the hallway.

Full of misery, he sat on the edge of the bed. After he told her about his failed marriage, after she knew it was the reason he'd been involved in a pseudo-relationship with Holly, he'd never see her again.

She would dump him on his ass the way he deserved.

"Dane!"

He blinked as a tiny woman raced across the patio and flung herself into his arms. With her legs wrapped around his hips, her arms around his neck, she exclaimed, "I'm so happy to see you!"

Other participants of the retreat looked on in amuse-ment, and Dane, grateful he hadn't a glass or a plate in his hands, gave Marta Braddock a bear hug in return, spinning her in a tight circle.

"Hey, Marta, glad to see you, too."

Marta jumped from Dane's embrace and bounced on her toes. With her brown eyes twinkling, she stuck her hand out to Nikki. "Marta Braddock. I organized this shindig. How do you like it so far?"

"It's great," Nikki said. "We appreciate the chance to come out. It's gorgeous here, and our room is fantastic. I'm looking forward to the runs tomorrow and listening to Tiff Sorenson speak. I've read her book, and it was very helpful."

"What do you run?" Marta asked, though she eyed Dane.

"A few half marathons here and there, a lot of 10ks. I run more for recreation. I know you met Dane and Brett running track at school. I've never been that hardcore," she said, and then took a sip of her wine.

"Sometimes it's fun to run, you know, for the run." Marta agreed, nodding. "I was surprised to hear you opened your own store, Dane. I'd kind of forgotten about it until you created your Facebook page. I never got a chance to tell you I was sorry to hear about you and Li—"

Dane took a step back and made a slicing motion across his throat with his finger.

"I'm sorry Brett couldn't come out with you," Marta said, covering her tracks, turning pink. "It would have been nice to see him, too."

Gratefully, Dane smiled at her and wrapped an arm around Nikki's shoulders. He needed to tell her about Liz before Marta slipped again.

"You know how it is. Brett's busy with the marathon, and it gets bigger every year. I've been helping where I can, and I've been training Nikki to run the store so I can give him more of my time."

"How's he doing?" Marta asked, picking at her watch strap.

Telling her the truth he said, "You know, same as always."

Marta frowned. "I wish he would find a woman and settle down. He needs someone in his life."

"Are you still in touch with him?" Nikki asked.

"We chat here and there on Facebook." Marta's eyes flattened. "I should mingle with the other guests. What are you two running tomorrow?"

Nikki wrinkled her nose. "I'm not one for early morning runs. I'll be doing the late afternoon trail run before the banquet. Luckily, our flight isn't that early, and I'll be going on the last run of the retreat, too."

"Well, I know Dane loves to run before the sun comes up. Be my running buddy in the morning?" she asked with a grin. "I kind of have to be there."

"Is that okay?" He nudged Nikki's shoulder.

He'd followed Nikki's advice earlier and had taken a short nap while she went downstairs to help herself to the complimentary coffee available in the lobby.

Lying there, feeling ashamed he let his past relationships interfere with what a good thing he had going with her, he drifted off. He woke to her sitting on the balcony reading her book from the airport, waiting for him so they could attend the meet and greet together.

She'd looked worried about him, and not once did she bring up how he manhandled her.

Nikki laughed. "I'll be sleeping. You do what you like."

"You're on. I hope you didn't get too slow in your old age," Dane said to Marta.

Marta laughed. "I've always been faster than you. Enjoy the rest of your evening. Nikki, I'll catch up with you tomorrow, and we can chat more before you guys leave. It was nice meeting you."

"And you," Nikki said, nodding at Marta before the petite woman dashed off to greet other participants. "I bet she can run a mile a minute," she murmured as Marta darted enthusiastically from group to group.

"She can," Dane said, snagging Nikki's wine glass and taking a sip of her Merlot. "She missed the Olympic trials by a few seconds."

"She seemed sad about Brett."

"Yeah. No one knows what happened. It has always been between the two of them." He handed the glass back to Nikki. "You know, I think I'm going to go up."

Nikki set her glass on an empty table. "I'll go with you."

Dane held her hand in the elevator, and anticipation crackled between them.

His hand trembled as he used the keycard to open the door to their room. As soon as the door shut behind them, they stood in the dark for a moment, their eyes adjusting.

Before he could reassure Nikki he didn't want anything from her, she flew into his arms, her lips were on his, and there was no way he could have denied her.

"Now, we've waited too long," she moaned against his throat, reaching for the belt buckle of his cotton khaki pants.

"Are you sure? I don't want to rush you."

His question was answered when her hand found his erection, and he released his breath in a loud hiss. This wasn't the way he wanted to first take her, in the hallway of their room, against the wall, but desire consumed him, and he couldn't think of anything but the way his cock throbbed cupped in her hand.

"Please," Nikki whimpered.

Dane pulled her hand from his pants and crouched in front of her, running his hands up her slim, firm thighs.

Hooking her lace panties with his thumbs, he pulled them down her legs. As he stood, he pushed up the hem of her sundress.

He lifted her up, his hands under her ass. Even though she stood taller than Liz or Holly, Nikki didn't weigh that much, and he easily held her steady. Thank God. He didn't need to look like a weak-ass during their first time. Maybe later he would admit he hadn't had sex anywhere that wasn't a bed in so long he couldn't remember the time or place.

"Wrap your legs around my waist," he said, bracing her against the wall. "Are you sure?" he asked again, his cock ready to slide inside her, the tip fitting snugly against her slit. He groaned when she wiggled.

"Now," she panted and pushed herself down slowly, taking him in.

"You're so wet. God, you're tight. How long has it been for you?"

"A while," she said, licking his neck. She moved her mouth along his throat, along his jaw.

Her answer excited him. She hadn't had one last little fling with Eric the night he took her out. Dane hadn't wanted to consider the possibility, but Nikki wouldn't have been the first to engage in goodbye sex with an ex.

He thrust up.

"More. I need more," she begged, resting her head against the wall.

He gave it to her, in steady, forceful thrusts.

Dane felt her contract around him, and he came inside her, unable to hold back. He braced her against the wall as he emptied into her, claiming her as his. He filled her with a part of himself, and now she belonged to him.

Nikki relaxed in his arms, and she rested her head on his shoulder.

He sank on the carpet with her in his lap, his runner's legs steady carrying her weight, and her thighs straddling his hips. When she wiggled to make herself comfortable, his cock slipped out of her.

She pressed herself into his chest as she nipped kisses along his jaw.

His hand slid up and down her leg, moving closer to the apex of her thighs with every stroke. Dane wanted to touch her, and his fingertips whispered over the delicate skin of her clit. She shivered and rose on her knees to give his hand more room between their bodies. He captured her mouth in another kiss as he slid his finger inside her.

She was wet . . . maybe too wet.

Shit.

"I didn't protect you. We, I, we were in such a hurry, I didn't use anything." He hadn't wanted to use anything, and now with the haze of lust dissipating, his mistake and its consequences slammed him over the head. He was a selfish asshole. "God, I am so sorry."

He couldn't get anything right.

"It's okay. I'm on the pill, and I'm healthy. I haven't been with anyone since Eric." Nikki rubbed her cheek against his.

He sighed. "I've only been with Holly, and we were faithful to each other. I swear I'm healthy, too. I would never hurt you. I keep saying that, and I keep doing it. I'm sorry."

"I know. Besides, this was my fault. I couldn't wait." She laughed. "I wanted this the night we came back from the park, but you were such a gentleman, I didn't want you to think I was some kind of . . . whore."

She took his mouth with hers, and he moaned with renewed arousal and relief he hadn't fucked up as much as he thought he had.

"You were only thinking about me because of the night at the store, but maybe the wait made it better." She pulled back and rubbed his nose with hers.

"I wanted you the day we met. Your legs drive me crazy." He slid his hands from her ankles up to her thighs.

"Now what?" Nikki wiggled on his lap.

"How about a hot shower?"

Nikki moaned. "Perfect."

Dane ran his hands under her dress, over her waist, up to her breasts which were held in place with a strapless bra. "I can't stop touching you."

"If you keep doing that, we'll never get a shower," Nikki said, unbuttoning his dress shirt. She lightly rubbed her thumbs over his nipples. When he hardened, she shimmied and slipped him inside her.

"Twice in the hallway?" Dane panted. He unhooked her bra, pulled it from under her dress, and tossed it onto the floor. He filled his palms with her breasts, and he flicked her nipples with his thumbnails as she started to move.

"Are you complaining?" she asked, increasing the tempo, her strong runner's thighs doing all the work.

"I don't think so," he murmured into her neck, sliding into oblivion with her.

AFTERWARD, IN THE shower, Dane gently soaped her,

running his fingers lovingly over her peaches and cream skin.

The mark he'd put on her arm disappeared.

He washed her hair, and his lips against her slippery skin followed the water as it rinsed the shampoo away. Holding her as if she were a fragile, hand-blown glass figurine that would shatter into a million pieces if he dropped her, he rasped close to her ear, "Let's get out."

He wanted, no, he *needed*, to get this over with. The weight of what her reaction could be was too much for him to bear. He'd waited too long to say something, and the expectation had grown into a fever pitch making him want to tear at his skin.

"Wait. I need to put conditioner in my hair or I won't be able to brush the knots out. You go. I'll be there in a minute."

Dane nodded and grabbed a bleached-white towel hanging from the rack outside the shower stall. He wrapped it around his waist and slipped on one of the complimentary robes before shutting the bathroom door behind him.

Nikki waited until the door closed before leaning against the slick beige wall in defeat.

She closed her eyes and tears started streaming down her face, mixing with the warm spray. She couldn't stop thinking about the tortured expression in his eyes, the pain radiating off him as he held her.

After he told her this wasn't working, she'd have to quit his store.

Already in love with him, she wouldn't be capable of

seeing him every day, wouldn't be able to tolerate being around him and knowing he wasn't hers.

If he started dating someone else, oh God. No, she would have to leave TCRC; she would have to leave her building. Every nightmare she feared starting a relationship with him was coming true.

Quickly, she drenched her hair in conditioner and rinsed it out as fast as she could, hoping she did a good enough job. With shaking hands, she took the time to dry her body, prolonging the inevitable. She slipped into the remaining white terry cloth robe and found her wide-toothed comb in her cosmetics bag.

Dane looked away from the muted TV and met her eyes. "Let me do that." He guided her onto the bed and started to untangle her hair in long, even strokes.

Tears wet her cheeks as he pulled the comb through her damp strands. A man had never brushed her hair before, but she couldn't take pleasure in it.

When he finished, he kissed away the wetness on her face. "Nikki, don't cry, baby." He untied the sash at her waist and exposed her breasts. "You are so gorgeous." He drew one of her nipples into his mouth.

She moved farther up the mattress, and she moaned when his fingers found her core. Her hips moved in rhythm to his touch. "Dane," she whispered, "please."

Dane shed his robe and moved over her. Sliding inside her he said, "Don't cry. I don't know how, and I don't know when, but somehow you've become my whole world."

Nikki accepted his tender kisses, and she wrapped her legs around the backs of his thighs, pulling him to her as closely as she could.

She came with a small cry, and he followed a few moments later, pulsing inside her.

While she caught her breath, she buried her face into the curve of his neck. He smelled of sweat, hotel soap, and sex.

After giving her a kiss, Dane slid off her and pulled back the heavy gold bedspread.

Nikki pushed off her robe and crawled into the sheets with him, wrapping her body around his for warmth. She melted into him when he put his arm around her.

Dane was silent for a moment and she held her breath, preparing for the worst.

"I've been married."

She tensed. That was far from what she thought he was going to tell her.

Margie never alluded to him being married before. But she relaxed and shifted, lying half on top of him, her head on his chest, her wet hair dampening his skin.

Comfort. She wanted to give him comfort because he desperately seemed to need it. By the sound of his voice, Nikki guessed this was a painful topic. But being married and then going through a divorce, that didn't seem like such a big thing.

She was at an age where some of her friends had tried marriage too young, and it didn't work out.

Dane wasn't the only one she knew who was divorced. She hadn't been married or even engaged, but she wouldn't judge Dane for a mistake.

"I married her right out of university. She knew Brett and Marta; the four of us hung around together. Marta and Brett didn't work out, but Liz and I got married, bought a house. She majored in marketing with a minor in fashion design, and now she's a buyer for a big department store in one of the malls. Liz was ambitious then, still is from what I've heard, and she was drawn to my business major. She encouraged me to take the job at the bank, and we were happy. I loved her, and I thought that was my life, that we would be happy for the next fifty years."

Nikki made herself keep quiet. He wasn't done, not by a long shot.

"But as the months went on, she wasn't happy. She wanted me to get promoted faster, she wanted me to make more money. We were only married for three years before things got bad. She hated the way we lived. She wanted a bigger house, new cars. Liz didn't want kids because it would ruin her figure. She always wanted to go to parties, or to the symphony, the opera, to network, to climb the social ladder. Ambitious and power hungry, she was greedy, and even with the money I was making, I made her miserable."

She kissed his cheek. She didn't want to break the spell, the quiet enveloping them in the darkness of the room. He pulled her closer, and he continued.

"I *was* getting promoted, working sixty, seventy hours a week. Her temper started getting shorter and shorter, and I couldn't please her. Nothing I did was right. She started cheating on me, and I didn't even know because I was never home, I was always at work. I didn't see Brett because I was exhausted all the time.

"I couldn't take Liz to all the events she wanted, needed, to go to because I worked twelve-, thirteen-hour days, sometimes more. She hated me for trying to make enough money to please her. Finally, I realized I never could. I had high blood pressure, and my doctor said stress would kill me.

"Without asking her, I quit my job and bought the store. That made her even more furious with me, if that were possible. I moved out and served her with divorce papers. I had to choose between my happiness, my sanity and health, and my marriage. God, please believe me, it was the hardest choice I've ever had to make in my entire life."

"Your marriage should have made you happy. You shouldn't have had to make the choice at all," she whispered, and Dane ran his hand up and down her spine, making her shiver.

"My marriage to Liz is the reason for a lot of things. My parents stopped talking to me after I divorced her. They've been married for thirty-five years and thought since I had chosen her I should have stuck it out. Maybe they didn't understand how miserable we were, or how much she'd changed after I put a ring on her finger, but they took her side. They told me it was my responsibility to make her happy. They didn't understand I couldn't. There was no way, and I know because I sure as hell tried.

"I met Holly the night my divorce was finalized," he whispered. "The fight in court took almost a year. Liz sued me for all I had, and she won. She took the house and, thankfully, the mortgage that went with it. She took our cars and what little savings we had. By then she'd started dating a lawyer and the judge was his close friend.

"I was at a bar licking my wounds when Holly came in with some of her friends. She took me home with her. The next morning, I told her I couldn't be with a woman that way, couldn't start a relationship because I was still too raw. She had some fucked-up idea she could save me, put me back together, and I'm ashamed to say I let her try."

Dane rubbed his eyes. "I was always honest with her, always. I never made any promises, never indicated there would be a future between us. Our relationship was day by day, hour by hour.

"I was hard, my feelings were shut down. If I didn't feel

like seeing her, I didn't. I avoided her when she had bad days because I couldn't deal with it.

"She stuck by me, and eventually, I calmed down. But I still didn't make any promises, and she understood. I saw her off and on for two years. I never thought of her as a girl-friend or a potential wife. I never loved her.

"My feelings for her would never have turned into love, even if I wouldn't have met you. Maybe she helped me heal, maybe she didn't. I suppose with time I would have alone, but I can't lie, it was nice to have companionship without strings, without the pressure of having to give something back."

She bit her lip. She didn't want to ask questions if the answers weren't any of her business, but she needed to know what happened earlier. "I don't understand what this afternoon was all about. You expected me to be angry about the room, that makes sense now, but what did you mean when you said the mistake wouldn't have been made if you would've paid? Mistakes happen all the time, I don't under-stand what money has to do with it."

With her fingertips, Nikki made sweeping loops on Dane's chest and glided lightly down the ridges of his ribs.

Dane sighed. "Liz liked to tell me I was stupid for not being able to make any money. I equated the mistake to Marta comping our room. Somehow, if I would have been able to afford this retreat, and God knows I'd never be able to afford something like this right now, everything would have been perfect. It will always be money. The store may be in the black, but I sink all I can into the loan. I want to blame Liz, and I could. The divorce certainly didn't help, the attorney fees I paid were astronomical. She took me for all I had and I let her to get rid of her, but I made more working at the bank than I do owning the store."

"But you weren't happy there."

Dane didn't answer, but he didn't need to.

The minutes ticked by, and Dane stiffened when she whispered, "I don't know what you want me to say."

Nikki rolled onto her back, and she reveled in the heat radiating from his skin as he pulled her close, covering her mouth in a soft kiss. "Tell me you can see past my divorce, tell me you don't hate me for my relationship with Holly."

Framing his face in her hands she said, "You're a good man, Dane Montgomery. Liz didn't deserve you, and I'm sorry she put you through that. You'll repair your relationship with your parents because one day you'll remarry, have kids, and they'll want to be a part of that. The store is doing great, and you won't pay on that loan forever. You have a lot to give."

He wasn't ready to hear she would support him in every way she knew how. He wouldn't believe she would be there to take his heart when he offered it to her. They'd only known each other a few weeks, and trust took longer to build, to earn. She wanted his trust, his love, and until he believed he could give them to her without fear of her demanding in return more than what he could give, patiently, she would wait.

CHAPTER SIX

AFTER A KISS to Nikki's shoulder, Dane crawled out of bed, threw on his running clothes, and met Marta in front of the resort for their long run. Others were waiting as well, and after Marta took a head count, they started down the darkened road winding its way through the vineyards of Napa Valley.

Marta paired up with him like she promised, and they ran quite a distance in silence letting their muscles loosen before she finally spoke. "I'm sorry to hear about you and Liz. Brett told me a little about what happened. It's hard to believe she could change like that. She seemed . . . I don't know . . . nice, when we were at school."

Dane grunted. "Trust me, if she had shown her true colors at school, I never would have touched her, let alone married her. She duped us all."

"So, you and Nikki?"

"I don't know. She didn't know about Liz when you met her yesterday—that's why I had to cut you off—but I told her last night after the meet and greet. She listened to what I told her, but she didn't have much to say."

"Have you been dating her long?" Marta nodded to another runner who passed her to catch up with a friend.

"We're not dating, not really. Mostly just hanging out. I told you last night she's the new manager of my store. I finally made room in the budget because Brett's been bugging me to help him with the marathon."

"Oh. It seemed like you two were closer than that. There was this . . . feeling about you two when you were standing together."

"I'm in love with her."

"Dane," Marta said with a sigh. "That's wonderful. The way Brett talked, sometimes I thought you would never fall in love again. He made you sound so battle-wounded."

Dane looked down at the petite woman, her short brown hair pushed back from her face with a bright pink headband, her muscular legs pumping in black spandex shorts, her little feet wearing the shoes a shoe manufacturer gave her every month.

"You sure talk to Brett a lot for hightailing out of Minnesota like your ass was on fire," he said. He didn't want to talk about himself and Nikki anymore. She would either see past his mistakes, or she wouldn't and decide he wasn't worth the trouble.

"We're not talking about me," she said, but she quieted for half a mile. "Does she feel the same?"

"You can't help yourself, can you? Well, she didn't run away screaming after I told her about Liz and my relationship with Holly, which I'm going to assume you know about, too, because of Brett's big mouth. But she didn't say anything about how she felt about me, or give me any idea of where we're going. Maybe she doesn't know and needs to think. I did drop a bomb on her."

"How long have you known her?"

"A couple of weeks."

"I suppose you should give her some time, then. Does she like working at your store?"

"Yeah. She's great. It's one of the reasons I want to go slow. She didn't want to get involved with me at first because she didn't want to lose her job. Plus, she lives next door to me in my building. Holly said Nikki has a lot to lose if things don't work out between us, but it's hard for me to take it slow. I love her. I want to tell her, but I don't have anything to give. I'm a beat up, worn out man."

"You are so fucked up. You've been talking to Holly about Nikki? What the hell? You know Holly wanted to marry you, waited for you, and then Nikki comes along, and boom, you and Holly are done. Jesus Christ. You're lucky if Holly doesn't meet Nikki in a dark alley and beat the shit out of her."

Feeling like a stupid ass because Marta was right, he said, "That's not funny. Nikki interrupted a burglary at the store and got knocked around, so shut the hell up."

Marta lost her rhythm and fell back a step. After she caught up, she swore. "Fuck. I didn't know. I'm sorry. I've been busy putting this retreat together, and I haven't talked to Brett for a while. I'm sorry," she repeated. "I didn't know."

Dane sighed. "No, I'm sorry."

He tried to relax into the run, tried to let the footfalls and chatter of the other runners calm him. "You're right. I *am* fucked up, and Holly paid for it. But God. I met Nikki, and it was like you said, boom. I was gone."

"What are you going to do?"

"Nothing. Keep doing what I've been doing. Work with her at the store, spend time with her if she lets me. I can't pressure her into a relationship, and it's only been a couple weeks. I'm poor, she might not want me."

"There's more to life than money. I think everyone in the world knows that except Liz. Look, I bet you're not even paying Nikki that much. It wouldn't be hard for her to find something that would pay her more, so you know she took the job at your store for a reason. Be thankful for it and stop looking for reasons for her to quit."

Marta moved on to other groups of runners to chat and left Dane alone.

He was grateful for the silence. The worst was out there. He told Nikki all his horrible secrets, and while she hadn't proclaimed her undying love, she hadn't shut down like he feared she would. Liz taught him to look for the worst, and he needed to stop.

Right now, Nikki was sleeping in the bed where they'd made love, and she would be there when he came back. That should count for something.

Dane took the elevator and let himself into the room. Nikki still lay in bed surrounded by sheets and pillows. The bedspread was balled between her knees as if she had gotten hot and pulled one leg out to cool off. He smiled when he saw she moved to his side of the bed, possibly searching for him, for his warmth. He took a quick shower and dried off. With the towel wrapped around his waist, he sat on the edge of the bed and fluttered kisses up and down her arm.

Groaning, she flipped onto her back and opened her eyes into slits. "Morning. Did you have a nice run with Marta?"

Dane brushed his lips against hers. "Morning. Yeah, it was. This is beautiful country out here."

"Did you see any of it?" Nikki teased, propping herself onto her elbows. "It's still dark outside."

"How did I get caught up with a night owl?"

Nikki sat up, the sheet falling away to expose her breasts. "Lucky, I guess," she whispered, and kissed him, wrapping her arms around his neck.

"Yeah, I guess," he mumbled against her lips, pushing her into the bed to give her a proper good morning.

NIKKI MOANED WITH pleasure. It was almost as lovely as sex.

Almost.

After she and Dane had the best morning love-making she'd ever had, she'd taken a shower to shave her legs. On the patio, they'd eaten breakfast ordered from room service, and now she was spending the rest of the morning in the spa. Nikki signed up for the whole works: body wrap, facial, mud bath, and massage.

Since he'd already had his run for the day, Dane didn't have a plan for the afternoon, but that was one of the best parts of being in a healthy relationship. She didn't feel she had to report to him every second, and she was content to let him do whatever he wanted.

In fact, she had most of the day to herself. After the spa, she planned to grab lunch in the hotel's dining room then dress for her late afternoon run. She wished they could stay longer, but she already missed her kitten and Alyssa.

Thanksgiving would be nice. She needed to ask Dane if he'd remembered to invite Brett to share the holiday with them.

Nikki wanted to buy Dane a nice Christmas gift, too. It

couldn't be anything expensive because he would shun a gift she spent a lot of money on. It had inexpensive and meaningful, from her heart. For the remainder of the massage she thought about what she could give him for a holiday present.

Refreshed after her spa treatments, Nikki sat in the brightly lit dining room eating her lunch when Marta took the seat opposite her. "Having a good time?"

"Oh, my God, it's the best," Nikki said, looking up from her phone. "I was tweeting about how wonderful it is here. I've taken pictures and posted them on the store's Facebook page. It's incredible. I can't thank you enough." She laughed. "It's ironic though, I'm at a running retreat, and I haven't run yet."

Something dark flickered in Marta's eyes. "There's more to life than running."

Nikki's smile died. "Not much, though."

"No," Marta whispered. "Not much." She cleared her throat, breaking the tension, and ran a hand along the side of her face. "I'm glad Dane hired a manager for his store. He's put a lot of time and effort into it, and he needs a break. It's great to see it working for him. I have to say, I haven't kept in touch with him much, and everything I know comes from Brett." Marta blushed. "Anyway, where is Dane now? I'm surprised to see you sitting alone."

Nikki took a bite of her gourmet macaroni and cheese. "I don't know. I haven't seen him since he got back from his run with you. There are days I can barely keep track of myself. If Dane needs a babysitter, he's got the wrong woman. I'm not interested in keeping tabs on him every second."

"Are you the right woman, Nikki? Woman to woman, are you right for my friend?"

Nikki grabbed Marta's hand. "I hope so. I'm going to try my best. That's all I can do, right?"

"I've known Dane for a long time. He's going to fuck up. It's human nature, and boy, can he be an ass, I've seen it first-hand. You have to be able to look past it and forgive him. If you can do that, if you can be strong enough, that's all he needs." Marta pushed her chair away from the table. "I'll see you guys at the banquet tonight. We've got some great speakers. I would appreciate it if you would live-tweet their speeches. It will be great publicity."

"I planned on it. Can you message me the hashtag that you've assigned to the speakers? I'll use it in all my posts."

"Sure. That's a great idea."

"Thanks. And thanks for being a good friend to Dane. For wanting to check me out."

Marta's cheeks flushed. "Was I that obvious?"

"Woman to woman? Yes."

***

DANE CUDDLED NIKKI while she settled into the airplane's chair, the book he'd stolen from her on the flight to California sitting in her lap.

He sat back with a contented sigh, and she leaned into him resting her hand on his leg.

In only three short days their relationship had evolved into something completely breathtaking, and he had trouble wrapping his mind around it. He'd told her his secrets, and she hadn't turned him away.

Holding her close as she watched the clouds as the plane flew by them, Dane thought about how far they had come, not only emotionally but physically. It seemed he couldn't get enough of her, but once they arrived in Tower City, things would go back to the way they were.

He'd have to give her space, give her time. He hadn't told her he loved her, and even though he wanted to, he would wait.

The remainder of their stay had gone smoothly, but quickly. The banquet had been fabulous, the meal a seafood lover's delight of shrimp, crab cakes, and lobster. He and Nikki had their pictures taken with the guest speakers, and Nikki posted them online.

He'd been anxious when he'd shown up to their room, and he found her doing her hair and makeup for the banquet.

While she visited the spa, he'd been at loose ends. He stumbled into a running seminar and lost track of time during the breakout sessions.

In a blur, the afternoon faded away. After realizing the time, he panicked and trotted back to their room. He worried how angry she would be at him for disappearing.

Liz had needed to know what he was doing every moment—which had been fucked up because he was always working—but his explanation stuttered to a stop when she only continued to apply her mascara.

"You're not angry?" he asked, surprised.

"Of course not. I was doing my thing, you were doing yours. I had lunch with Marta after my spa visit, and then I went for my run with the group." She leaned her belly against the bathroom sink, peering into the mirror.

"Come here," Dane murmured and pulled her into his arms. He still couldn't get used to her being as agreeable as she was.

Little things that would have set Liz off in a stream of hysterics didn't give Nikki a reason to even shrug. He thought Holly had cured him of his whiplash reaction to these kinds of situations, but he'd given Nikki power over him when he'd fallen in love with her.

He lifted her onto the counter near the sink bowl and ran his hands up her thighs. "Nice dress," he said, playing with the dark purple hem. He wanted to thank her, worship her, love her.

"We don't have time for this," she said, but she didn't push him away.

Dane shoved his running pants down his thighs and freed his erection from his briefs. "I'm so hot for you, we only need a few seconds." He slid her black lace panties from her legs and let them drop to the tiled bathroom floor. After spreading her legs, he slipped a finger inside her, making her moan. "You're hot, too," he said, positioning her near the counter's edge.

Nikki widened her thighs and gasped when he pushed himself into her.

"Come for me."

She leaned back on her hands and rested her head against the mirror. "Dane," she breathed. "Oh, God, harder. I need it harder."

Complying, he rammed himself into her as forcefully as he dared; he didn't want to hurt her. He'd already done enough of that with his insecurities. He gripped her hips, and he came, filling her completely.

Taking a moment to catch his breath, he hugged her to him, pressing his lips to her temple. "You didn't come, did you?"

"No. It must be the position. I've never done it like this before."

"It's no problem." He adjusted his pants, and he knelt in front of her. She glistened, his scent lingering on her skin. It turned him on and made him hard again. "I love looking at you." With his thumbs, he spread her open and found her pink shining nub. "So gorgeous." Dane touched his tongue to her. He couldn't remember the last time he'd gone down on a woman.

Liz hadn't liked it, saying it was disgusting, but one day during an impersonal bout of sex, he realized it wasn't the act that disgusted her, it was him.

He'd never kissed Holly that way because it was too intimate, and he hadn't wanted to make her any promises or take their relationship in a direction he didn't want to go. She never asked him about it, and thankfully, he hadn't needed to have that conversation with her.

With Nikki, it felt right to taste her, to bury his face between her legs and claim her. "You taste amazing. I love kissing you here." He lapped at her like a cat gorging on a bowl of cream.

Nikki leaned onto the counter, propped on her hands, the arches of her feet fitting into the curves of Dane's shoulders. "Dane, oh God."

He suckled and licked.

"Yes, yes," Nikki panted.

Dane shoved his fingers into her, coating them with his own come. It turned him on knowing he'd left part of himself inside her. Her muscles clutched at his fingers, and he thrust them in and out while she pulsed with pleasure beneath his lips.

When she quieted, he nibbled the inside of her thigh and smiled against her skin when she giggled.

"Now we're going to smell like sex at the banquet."

Dane kissed her lips, his flavor and hers mingling in his mouth. "Let's go make 'em jealous."

NIKKI CURLED INTO Dane's side on the plane, her legs already sore from the long run she'd shared with him that morning before checking out of the retreat to catch their flight.

They'd been out longer than planned because somehow, they'd started talking about their exes.

"Have you heard anything about Daniel?" Nikki had asked as they ran along a trail near one of the vineyards close to the hotel.

Sweat ran down her back and her sunglasses kept slipping down her nose. This was their only run together during the retreat.

Marta had hinted at joining them, and Nikki was glad Dane turned her down.

"No, I haven't thought to look into it, but Holly called me, the morning after. The robbery made the front page of the paper. I forgot to tell you."

She already knew; Margie had shown her the paper, but she frowned at the mention of Holly's name. "Does she call you a lot?"

Holly knew all of Dane's secrets, and she'd still wanted him. He'd kept his secrets from her fearing she'd turn him away, and she tried to control the jealousy.

He hadn't cared what Holly thought, she reminded herself, focusing on the run to keep pace with him.

"No. Just that one time. You don't have a problem with it, do you? I don't expect to talk to her on a regular basis."

"No. I mean, Eric called about it, too. To make sure I was alright. I guess I shouldn't say anything."

Dane stopped running, and she trotted a few beats

ahead before she realized he was no longer by her side. "What?"

"What do you mean, Eric called you?" he demanded, hands on his hips, his chest heaving as he tried to catch his breath.

"He called the night before we left. You said you and Holly broke up friends, and well, I guess Eric and I did, too. He felt guilty for leaving me in the parking lot alone, and he called to apologize."

Dane rubbed the sweat from his forehead and rolled his shoulders. "I told you I wouldn't share you."

"Talking on the phone with a guy isn't sharing me. And what about Holly? You were with her for a lot longer than I was with Eric. She thought you were a sure thing—it must have killed her to watch you walk away."

"I never gave her any reason to hope," Dane said, pulling her onto a patch of grass allowing the other runners to run by them.

"*Eric* broke up with *me*," she reminded him.

"Something he regrets," Dane shot back.

"He knows I met someone, and I hinted I wasn't coming here alone. What did you tell Holly?"

"I didn't tell her anything. She said she was sorry, I said thanks, and we hung up. All I could think about was you." Dane lifted a hand to her face.

"And all Eric said was he was glad I wasn't hurt, apologized again for not seeing me home, and we both said goodbye. All I could think about was you." Nikki pressed her lips to his. "Was that our first fight?"

"Hmmm," Dane said, twisting his fingers through her ponytail. "I guess it was. Let's not do it again."

"Deal."

Now, as the plane flew them home, she worried how the

evolution of their relationship would translate into the real world when work and other responsibilities crowded into the time they could spend together. She grew quieter as the plane descended into Tower City.

They pulled their carry-ons from the overhead compartment, and they waited for everyone to deplane before thanking the flight attendant and walking through the airport full of people traveling for the holidays to celebrate an early Thanksgiving.

Nikki didn't see any of them, didn't feel the cold November afternoon as they stepped through the airport's sliding doors and trudged through the parking lot to Dane's truck.

On the drive to their building, she fidgeted with her bag.

She didn't want to go home.

Dane sat for a moment after parking his truck in his space, his hands resting on the steering wheel. The engine clicked as it cooled down, the sound invading the small space of the cab. "What is it?"

"I don't know!" She buried her face in her hands. "I don't want things to change now that we're home."

"I know." Dane released his seatbelt and wrapped his arms around her. "We got a lot out into the open, and things are better than ever. You love your job, I love having you there. You live next door to me, honey. If I need you, I know where to find you. And I need you. Don't ever think I don't."

She pressed her face into his winter jacket and tried not to cry.

Silently, Dane coaxed her from the truck and helped her with her carry-on.

While she unlocked her apartment door, Princess

Snowflake mewed on the other side, and Nikki's lips quirked at the lonely sound.

He gave her a tender kiss, and she leaned in, warming his lips with hers.

Gripping the handle of his carry-one, Dane said, "I'll see you tomorrow. Call Alyssa and your parents and let them know you're back safe and sound. Go to bed early, okay? It's late, and it's been a long day."

"Okay," she whispered. "Have a good night. I'll see you tomorrow."

She stepped inside her apartment and leaned against the door for a moment. She missed him already, and the night loomed in front of her like a large black lonely hole. It hd been too easy to get used to spending the night with him.

With tears welling in her eyes, she wrenched the door open, slamming it behind her. She pounded on Dane's door, and immediately, he flung it open.

The same lonely expression shadowed his face, and when she propelled herself into his arms he muttered, "Jesus Christ," into her hair.

"A few more seconds," she whispered, "a few more minutes." She pulled his t-shirt up and rubbed her hands over his chest. "A few more hours."

"Only my life," he said, grabbing a fistful of her hair and pulling her in for a kiss.

He carried her to the bedroom.

"COME HERE AND look at these, Nik," Dane called from his office. He leaned back to watch her, balancing on the two hind legs of his chair; he loved seeing her dressed in her black spandex running pants and black TCRC polo.

He liked her dressed up too, in her dresses and stilettos, with her hair pinned up. But this way, dressed as she was now, made her a part of his world. He wanted to keep her there, where running shoes ruled, where putting on a TCRC shirt wrapped him around her.

"What is it?" she asked, sitting in the chair next to his. She studied the screen.

He draped his arm over the back of her seat, but resisted pulling her close. They were at work, and he did his best to act professionally since it meant so much to her.

She'd twisted her curls into a thick braid, and it started above her ear, snaked along the back of her neck, and ended in a tail that flopped over her shoulder.

He itched to run his lips along the tender skin of her nape. She shivered when he kissed her there, and his cock hardened thinking about his affect on her.

He shifted his attention to the computer monitor. "Brett sent proofs of the logo for next year's race. He needs to okay one soon. He's a bit behind this year because of some problems he's been having."

Nikki studied the neon logos, each differing slightly in either font, color, or other detail. She wrinkled her nose.

"You don't like any of them?" Dane gave in to touching her and ran his fingers along the ridge of the braid. He barely touched her skin.

"They're so garish. I know it's supposed to be eye-catching, but I'm a girly-girl. I like elegant. I like pink and silver and sparkles. I want tiaras handed out at the race finish, not another medal."

Dane laughed. "Fair enough."

He texted Brett. *Nikki wants a women's race.*

Brett's reply appeared on Dane's cell phone screen.

Great idea. She's in charge. I'll come to your office tomorrow to talk to her about it.

"Are you sure you want a women's race?" Dane asked.

"I think it would be great for the community. And oh, my God, it would be so much fun! We could do things Brett can't do for everyone, like the tiaras. Maybe at the expo we could have a fashion show featuring women's running gear. The proceeds from the tickets could go to charity," Nikki said.

"Well, it's great you're that eager because Brett just made you the director."

"What?"

He showed her Brett's text. "You shouldn't have opened your mouth."

"I can't believe it!" Nikki squealed, doing a little dance around the tiny office. "I'm going to put on a women's race!"

She grabbed his phone. *Thank you, thank you! Are you coming to Thanksgiving? This is Nikki, btw.*

Dane is making me go. What do I need to bring? Brett replied.

Nothing. Just yourself! See you tomorrow :) Nikki texted and handed the phone back to him.

"He's coming to Thanksgiving too. Oh, you don't mind, do you? About the race?" Her face fell in disappointment. "You hired me to be here at the store."

"I don't mind," he said and gave her a peck on the lips, thinking she'd forgive him since she was in such a good mood about the women's race. "It's great how easily you've fit in here, at the store . . ."

In my life.

". . . and doing things for the marathon. I was damn lucky all around I hired you. You've changed my life in ways I didn't think a woman could, ever again."

And she did, Dane thought, going for a quick run the evening before Thanksgiving while Nikki shopped with Alyssa for last minute things to serve with their meal.

He and Nikki spent all their free time together. Most nights it was dinner in with Flix Roulette, and sometimes they skipped that all together and ate in bed after making love.

They grocery shopped and went to the store for mundane things like laundry detergent. Winter was holding off, and they drove out to Eagle Pass State Park to run the trails. He huffed out a laugh thinking of them making love on a deserted hiking path. They'd almost frozen to death, half naked while their panting had turned white from the chilly air, but it'd been worth it. These past few weeks with her had been blissful, and he was looking forward to Thanksgiving Day.

It had been a long time since he'd looked forward to the holidays. For Liz, all she'd been concerned with was what he was going to buy her for Christmas, what jewelry for Valentine's Day.

It made him stressed about Nikki's Christmas gift. He couldn't afford much; there was no way he'd be able to buy her diamonds to put under her tree like Mr. Rolex.

Christmas plans were up in the air. He wanted to ask her if she would share the holiday with him, but her parents lived in Tower City, and the only reason she was with him for Thanksgiving was because they were on a cruise.

That wasn't true, and Dane felt guilty for thinking it. She wouldn't leave him hanging for Thanksgiving.

She would have invited him to her parents' house, he was sure of it.

Tomorrow worked for him though, to share the holiday with her, Brett, and Alyssa. Maybe next year, if things went the way he hoped, they would be married or engaged and they would do the two-family holiday thing.

If he married Nikki, he wondered if his parents would finally forgive him.

Nikki seemed sure they would, when he got married and started having children.

She hadn't alluded to herself in the role of his wife, but starting a family with her was a new dream. Living under one roof instead of splitting time between their apartments. He wasn't sure how they could afford kids, but he would do it, for her, if she wanted it. He would do anything to make her happ—

Nikki wasn't Liz, he told himself firmly, running along his favorite loop in the park behind his apartment building.

She wouldn't change when he married her.

He had to trust someone sometime or he would spend his life alone. Nikki had proven time and again she wasn't like his ex-wife. She was happy with how they lived. She didn't make any snide comments about always staying in, lying on her couch, Princess Snowflake cuddled in his lap.

When he asked her to stop dating other men, she had. He knew she had because they were always together. If she wasn't at the store, she was with him at her apartment, or they were at his.

Sometimes he went out with Brett, and she went to Alyssa's, or she went out with Alyssa and their other friends.

He encouraged that.

He valued the space she gave him when he wanted it, and he did the same for her, even if it did make him nervous as hell when she went out dressed in her ass-hugging jeans and sparkly tops. But to be fair, she never said anything about him hanging at the bar with Brett, though she didn't know women didn't make an appearance at the little bar all that often.

She loved him. She hadn't said the words yet, and he hadn't told her he loved her, either, but it was there. It was there in her touch, in the way she kissed him, in the way she always had his favorite beer in her fridge. In the way she searched his eyes, looking for the sadness that had always been there since they first met.

The unhappiness and pain were slowly going away. The wounds to his heart were finally healing. He only needed two more things: a truce with his parents and a ring on Nikki's finger after she told him she would marry him.

Life was good now, but if he had those two things, life would be damn near perfect.

He was cooling down in a slow trot heading toward his apartment through the chilly wind when his phone chimed with a text. His fingertips tingled when he took off his running gloves to look at his phone.

Lucky I bought the turkey last week. A picture of an empty bin at the grocery store popped up. *Store is crazy. Going to Alyssa's to read part of her new book. Don't wait up. See you tomorrow <3*

Dane was disappointed he wouldn't be sleeping with her tonight, but the heart at the end of her text made him smile. He pulled up Brett's name. *Free man tonight. Madden?* Dane asked, mentioning one of their favorite video games.

Sure, come over. Bring beer. I'm out. Brett's text came back immediately.

Dane texted him back with, *Will do, give me 30.*

To Nikki, he wrote, *Going to Brett's to play video games. Have fun at A's. See you tomorrow. <3 you too.*

He slipped his phone back into his running jacket to protect it from the chilly temperature and finished his cool down, his hot sweat now chilling his skin.

That kind of exchange with Liz would have been impossible. She wouldn't have allowed it. It was further proof Nikki wasn't his ex-wife. She was her own person. The right person. For him.

"THAT WAS A pain in the ass," Alyssa grumbled, pushing the door of her apartment loft open.

"Oh, my God, we were fools to go to the store today," Nikki said, pulling off her gloves and the black beret she wore in lieu of a hat. It did absolutely nothing to keep her warm, and her ears stung from the frigid wind.

Alyssa set two paper bags of wine and champagne on her kitchen counter before taking off her parka. "I'm glad the liquor store was still stocked."

"You certainly took advantage of their sale."

"Ha! So did you!" Alyssa said, shaking out her hair. She'd worn a proper hat to ward off the chill. "If we drink everything you bought, we'll be too drunk to eat."

"It's the holidays, why not?"

"Pour some of the champagne, and we'll start early." Alyssa hung her jacket in the front closet. "You and Dane are doing pretty well, huh?" she asked, digging into the bags to start putting things away. "How was the retreat?"

"The retreat was awesome! California's weather was magnificent, and I met Dane and Brett's old friend from college. She's nice, and I guess she and Brett have a history that they haven't told Dane about. The speakers were infor-mative, and the food was wonderful."

"Did you do any running?" Alyssa asked wryly, grab-bing the flute of champagne she poured. In invitation, she tilted her head in the direction of the stairs leading to her loft.

Nikki laughed. "You're so funny. Yes, we did. I ran in a group run, then one with Dane the day we flew back."

Her smile dimmed, and she took a sip of champagne to hide it, only her friend knew her too well.

"What? I know that look. What happened?"

Nikki wandered the office she'd seen a hundred times before. "Well, on our run, Dane told me Holly called him to tell him she was sorry about the store being robbed."

Taking a seat behind her desk and bringing her computer to life, Alyssa said, "That doesn't seem like a big deal."

"I guess not, but I got nervous they talked, then I had to tell him Eric called me about it, too."

Alyssa glanced up from her monitor. "He did? You didn't tell me that."

"Yeah. After you left the night before Dane and I flew to California. He called to see how I was doing."

"Do you think he still wants more?" Alyssa asked. She took a sip of champagne and leaned back in her chair.

"Yeah, he as good as said so. When we talked, he mentioned us taking a vacation together to help me get over the robbery. And he asked me to consider going back to Shine. I told him no to both things, but when I came back from the retreat, I found flowers in my kitchen. There must have been about four dozen roses. The only thing I can think of is he sweet-talked the building manager into letting him into my apartment. I had to sneak them to the dumpster in a garbage bag so Dane wouldn't see them. I know he would've flipped out."

"That's creepy." Alyssa frowned. "You should complain because that's not right. Eric could have been some perverted creep who wanted to steal your underwear."

Nikki stared out the window. All the trees were bare now, the sky a continual dreary grey. "I didn't call to thank him or anything, and I hope that's the end of it."

"Did you tell Dane about the flowers?"

Nikki settled into a loveseat under the window. "No. At the retreat we kind of fought about Holly and Eric a little, and I didn't want to add to it. I'm sure Eric will leave me alone now. He can have anybody."

"But not you. Look, I did a little research on stalkers for *Watching You*, and it's some spooky shit. A lot of times the victims can't do anything. Be careful. And complain to your landlord. Them letting in anybody, that's garbage."

"Well, it's the holidays, and Eric will be busy with parties and stuff. He won't give me another thought."

"I hope you're right. Now come here and tell me what you think of this opening scene. Something is off, but I don't know what."

Relieved Alyssa shifted the conversation away from Eric, Nikki sat next to Alyssa and started to read.

RUBBING HER EYES, still tired from staying at Alyssa's until later than she should have, Nikki opened the door to Dane's knock the next morning.

"What are you doing here so early?" she asked, squinting, the hallway light shining behind him.

"It's not *that* early, and I wanted to see if you needed

help . . . and to do this." Dane swept her into his arms and gave her a kiss.

His kiss made her shiver, and she sighed as he ran his tongue over her lips. She opened her mouth to let him in, and she smiled when she tasted toothpaste. He'd woken her up, and her own mouth tasted like glue in comparison.

"Mmm. You look nice."

He was dressed in a dark pair of jeans with a dark brown and cream sweater. The collar of a cream dress shirt peeked from the sweater's neck.

"Too much, do you think?"

"No, not at all. I haven't showered yet. I crawled out of bed to go to the bathroom. How was Brett's last night? Sorry I flaked on you. Alyssa wanted my opinion on the beginning of her book, but I think that was just an excuse. She kept me for a lot longer than I thought she would and I didn't get back until after two. She's lonely—the holidays bring her down."

She pulled a container of orange juice out of the fridge. "Can you grab the champagne out of the cabinet?"

"I don't know why she's not with someone. Alyssa's great."

"What she said at the Whine and Wine Wednesday you crashed is true. At some point, the men she dates try to change her. I've known her since we were little kids. I've seen it happen, how they end up treating her."

Dane handed her the champagne and she fought with the gold foil glued around the neck of the champagne bottle for two seconds before he took it back, chuckling.

"Let me make the mimosas, and you go take a shower."

Nikki leaned up to kiss him. "Thanks. When you're done, put the pitcher in the fridge to chill, okay? I'll be out in a little bit. Happy Thanksgiving." She wound her arms around his neck and whispered, "I'm glad you're here with me."

He brushed the hair from her face. "Me, too."

Nikki heard the front door open as she stepped out of the shower. She didn't know who had arrived, but she wanted to take her time getting ready. Today was a special occasion—their first holiday together.

She dried her hair the best she could with a towel, then spread lotion all over her body. It smelled like pumpkin pie, and she wondered if later Dane would eat her up.

As she capped the lotion, she laughed. God, things were fabulous, and telling Dane about the flowers Eric put in her apartment would ruin it. Bringing it up would be pointless and only cause friction.

They were always on the same page about everything, and she wanted to keep it that way. Unlike some of her past boyfriends who only wanted her at their beck and call, she didn't have to be afraid Dane would get angry if she wanted to spend time with her friends.

Eric was more like her exes than Nikki realized. She hadn't expected him to be so forward, delivering flowers to her that way, but luckily, he hadn't contacted her again. It was rude not to thank him, but she didn't want to encourage any communication between them. He was used to getting what he wanted—Alyssa was right about that. She didn't want to lead him on, in any way.

Soon she'd need to ask Dane what his plans were for Christmas. She wasn't sure how she would fit him into her family drama, but she wanted to celebrate the holiday with him, somehow.

Nikki hadn't decided what she would buy him, but it would be something simple.

Maybe she would ask Alyssa to take a nice picture of

them, and she would print and frame it. The gift would be inexpensive, but it would mean something.

He could put it on his desk at the store. It irritated him she kept to herself while they were working, and she promised herself she would try to lighten up. It's not like their being together was a secret. Margie had known from their first kiss.

Proud of the idea, Nikki tugged on a pair of jeans then looked through her closet.

He was wearing brown and cream. If she wanted to complement him in the picture she could wear . . . hmmm. She pulled out a cream short-sleeved blouse decorated with gold sequins. Festive, and it matched the cream in Dane's sweater.

She wound her hair in a damp bun and applied a hint of makeup. The bruise on her face had faded, and she hadn't thought about that night for a long time. Thankfully, she hadn't been uncomfortable in the store like Dane feared she would. She added some mascara and dotted her lips with gloss. His presence at the store erased any bad feelings she could have had.

With Princess Snowflake following at her heels, Nikki made her way into the kitchen and Dane handed her a mimosa.

She greeted Alyssa, who was sitting at the table, and gave her a hug. "Happy Thanksgiving. I'm glad you're here."

"Me too, considering I was the one who picked out the pumpkin cheesecake we're going to have for dessert."

"I'm going to put the football game on," Dane said, grabbing the remote from the back of the loveseat. "The pre-game show should be playing."

"What if we wanted to watch the parade?" Alyssa asked, tamping back a laugh.

Dane tilted his head. "Seriously?"

There was a knock at the door, and he shoved the remote into the back pocket of his jeans. "I guess I'll answer the door instead, but that doesn't mean you have control of the TV."

Nikki laughed, and Dane winked at her.

"Right on time," Dane said when he let Brett inside, and Nikki poured him a mimosa.

Dane took the bottles of booze Brett held out, and Brett hung up his winter coat. "You brought Jack," Dane said, amused.

"Couldn't leave him behind," Brett said, walking into the kitchen. "He's a tradition." He hugged Nikki. "Thanks for having me, Nik."

"I'm glad you're here, Happy Thanksgiving," she said, handing him the orange, frothy drink. "This is my friend, Alyssa."

Brett shook Alyssa's hand, but he didn't seem interested in speaking with her and instead, quickly joined Dane in the living room.

After the men settled in front of the TV, Nikki puttered around the kitchen with Alyssa, talking about her parents and the fun they were having on their cruise, and if Alyssa was going to fly to Florida to spend Christmas with her mom and dad.

"It wouldn't feel like Christmas without snow," Nikki said, carrying a tray of meat and cheese into the living room. "If you guys are hungry, this will keep you from starving to death. The turkey will be another two hours or so."

Dane snared her waist and pulled her into his lap. "It's hot in here." He playfully panted into her ear.

"Dane!" Laughing, Nikki steadied the tray in her hands. "You're lucky I didn't drop this. If you're that hot, you can open the open the balcony doors. Let me up now. I have things to do. Unless you want to help?" She nipped at his neck.

He caught her in a a quick kiss before she set the tray on the coffee table. "Nope. I'm fine where I am."

"Ah-huh. You look like it."

At the sink, she started to peel potatoes for the pan of sour cream potato bake she was going to serve with the turkey and gave her friend the side-eye as Alyssa lounged at the table sipping champagne.

"Why aren't you helping?" she asked Alyssa, almost taking off a nail with an aggressive swipe of the potato peeler.

Alyssa stuck her tongue in her cheek. "I'm a guest."

Nikki grunted.

Standing from the table, Alyssa said, "Can you believe Kayla's having her wedding on the Saturday after Christmas? God. I'm going to freeze at her bachelorette party. Why couldn't she have gotten married in June like everyone else?"

"The church will be beautiful," Nikki said in Kayla's defense. "All the poinsettias and twinkle lights. And she decided to have a candlelight ceremony. It'll be gorgeous. Did you see the pictures she sent everyone of her dress? It's amazing. She's going to wear a cape, and she has a matching hand muff. I'm glad we're not in her wedding party, though. The dresses suck, as usual." Nikki finished another potato. "Do you have a date?"

Alyssa drained her glass and reached into the fridge for the champagne bottle. "Of course not. There's nothing worse than trying to find a date for a wedding. Can't I hang out with you and Dane?"

"I haven't asked him to go with me yet."

"He'll go with you. You two will probably be taking notes for your own wedding."

"We've only known each other a couple months." She lowered her voice, though she didn't think the men would hear her over the roar of the game. "He hasn't even said he loves me."

"I'm pretty sure that's a technicality at this point," Alyssa said, grabbing the cutting board Nikki stored by the microwave.

"I don't know. I don't want to assume anything."

"Well, I'm your third wheel for the wedding, and I'll pick you up for the party. What's the date for it again?" Alyssa asked, dumping the cubed potatoes into a large pot. "I keep getting the Saturdays mixed up."

After drying her hands, Nikki grabbed the invitation stuck to her fridge by a magnetic rabbit clip, its large teeth clutching the edge of the fancy paper stock. "The thirteenth. But you don't have to pick me up, remember? Kayla's maid of honor hired a limo."

"No way I'm riding in it," Alyssa said. "I'm not depending on someone to bring me home. I might need a quick escape, especially if they want to go to a strip club. That's the last thing I want to do with my time and cash."

Finishing the potatoes, Nikki said, "Good point."

When she was single she wouldn't have minded doing something like that, but now she had Dane and going to a strip club didn't sound fun to her, either. "But . . . limo. When will we have another chance?"

"You can ride in it, and I'll bring you home if you want to leave early with me."

"No," she said with a sigh, "I'll ride with you. You've never been wrong. Help me with the sweet potato pie, now, will you?"

"THAT DIDN'T GO well," Nikki said, shoving some the leftover turkey she couldn't convince Alyssa and Brett to take home into her fridge.

Dane took a bite of cheesecake as he leaned against the humming dishwasher. "Brett's pretty abrasive. I guess with Alyssa being so sensitive, they're like oil and water."

"She may be sensitive, but not that much. They barely spoke during dinner. Oh, well. They won't have to see each other ever again." She flicked a glance at Dane. "How many miles are you going to run tomorrow? That's your third piece of cheesecake."

Dane set the plate in the empty sink and dusted his hands on the thighs of his jeans. He pulled Nikki into his arms. "How about," he purred into her ear, "we go work off some calories right now, and I'll tell you how thankful I am you're in my life. You know, in the spirit of Thanksgiving."

Nikki stood on her tiptoes to meet his lips with hers. "That sounds wonderful, but I don't care how much you beg, I'm not going running with you in the morning before we open the store for Black Friday."

Dane groaned in mock frustration as she pulled him to the bedroom.

Nikki laughed until Dane wouldn't let her laugh anymore.

While driving Nikki home after a long shift at the store, Dane breathed a contented sigh. Last year, if someone would've said he would be this happy, he never would have believed it. Yeah, he'd been dating Holly, and while she'd been a catalyst in helping him after his divorce, it had been Nikki and her love that healed him.

In his apartment on the evenings Nikki went out with her friends or worked the night shift at the store, he shopped online for an engagement and wedding ring set he could afford.

He wasn't sure when or how they would celebrate Christmas together, but he was going to ask her to marry him. There were a couple weeks before the holiday, and he'd narrowed down the rings to a few he liked.

Tonight he was in the Christmas spirit, and he wanted to take her for dinner. "Let's go out."

"Go out?" Nikki asked, confused, opening the door to his truck.

She finally agreed to let him take her to and from work, and it made him happy.

It was coming nearer to the time he wouldn't go in at all, and he winced.

The reason he hired a manager was to free up time to help Brett with the marathon. Now he wanted to spend time with Nikki, but she was at the store forty to fifty hours a week.

Brett knew the holidays were a busy time for him, but that excuse wasn't going to last long. When January arrived, there would be no getting around helping Brett at marathon headquarters, when the race loomed as May's largest Tower City event.

If Nikki said yes to his marriage proposal, he would talk to their landlord and ask if he could break his lease. Nikki signed hers not long ago, and his didn't expire until the summer. He didn't want to wait that long to move in with her. He already slept there most nights anyway. Sleeping in her bed every night would be a small consolation for giving up his days with her.

And if she said no, well, he wouldn't think about that right now.

Over dinner he would feel her out, try to get an idea of how she felt about marrying him. "

Yeah," he said, rounding the box of his truck to take her hand. "You know, get a little dressed up, go out to eat. Let's go downtown; the streets are decorated for Christmas. I know an Italian place with great manicotti. It's near a club that plays live jazz. You like jazz?"

"Sure, it sounds great. But we haven't gone out since we've started seeing each other. We don't have to—"

Dane interrupted her with a kiss. "I want to. I've kept you to myself all this time, but it will be nice to go out, too."

Eyes shining, she kissed him back. "Okay. If you're sure. I need to change and freshen up. I'll probably take longer, so come over when you're ready."

After he changed out of his work clothes, Dane sipped a beer, leaning on the doorjamb of her bathroom while he waited for her to finish reapplying her makeup. "You don't need all that mess, you know."

She wrinkled her nose at him in the mirror. "Thanks. But even if men complain about it, I'm sure they appreciate it more than they think." Nikki added more gloss to her lips. "I'm all set."

On the drive, large snowflakes started drifting from the sky. He parked, and they landed on the windshield covering the glass in seconds.

"Sorry. This is the closest I can get tonight. A lot of other people must have had the same idea."

"That's okay. Walking around is part of the downtown experience."

She carried her purse with the strap crossed over her body, and she wound her arms around one of his and rested her head on his shoulder as they walked to a small Italian restaurant.

He pressed a kiss to her head, snowflakes chilling his lips.

The scents of basil and garlic met their noses, and he breathed in deeply. Decorated for Christmas, candles and twinkle lights sparkled in the restaurant's darkened dining room. Patrons, speaking in hushed but cheerful tones, dined on pasta and drank wine and cappuccinos.

A hostess wearing a black dress and a string of pearls led them to a table, and Dane took off his jacket while Nikki shook out her coat and hung it on the back of her chair.

Nikki had dressed in black as well, and Dane eyed her clothing with appreciation. Her light blue skinny jeans molded to her ass perfectly, and she'd tucked them into black high-heeled boots. Her black pea coat jacket matched her black turtleneck sweater. She'd pulled her hair into a low side ponytail, and large gold hoops hung from her ears. She looked amazing, and it had only taken her a couple minutes.

For a night out like this, Liz would have taken hours to dress, and her blouse would have cost him three times their restaurant bill. She also would have been scouting the customers, looking to see whom she knew and trying her best to be noticed.

All Nikki did was reach for a menu.

"I've never been here before. I don't come downtown

very often, and I forgot how charming it is. Maybe I'll see if Alyssa wants to do a little shopping at the shops here for Christmas; we always go to the mall."

"Brett and I drink at a bar a few blocks from here when we go out. I can show you where it is, if you want to take a walk after dinner. It's not much, but we're friends with the bartender and don't hang out anywhere else."

The waitress stopped by their table to take their drink orders, and Dane threw a worried glance Nikki's way. He didn't want to add an expensive bottle of wine to their bill.

He bit back a sigh.

If he was going to have a future with Nikki, he'd need to think about his finances, his bank loan, amend his personal budget. They hadn't talked much about their future, preferring to take things day by day.

When she ordered coffee, he shook the tension from his shoulders. He should have known he could count on her to make things easier for him. Sometimes he thought he would never get used to it.

"I'll have the same," he said, nodding to the waitress.

He picked up a sugar packet and started flipping it between his fingers. "What are your plans for Christmas?" he asked, studying the red and white checked tablecloth.

He didn't want to assume they would be spending Christmas together, but he hoped, and he was nervous about what she thought.

"You're not going to see your parents at all?" Nikki asked. She smiled her thanks to the waitress who set thick white mugs of coffee in front of them. She added cream to hers and took a sip.

He cleared his throat to give himself a few more seconds. "My parents pretty much cut me off after my divorce. I tried the first year, when the divorce was going through the courts, when Liz was suing me for all I had. I needed . . . support from them, but they made it clear they wanted nothing to do with me. I stopped trying, and I haven't spoken, I mean, really spoken to them, since the divorce went through."

They gave their orders to the waitress, and Nikki picked at a piece of bread the waitress set on the table before she walked away.

"My sister is driving from Chicago with her husband."

"You know, for all the time we spend together, I didn't know you had a sister."

"She's a little bit older than I am. She got married a few years ago, and her husband is an architect. He took a job in Chicago, and they've been living out there."

She nibbled the bread and swallowed before continuing.

"They're having problems conceiving and every year we see them the stress is worse. She wants a baby desperately, and the doctors can't figure out what's going on. They both checked out. She's fine, he's not shooting blanks." She laughed at Dane's pained expression. "Nothing is working for them."

"Sounds rough," he said, taking her hand. The coffee mug had made her skin warm.

She squeezed. "Yeah. So, I'm leaving it up to you. Meeting parents is stressful on a normal day. Mixing my sister's infertility and a holiday together doesn't seem like the best situation. Don't feel bad if you don't want to. We can celebrate New Year's together."

Dane didn't want to meet Nikki's parents under those conditions, and he was grateful she was leaving it up to him and not making him feel like an asshole in the process.

"We would still do a little something, wouldn't we?" He brought her hand to his lips and kissed her palm.

"Of course. I have to give you your present."

"Nikki—" Dane started.

"I know you wouldn't want to spend much. I promise. I paid . . ." She looked up at the ceiling while she thought, and he wondered for a split second if she was thinking up a lie. "I paid ten dollars. I swear."

"Ten dollars?" he asked skeptically, lifting his eyebrows.

Nikki waited to reply until after the waitress finished setting down their plates of steaming pasta and asking them if there was anything else she could do for them before drifting away.

"I wouldn't lie to you. I promise. Ten bucks. You can spend ten bucks on me, or less. It will be a Christmas tradition. Even if we win the lottery, even if your store takes off and you open running shoe stores in every state, every Christmas, ten bucks."

"You see a lot of Christmases in our future?" He met her eyes over the flickering candle.

"I do," Nikki said, returning his gaze.

Dane hoped to hear those words from her mouth while they stood in a church, at the altar, with everyone who meant something to them looking on.

Soon.

But for now, he leaned over the table to kiss her, and with his heart pounding, asked the waitress for more coffee.

NIKKI TUCKED HERSELF under Dane's arm as they walked the streets downtown.

It was still snowing, big wet snowflakes slowly falling

from the dark sky. The streetlights were sparkling with white twinkle lights wrapped around their poles. The stores had decorated their window displays with gift ideas for the holiday: everything from wine and wine glasses to toys for children to holiday lingerie.

"I need to do a little shopping for my family," Nikki said as they passed a window showcasing men's scarves and wallets. "We don't go all out, but we exchange little presents. We should buy Brett something. And I always give Alyssa a gift."

She stopped in front of a party display. "I wish Alyssa and Brett got along better. We could have invited them over for New Year's. But I don't want to force her to spend time with him."

Dane backed her up against the window of a store closed for the evening. "I think I'd like to bring in the New Year with only the two of us, anyway. We could watch a movie we both choose, not Flix Roulette. We could make dinner, make love, make plans for the year."

Nikki covered her heart with her hands and gasped. "No Flix Roulette? Hmm," she sighed when he tipped his head closer to hers. His lips were cold against her cheek, and she smelled the faint scent of coffee and sugar on his breath.

"Nikki, I want to share my life with you." Dane framed her face with his palms. "I've wanted to tell you for a while now that I lo—"

"Well, isn't this cozy?"

Nikki jerked away from Dane. A distinguished man and an elegant woman approach them. The woman's eyes glittered black, and even in the faint glow of the streetlights, Nikki could see the unhappiness and anger on her face.

She could have been beautiful. Nikki tried to look past

the lines of dissatisfaction marring her skin, through the bitterness pulling her mouth down into a perpetual frown. Her hair, falling around the shoulders of an expensive black leather jacket, sparkled with snow. Leather gloves covered her hands that were balled into fists. Nikki recognized the logo of an expensive brand decorating her purse.

Dane stiffened. "Liz." He tightened his grip on Nikki and tried to pull her away. "Let's go."

"But we haven't caught up," Liz said, stepping away from the man she was with.

Nikki assumed he was Liz's husband, but she couldn't remember if Dane told her Liz had remarried.

"How long has it been?" Liz asked, stepping too close into their personal space for her liking. "Are you doing any better? Have you been able to trade in your piece of shit truck? Do you still live in that little godforsaken apartment?" She smirked. "Are your parents speaking to you yet? They know what a loser you are. They disowned their only child because you weren't man enough to keep your wife happy."

Dane emitted a strangled sound from the back of his throat, and the blood drained from his face. Trying to soothe him, Nikki patted his back.

"Liz, this isn't necessary," the man said, pulling on her arm. "He's in your past. You should leave him there."

Nikki flinched when Liz's eyes turned to her.

"But I need to warn her," Liz said, yanking her arm from her husband's grasp, her breath streaming in angry puffs, turning white in the frigid air. "Listen, honey. Get out while you can. Dane doesn't have anything for you. He can't take you on vacation, he won't buy you jewelry. You'll never drive a new car. Do you even know how much he makes a year?"

"Yes, I do," said said, lifting her chin, relishing the chance to tell his vile woman off. "I've seen the store's books. I know exactly how much he makes every year."

Liz looked taken aback for a moment, and Nikki felt a momentary sense of victory.

"Then you know you can do better, hon. Trust a woman who knows." Liz pulled off the glove of her left hand. A huge diamond glinted on her ring finger. "Take a good look. You'll never wear a ring like this if you stay with him. Dane Montgomery is worthless."

"Enough," Liz's husband growled, putting an arm around her shoulder. He turned to Nikki and Dane. "I'm sorry, she had too much to drink at dinner. Have a nice evening."

It was too late.

The lights had lost their twinkle, the promise of the New Year drifted away, and Nikki fought to head off the sadness radiating from Dane's body.

"Don't listen to her," she said, wrapping her arms around Dane's neck. "She'll always be unhappy. All those things she said I would never have, she has them, and she's still unhappy. Don't listen to her."

Desperately, she pressed her mouth to his, pushing herself into him as closely as she could, but he didn't return her kiss. "Tell me what you were going to say before she interrupted us. Tell me."

Shadows hid half of Dane's face, and her heart skipped painfully in her chest. Liz had caused damage, but time would only tell how much, and how much work it would take her to fix it.

Dane pressed a kiss to her forehead. "We should head back. It's late. I promised Brett more time before Christmas, and I'll be spending all day with him at headquarters."

The back of her throat burned. The sad change in him made her want to cry. How stiffly he held himself now, how he tucked his hands into his pockets to avoid her touch. He wouldn't look at her, didn't notice when she lagged two steps behind.

What a hateful, horrible woman. It was no wonder he hurt.

She would help him forget; she would help him move forward.

She was sure before Liz interrupted them he was going to tell her he loved her. She wanted to hear it, wanted to say it in return, but if she said it now, he would think it was in sympathy or pity, and he wouldn't believe her.

Eyes on the snow-covered sidewalk, she wiped a tear from her cheek as she hurried past the windows beaming holiday cheer.

When Nikki looked up, Dane was gone.

Turning in a circle, she searched for him. She hadn't paid attention where he'd parked his truck, and now he'd disappeared, leaving her lost.

Standing on the empty sidewalk, she was alone but for the falling snow.

As her panic heightened, Dane appeared behind her.

"Hey, what happened to you?"

"I lost you."

She meant it in all the ways possible. After Liz's husband led her down the sidewalk, after Dane pulled away from her embrace, he was gone. His mind, spirit, and heart had disappeared.

"No, you didn't. I'm right here." Dane pulled her into his arms and pressed his lips to her temple. "Let's go home."

Nikki tried to relax after he rescued her from the empty

street, but the spark that had been in his eyes during their romantic Italian meal was missing.

He didn't speak on their drive to their apartment building, holding her hand, and he dropped her at her apartment door, chastely kissing her goodnight.

"But I wanted to—"

Dane shook his head. "I'm not good company tonight."

She nodded and watched him unlock his door and step inside, closing it with a soft click. There was no way she was going to leave him alone. If he wouldn't let her in, she would call Brett.

She didn't like the way Dane was acting, and she wouldn't let him hide.

Nikki combed out her hair and took off her makeup. She brushed her teeth and changed into her boxers and tank top, then slipped a robe over her pajamas.

Self-consciously, looking down the empty corridor, she tapped her knuckles on his door. It would be embarrassing to be caught in the hall in her night clothes, and she hoped Dane wouldn't ignore her.

She breathed a sigh of relief when he answered.

"I told you I didn't want company."

Nikki ignored his protests and stepped inside his apartment. "You mean you don't want company besides Jack. I'm not going to let you sit in your apartment and get drunk because of some stupid, heartless woman. You mean more to me than that. I want to spend the night with you."

"No. Go home."

She narrowed her eyes and crossed her arms over her breasts. He didn't scare her and she wouldn't budge.

"No."

Dane closed the door and locked it, the snick of the bolt sliding into the lock the only noise in the entire apartment.

"You really want to go head to head with me?"

"You would never hurt me."

He fisted her hair, making her gasp. "Are you sure? Do you want to test me? Go home."

They stood in the little hallway, his kitchen to one side, two bedrooms to the other. An empty coat closet took up the hallway wall. His scent consumed her. He didn't cook here; if he made a meal, he did it in her kitchen.

Home.

It wasn't her apartment or his apartment. It wasn't even this building.

His grip loosened when she began to speak. "Don't you get it? Don't you understand? It doesn't matter where I am. It only matters where you are. Home is with you, Dane. Home is with you."

"God," he moaned, pulling her to his bedroom. "Didn't you hear what she told you?"

They stepped into the dark, and Nikki helped him slide off her robe. She pulled her tank over her head, pushed her boxers over her hips, and kicked them off her feet. Naked, she pushed her lips to his and tugged at the waist of his shorts.

He dragged his lips from hers and pushed his shorts down. "Didn't you hear?" He fluttered kisses over her face, down her neck, and over the tops of her breasts before taking a nipple into his mouth.

Nikki moaned and forked her fingers through his hair. Yes, yes. This was much better than sitting in her apartment, worrying about him. This was better than him getting drunk, thinking of the past, and how it wouldn't let him go, no matter how fast he ran.

"Worthless," he mumbled against her lips, pressing her onto his bed.

Nikki opened her mouth for him, and their tongues danced together as Dane pulled her closer, his erection pressed against her leg.

"Kind," she whispered, kissing his neck and at the same time arching her hips, inviting him closer, inviting him in.

"Loser," he said, running a hand along the inside of her thigh.

"Hero," she murmured, thinking of the food drives the store held, the giving tree she decorated in the store that would collect toys for impoverished children.

Dane pushed his fingers into her, and she cried out. "Poor," he muttered. "I have nothing."

"Rich. Love me, Dane. Give me all your love."

Dane propped himself on his hands and pushed into her hot core, carefully, slowly, shuddering until he was fully sheathed inside her.

Nikki smoothed her hands over his arms and chest. He was so beautiful, this man, inside and out. How Liz could have thrown him away she didn't know, but it was the best thing Liz had ever done because it meant Dane was with her now.

He rolled to his back, and she sat on top, riding him. She moaned when he slipped a finger between their bodies and feathered his fingertip over her clit. The pleasure and the tension grew as she reached her peak.

Dane increased the tempo and thrust deeper, harder, than he ever had.

Nikki contracted around him, and she smiled when Dane groaned. She pushed herself closer to him as he throbbed inside her finding his own piece of heaven.

Oh yes, this was better than spending the night alone. If it were up to her, she and Dane would never spend another night apart.

She lowered herself onto his sweat-slicked body and with trembling lips, kissed his mouth.

He pulled at his comforter and wrapped it around them.

They lay quietly, the blackness consuming them, no light from anywhere to penetrate the darkness of the room.

"You really won't be at the store tomorrow?"

DANE LAUGHED. HE couldn't believe that after all that happened, the only thing that concerned her was that he wouldn't be at the store the next day. And really, he only said it because Liz pissed him off.

"It's not funny," Nikki pouted, lifting over him to lick his sensitive nipples.

"That's all you have to say about tonight? Goddamn Nik, if I had it my way, you never would've met that harpy."

"You know what I was thinking about when we were making love?"

Dane kissed her hair. "I hope making love, and how excellent I am."

"Yeah," she said, and he imagined her rolling her eyes, but he heard the laugh in her voice, knew she was smiling, even though it was pitch black in his room.

He didn't care about this bedroom anymore; he was rarely there. He would've been here alone, too, if he would have had his way.

Thank God Nikki was so stubborn.

"No, really. I was thinking if you and Liz would have worked, if you would have still been married, I wouldn't be here. I know that's selfish, but I can't help it. You've become such a big part of my life, sometimes I forget what it was like without you in it."

Dane pulled her closer and lost his chance to speak when Nikki's breathing evened out. It had been a long day for her, and there would be more. The holidays were in full swing.

She called him a hero. No one had ever called him that before.

He hoped he would always be hers.

CHAPTER SEVEN

S TARING INTO THE mirror in her bathroom smoothing glittery blush on the apples of her cheeks, Nikki was flying high.

Dane seemed to have forgotten their encounter with Liz, and he acted as if he found some of the Christmas spirit that had disappeared after that fateful evening.

Several times he went ice skating with her at the city rink and drank hot chocolate in the warming house. They rode in his truck and looked at Christmas lights while she fed him French fries from a fast food joint. They took a sleigh ride through Eagle Pass State Park and afterward, they had to stand under a hot shower to thaw. That had been the best part.

When she wasn't with him, she was Christmas shopping with Alyssa. One afternoon they braved the mall to find dresses for Kayla's bachelorette party, finding amazing sales on discounted holiday dresses.

Alyssa asked her if she'd heard from Eric again, and she was relieved she could say no. Eric had given up, and the subject dropped when she spotted a beautiful pair of heels marked on clearance.

She talked with her sister and mother about Christmas plans.

One evening she baked with Alyssa, and they ate more of the cookies than they saved for the holiday. They drank too much wine, and the next morning Nikki woke up sick on a sugar and alcohol overload.

After a busy shift at the store, she wrapped the picture Alyssa had taken of her and Dane on Thanksgiving Day.

She studied it, running her finger down Dane's cheek through the glass before covering the frame with silver and blue wrapping paper.

They looked happy together. He sat on her couch, his arms wrapped around her, his feet propped up on her coffee table while she cuddled in his lap. Their clothes were a perfect match —their jeans the same shade of blue, her cream blouse complementing the cream in the argyle pattern of his brown sweater.

And of course, through it all, they ran.

She and Dane ran through the scattering of snow falling almost every day.

Nikki smiled as she remembered going out to Eagle Pass State Park and running the snowy trails.

After they finished, Dane lobbed a snowball at her and accidentally hit her square in the face. He'd been worried she was angry, and he held her close, apologizing profusely, concerned he'd hurt her.

She took the opportunity to shove a handful of snow down his running shirt. She giggled at the memory. When they were home, she warmed him up in a hot shower.

They'd been taking a lot of those, lately.

It felt as if nothing could go wrong, and she sang along

to music on her phone as she dressed for Kayla's bache-lorette party.

She hated they would be apart for Christmas Day. She would find a way to make it up to him, and she thought up ways to make New Year's Eve and New Year's Day extra special for them.

After she finished her makeup, Nikki double-checked her reflection in the mirror. She loved the dress she'd found at the mall. It was fun without being too slutty, and she admired her butt in the mirror. The dress was made of bright pink lace, a large satin bow resting above her ass near the small of her back.

She wound her hair in a topknot, allowing some tendrils to escape sexily around her face.

Luckily, she already owned black and pink stilettos, and she wore a touch of matching lipstick, not too bright.

She didn't want to look like a hooker, even if it was for a bachelorette party. She hoped they didn't get too wild tonight. She worked the short shift at the store tomorrow, only six hours, but she didn't want to go to work hungover.

Nikki spritzed on some perfume, then checked the time. Alyssa would pick her up soon, and she wanted a minute to say goodbye to Dane, and maybe show off her dress, too.

She grabbed her powder blue dress coat and purse, made sure she had her phone, and stepped into the hallway.

DANE HAD ASKED Nikki to tell him goodbye before going to the bachelorette party, and when she knocked, he opened the door with a smile, eager to see her dressed up for the evening.

But she wasn't standing in front of his door, and Dane stepped into the hallway, confused.

Nikki leaned into another man's embrace, and through the red haze of fury, he recognized Eric.

She hadn't mentioned Eric since the day at the retreat when she confessed he called her, and it had only been after he told her about Holly's phone call.

He doubted she would have confessed if he hadn't said something first, and he wondered what else she'd been keeping a secret.

Nikki had been playing him for a fool all along, and anger and shame he'd been played again twisted his gut. "You couldn't stay away from him, could you?" he said, his voice surprisingly calm, pleased when she jerked her mouth from Eric's in surprise.

Eric met his eyes, and the fucker smiled at him.

"You had to know you couldn't keep her," Eric said, his voice smooth like the engine of his expensive Mercedes.

"Eric! Stop! Please, Dane, I didn't—"

Teetering on her heels, Nikki pushed away from Eric, her eyes frantic, her lipstick smeared.

"Don't bother with an explanation. I get it. He can give you more than I ever could. Houses, cars, clothes, diamonds."

Dane blinked, determined not to let the tears streaming down Nikki's face persuade him into giving her a chance to explain.

Gullible and in love, he would believe anything she said.

"No! Eric came here and—"

"Don't bother making excuses. You got caught, own it like an adult. Have a good time, have a nice life. Get out of here."

When Nikki only stood crying, he roared, "Get out of here!"

Sobbing, Nikki bolted from Eric's side and stumbled through the fire door.

Eric smirked, and Dane's heart stuttered to a stop.

Someone had knocked on his door, but it hadn't been Nikki.

He'd been set up, and he'd taken the bait, hook, line, and sinker. He was such a fool. Dane started to go after her, to apologize and beg for forgiveness, but Eric's words stopped him cold.

"She's out of your league. Let her go."

He didn't turn around. "You planned this."

Eric sniffed. "Not entirely. It worked better than I could have hoped. She didn't want me, choosing you, some scumbag loser, over what we could have had. And well, I figured, if I couldn't have her . . ."

Finally, Dane looked at Eric who was leaning against the cream-colored wall, his arms and ankles crossed. A burgundy scarf hung from his neck, an expensive-looking coat fitting him like it was custom made.

". . . But you exceeded my wildest dreams. I thought maybe you'd fight for her, and one of us would walk away with a black eye, at the very least. It never occurred to me you would blame her, as if you *expected* her to cheat on you."

Eric huffed on the fingernails of one hand and ran them over the lapel of his jacket.

"I realize now if I had been more patient you would have done this on your own, without my help, and I could have swooped in with a shoulder to cry on, her knight to the rescue. But she loves you, and in the long run, it wouldn't have made a difference. She never would have chosen me, even when you hung yourself on your cute little insecurities."

Dane swallowed back the bile rising in his throat.

Eric waved a hand in the air. "Nonetheless, I accomplished what I set out to do. You'll never get her back, not when she knows how little you think of her. You know that, don't you? You fucking moron."

Whistling, Eric walked down the hallway in the opposite direction Nikki had gone, his fingers skimming the textured walls until he disappeared down the stairs and out of Dane's sight.

Nikki ran through the fire door at the top of the stairs and stumbled down the stairway. She slammed through the glass door to the parking lot and fumbled with her key fob to unlock her car.

It took her several tries to open the door, and she propelled herself inside, her hands shaking so terribly she could barely shove the key into the ignition.

She didn't feel the chill from the December temperatures. No, the shaking, the trembling, was from Dane's hateful words.

He thought she'd been kissing Eric.

Voluntarily.

He thought she was meeting him and had been sneaking off to do it.

She rested her forehead against the cold glass of the driver's side window and tried to steady her scrambled thoughts, tears dripping down her cheeks.

She couldn't go to Kayla's bachelorette party now.

It took her several tries to text Alyssa, tell her not to

come for her, her phone's autocorrect making her text a jumble of incorrect words.

Not feeling well. Skipping party. Sorry for short notice.

Nikki breathed a sigh of relief when Alyssa responded only moments later. She couldn't let Alyssa see her this way.

I'm sorry. Is Dane with you?

Yes.

Nikki hated lying, but she had no choice. She didn't want Alyssa to check on her. She'd insist she stay with her, and Nikki didn't want to be around anyone right now.

Ok. Text me if you need anything.

Nikki replied with a quick, *Thanks.*

She couldn't stay here, but she didn't have anywhere else to go. Her parents were getting the house ready for Stacy and her husband's arrival for Christmas, and she didn't want to bother them.

Without a plan, she backed her car from her parking space, not sure what she should do.

The words looped through her head: *he didn't love her; he didn't trust her.*

Dane couldn't have believed in her or he would never have thought she could do such a horrible, selfish, despicable thing.

He wouldn't want the picture she made him for Christmas now, but she could give him something else, instead.

Determined to do one more thing for the man she loved, she grabbed her phone from the passenger's seat and called Information.

Dane looked wildly around his apartment. He couldn't sit there and do nothing. He would end up putting a fist through the wall if he stayed and stewed in his anger and disappointment in himself.

Nikki's tears were like hot pokers rammed down his throat.

He'd ruined his life with her, and he'd never forget the words Eric threw in his face.

I thought maybe you'd fight for her.

He'd turned on her like a rabid dog. Fighting for her was the last thing he'd done.

Dane grabbed his keys and took off for his truck and the bar.

Nikki skittered through the grocery store in her hot pink stilettos.

She must look like a hot mess, but she didn't care. Her eyes darted around the small floral department, and she chose the biggest poinsettia they sold.

After wrestling it into her car, she typed in the address she copied from Information and let Siri tell her the way.

She drove through a residential section, the houses smaller but nicely kept. Yards were decorated with huge evergreen trees strung with lights. Santa figures stood next to reindeer; lights dangled from snowy roofs.

Nikki stopped in front a white two-story house, the hedges glowing with blue Christmas lights.

She didn't know how long it had been since Dane had visited his parents.

He'd made it sound like they hadn't spoken for years.

For a moment she hesitated, unsure if meddling in his

relationship with his mother and father was something she should be doing, but they'd taken Liz's side.

After meeting Liz, she couldn't let them believe Dane had been the kind of husband they accused him of being.

She took a deep breath. If his relationship with his parents was as doomed as he thought, talking with them wouldn't hurt. She refused to believe they were the type of people who wouldn't listen or give Dane a second chance after knowing the truth.

They'd raised a kind and caring man; she could only hope they were as well, and that only a misunderstanding caused the rift between them.

Grabbing the plant, the red foil crinkling, she slid from her car, leaving her purse behind. She picked her way over a carelessly shoveled sidewalk and tip-toed up the steps of the porch. Pushing back her misery, she stood in the frosty air.

Dane said they were done; he'd given her no chance to defend herself.

He didn't love her; he didn't trust her.

Nikki rang the doorbell.

An older woman with short blonde answered the door. Her eyes were blue, lines crowding the corners from smiling, age, and sun. Slim, and shorter than Nikki, the woman wore black yoga pants and a light pink tank top.

Her lips parted in surprise.

She hadn't expected Dane's mother to look so approachable. The way he'd described her and his father, she'd thought they were as bitter as Liz, but the woman's eyes were sympathetic yet confused, her clothing casual and comfortable. The outfit was something Nikki would have worn had she been home and not standing on the porch of her ex-boyfriend's parents' house, freezing in the cold.

That's what Dane was to her now.

Her lips trembled, holding back a sob.

An ex-boyfriend.

Some guy she would bump into at the mall, make small talk with and move on. Some guy who would occasionally pop up in her news feed on Facebook because she wouldn't have the heart to unfriend him.

He would turn into some guy she would see at the race expos. He'd catch her eye and look away. Maybe he would have a new woman on his arm and he would smile, point out Nikki as an ex.

Tears leaked from her eyes.

"Do you have the right house, honey? Are you going to a Christmas party?" The woman opened the storm door and peered at her through the orange porch light.

"M-Mrs. Montgomery?" Nikki stuttered, trying to pull herself together.

"Yes. You have the right house, but I don't think I know you."

"I-I'm Dane's ex-girlfriend." Cradling the plant against her chest, she wiped her face.

"Who is it, Peg?" a man's voice shouted from another room in the house. "It's getting cold in here. Shut the door."

"We don't have anything to do with Dane," the woman said firmly, pulling the door shut an inch.

"Please," Nikki said, "I only need a moment." Her voice cracked.

"Peg, shut the door." A man walked up behind Peg and placed his hands on her shoulders. He resembled Dane, but his dark hair was greying at the temples, giving him a handsome, distinguished look. "Hello. Are you at the right house? We're not throwing a party."

"This woman says she's been dating Dane," Peg said. "We didn't catch your name, dear."

"Nikki."

"Let her in. It's cold out there."

"Thank you," Nikki whispered. There was no way she could hold the plant and bend over to undo the buckles of her stilettos to take them off. She wiped them on a small rug near the door and followed Dane's parents into a room where Dane's father had been watching Wheel of Fortune.

She handed the festive plant to Peg who frowned, but she accepted it and disappeared into another room.

"I'm Darren, it's nice to meet you, Nikki, but I don't understand what you're doing here. Have a seat."

Dane received all his looks from his father. The color of their hair was the same light brown and cut in almost the same style; they shared the same facial structure. Darren had added a bit of weight as he'd aged, but he still looked fit.

"Do you run?" she asked, making small talk. Now that she was here she didn't know how to say what she wanted to say, and her mind blanked.

"Not as much as I used to," he said, rubbing his stomach.

Carrying a tray, Peg came into the living room. "I threw this together. I don't know how you like your coffee. I'm sorry, you drink coffee, don't you?"

Nikki nodded and sniffled. "You didn't have to go through the trouble."

"I didn't. It was already made." Peg paused, about to pour. "You're here about Dane?"

At the sound of his name, Nikki turned her head and pursed her lips. This was not the way she wanted to meet Dane's parents.

She added a dollop of cream to her mug and picked it up, trying to steady her hands. The warmth felt good against her skin, but she doubted she would ever truly feel warm again.

"What can we do for you?" Darren asked.

"Yes, didn't you say you were his ex-girlfriend? If you think we'll be able to help you get him back, you're mistaken. We haven't spoken to Dane in years." Peg sighed and took a sip of her own coffee.

"I know. He told me. We, ah, had a falling out. I don't think we'll be getting back together."

Saying the words aloud made her sob, and she quickly put her mug down on the coffee table and covered her face with her hands.

Peg scooted closer to her on the loveseat. "Oh, darling," she said.

Nikki took a moment to compose herself; she was grateful Darren and Peg were being patient with her.

"I wanted to tell you Dane is hurting. He said you haven't spoken to him since his divorce—"

"That's none of our business," Darren said while handing her a tissue. "Dane's divorce is none of our concern."

Nikki wiped her eyes, sure her eyeliner and mascara were smearing everywhere. Not only did she feel like an idiot, but she probably looked like one, too.

"But he's been hurting, Mr. Montgomery," she said, showing respect to the man who would never be her father-in-law.

"That was his own doing. He chose Liz, he chose to say the vows, chose to have her as his wife until death. He didn't try to work it out, didn't try to meet her halfway."

Jumping to Dane's defense made Nikki forget her tears.

"Oh, but he did, sir. He did. He worked hard to make her happy, worked hard at the bank. He wanted to give her everything she wanted, but how do you give a woman every-thing she wants when she really *does* want everything? He told me about the cars, the house. If he would have stayed with her, he would have killed himself."

Desperately, she met Peg's eyes. "How do you keep a woman like that happy?"

Peg was more sympathetic than her husband, but it was evident she was on her husband's side in the matter. "Nikki, I don't think you know what you're saying. You've only heard Dane's side of the story."

Nikki was already shaking her head.

"Dane took me to dinner downtown not long ago, and we ran into Liz and her husband."

Nikki tried to push down her anger toward the other woman.

Liz had hurt Dane irreparably, and because of her, she and Dane would never have a normal relationship. He would never trust her not to be looking for something better. Never trust her when she told him he was enough.

Because he hadn't been, not for Liz.

"She's a horrid, horrible woman. The things she said makes me sick. She called him worthless, a loser. She accused him of being poor." Nikki took a sip of the cooling coffee. It washed some of the bad taste from her mouth.

Peg held Nikki's hand and rubbed her back through her jacket.

"She told me Dane would never be able to take me on vacation, or buy me diamonds, or designer clothes."

The things he accused her tonight of wanting.

"She spewed poison, and her husband stood by and let her. I don't know what kind of relationship they have, but he's not making her happy, either. You could see it on her face."

She met Darren's eyes.

"It wasn't Dane's fault. He may have chosen her, but that doesn't mean he had to put up with her for the rest of his life. He deserves someone who will make him happy. If anyone can. He's been suffering for a long time."

She realized Peg was holding her hand, and she clutched at the woman's hand in return. "I tried to help him, but in the end, he wouldn't let me. Or couldn't. I don't know. But maybe you can. He misses you very much, he talked about you all the time. He needs you. Especially now. We spent Thanksgiving together, but it's not the same as being with family."

"We never liked Liz," Darren said. "It's part of the reason we've been hard on him. We warned him to take it slow, to maybe have a longer engagement, but he was sure she was the one for him. During the divorce proceedings, we told him since he had made his bed, he needed to lie in it. I suppose that wasn't the best approach."

He took his gold-rimmed glasses from his face and rubbed his eyes.

"What do you want us to do?" Peg asked.

"Please talk to him. Give him a chance." The conversation was winding down, and she pulled her hand from Peg's grasp.

"Why do you care? Did he break up with you? Why are you here?" Peg asked.

"He broke up with me, yes. I'm the manager of his store, it's how we met. He hired me because Brett has been asking him to help with the marathon."

She pursed her lips against her tears. "I love him. We won't be together for Christmas, and I can't give him the gift I made, but I wanted to do one last thing for him."

"You were brave to come here, to introduce yourself to people who may not have acted kindly toward you."

Darren stood and helped her from the loveseat. But instead of shaking her hand like she thought he would, he enveloped her in his arms. He smelled like tobacco smoke, and for a moment it comforted her.

"We appreciate you coming. I think you've done more than help Dane. You said he misses us, and we've been missing him, too. We're grateful to you for coming forward this way. Is there a way to get a hold of you? To let you know how things go?"

Nikki shook her head and stepped out of the older man's embrace. "It's better to end things here. It was nice meeting the both of you, though I wish it had been under better circumstances. Thank you for the coffee."

Peg and Darren led her to the front door, and once again Nikki choked up. It would have been nice . . . if things had turned out differently . . . Nikki stopped her line of thought, Dane's accusations ringing in her ears.

"Goodnight and Merry Christmas." Nikki gave them a feeble smile and stepped onto the porch.

She didn't even feel the cold.

She was already frozen.

WHEN THE FRONT door of the bar opened letting in a burst of frigid air, Dane looked up from his empty beer bottle he held loosely in his hand. He tipped his head back in frustration and resignation when Brett glared at him from the bar.

Instead of walking straight to him, he spoke a few words with Ian, and he would bet his store Brett was cutting him off.

Ian probably called Brett in the first place knowing full well Dane wouldn't be able to drive himself home.

"Hey, buddy, what's up?" Brett asked, taking a stool at the high-top table they usually shared.

"What are you doing here?" Dane asked, but he knew it was to haul his ass home. Only it wasn't home. He'd never know home until he woke up in Nikki's arms again. "Leave me alone."

Out of beer, Dane raised a hand to get Ian's attention. He wanted more.

"No can do," Brett said, sliding off his winter coat. "Where's Nikki?"

"Fuck off."

Like hell he'd explain his own stupidity. Even Brett would say he deserved what he got.

"Did you guys have a fight? You're solid; you can fix it."

"Nothing will be able to fix it," Dane said, tears in his throat. "Can you fuck off now? I want to be alone."

"Nope," Brett said, shaking his head. "I can't leave you this way."

"If you won't leave me alone, I'll go. Jesus Christ, Brett, leave me alone." His voice cracked.

Brett sighed.

Through the buzz of alcohol, his skin prickled in embarrassment.

He'd never shown Brett this side of him before.

Near tears, so broken-hearted he couldn't think. And it was his own damn fault. Liz had been, too. His own fault, his own mistake, for rushing into things, sure she was who he wanted, who he needed. But at least he could blame her for changing, for not being who she'd promised him she was.

Dane only had himself to blame now.

"What happened?" Brett asked.

Dane wiped his face with his hand.

"Eric, one of Nikki's exes, was forcing her to kiss him in the hallway of our building. I was so pissed I didn't see her struggling to get away from him. I blamed her, and after she ran away Eric said he planned the whole thing to get back at me, and I fell for it. He said I deserved to lose her for not fighting for her, for not believing in her, and he's right. He was hurting her, and I was so wrapped up in feeling betrayed I never saw it."

"That's fucked up."

"I deserve everything I got. I'm too fucked up to keep her."

Brett poked at the little black bowl full of peanuts surrounded by Dane's empties in the center of the table.

"Come on, you need to go home. I'll drive you back, you're not fit behind the wheel."

Dane slipped on his jacket and pulled a stocking cap over his head. He nodded a curt goodbye to Ian who was already on his way to clear his table.

Brett led Dane onto the sidewalk and stuffed him into the passenger seat of his car.

He hunched over from misery and cold, and guilt ate at him during the entire drive.

His mind kept spinning back to Nikki in Eric's arms, and what a stupid, ignorant jerk he was.

He worried about Nikki and where she could have gone. Her parents' house, Alyssa's. Maybe she went ahead to the party, probably already sitting in some guy's lap, happy to be rid of him and his baggage.

Dane closed his eyes and the nausea heightened. Thinking those thoughts were what got him into trouble in the first place.

He didn't believe she could love him.

When Brett pulled into his parking lot, Dane's heart plummeted to his feet.

The space for Nikki's vehicle was empty.

Worry in the form of a headache gathered at the base of his neck. As they walked to the back door of the building, where he'd first met Nikki months ago, he called Alyssa.

Even though Nikki probably told her what an asshole he was, he hoped Alyssa would at least have the courtesy to tell him Nikki was okay, and he could stop worrying about her.

NIKKI COULDN'T GO home. Couldn't take the risk of bumping into Dane in the hallway or the parking lot. Her fears were coming true.

She drove aimlessly around Tower City, trying to puzzle out a plan.

Maybe she could try telling Dane the truth again—if he'd calmed down enough to listen to her and believe what she said.

Eric was a pig, forcing her to kiss him.

She couldn't believe what he'd done, and she would have bet her soul that he wasn't capable of doing something so cruel. She wondered what Eric said to Dane after she ran away. Dane would believe it easily enough.

He had no faith in her, no trust. He'd slapped her away the first chance he got, when she was the one who didn't want to start a relationship in the first place.

She slowed at a red light and eased to a stop. She thought maybe, by chance, she had been getting through, but they'd run into Liz, which had been inevitable.

Tower City wasn't a small town, but there was always

the chance of bumping into someone, be it in a store, or the movie theater, maybe the mall.

Their time to run into Liz had come a little sooner than she thought, but maybe it was for the best. Maybe it was for the best their relationship crumbled when it did, before they were married, before they had children who needed them.

It had been nice to imagine something, but if she were honest with herself, she had to admit she couldn't help him.

His parents were a big issue, and she hoped she'd fixed that for him.

They'd seemed open to speaking with him, and she prayed they followed through. To be punished for something that wasn't your fault . . . It must have been difficult for him to go through his divorce without the support of his family.

Nikki sniffled and checked her phone at another light. Alyssa tried calling a couple times, and she wiped her cheeks, sorry she was ruining her friend's time at the party. She could always join them, but her heart wasn't in it now and she'd lied to Alyssa, anyway.

Tears started dripping down her face.

She'd done a good job of keeping them in for a little while.

She drove by a Holiday Inn, and at the sight of the bright green sign, she inhaled sharply. The hotel was the answer she needed.

As she swerved onto a side road, her tires skid in the snow, and she yanked the wheel, turning into the parking lot. It was full, and she prayed they would have room for one more.

Nikki walked through the warm lobby scented with

lemon. She looked like a used-up whore, but she didn't care. She kind of felt like one. Used up, anyway.

Nothing left.

She handed her credit card to the young man working the front desk and pulled off her stilettos as he billed her card. With her shoes dangling from her fingers, she rode the elevator to her room on the fifth floor.

Five, she thought, her mind numb. They had lasted more than five weeks, less than five months. It would take her five minutes to write her resignation letter she would leave on Dane's desk when she worked her shift the next day.

Had Dane loved her for even five seconds?

She slid the plastic key card into the slot of her room door, and she dropped her purse and shoes in front of the bathroom. She collapsed onto the single queen bed and tucked herself into a little ball, making herself as small as she could.

Nikki didn't think she could cry anymore, but she did, long and hard, until finally, sleep took her.

HER EYES POPPING open in panic, Nikki woke with a splitting headache. She jerked into a sitting position and scrambled for her phone to check the time. The store was supposed to open at ten, and she needed to go home and shower and change into her work clothes first.

She breathed a sigh of relief; her cell read only seven-thirty. But the number of texts and phone calls she'd missed from Alyssa wracked her with guilt.

There was even one from Brett. Lord only knew what Dane told him.

Nikki read the last text she received from Alyssa: *Nicola Halstead if you don't call me I swear to God . . . I'm worried about you, hon. Where are you?*

Nikki called her, and she answered on the first ring.

"Nikki! Where the hell are you? You said you were with Dane, but I talked to him and he told me you ran off. Talk to me, honey. What the fuck is going on?"

"More than a fight," Nikki said, her voice rasping.

Raw from crying, her throat hurt when she spoke.

"Eric cornered me in the hallway when I was going downstairs to wait for you. Dane saw him kissing me, and he accused me of cheating."

The tears got the better of her, and she cried into the phone while she buckled her feet into her stilettos. Nikki grabbed her purse from the floor and left her plastic keycard on the desk. She didn't need to check out, thank God. She didn't want to walk through a busy lobby to reach the front desk. Not looking like this.

"Nikki, why did you lie to me? You should have told me, and I would have stayed with you." She paused. "Is Eric stalking you?"

"No, I don't think so—"

Alyssa's hiss of disbelief stopped her.

"No, really, I think he wanted to get back at me. I doubt many women have said no to him. Maybe I should have seen this coming, but he was such a gentleman when we were together. I have no idea what he told Dane after I ran off; it could have been anything."

Nikki took the stairs, and she leaned against the grey wall between floors four and three.

"But I didn't want to be around anyone. I didn't want to ruin the party for you, but I guess I did anyway. I . . . when I left I went to see Dane's parents. I don't know why, and I feel stupid about it now. I wanted to help him . . . fix . . . I don't know."

She started crying again and stumbled down the stairs, tears blurring her vision.

"Where are you? You need to explain to Dane it's not your fault."

Nikki let herself out of the hotel by a side door, the cold morning air slapping her face.

"Why should I have to defend myself? He doesn't trust me. He doesn't trust me not to cheat, not to try to find someone better, like his ex-wife did. I can't be in a relationship like that. I won't keep going through something like this. If it's not Eric, it will be somebody else, then somebody else."

She took a shaky breath and found her car. She slid in and turned the engine over, praying the heater would heat up quickly.

"I slept at the Holiday Inn because I didn't want to bother my parents, and I couldn't go home. I couldn't run the risk of seeing him, but I have to work today. I'm going home to shower and change. While I'm at work, I'll put in my notice. I can't be around him anymore."

Over Alyssa's protests, she said goodbye and tried to keep her tears in check and her attention on the icy roads.

Brett's car was parked in a guest space in the building's parking lot. They probably talked shit about her all night, and she hoped the early hour would prevent her from seeing either one of them.

A hot shower did nothing to alleviate the pain in her head. She took two ibuprofen tablets with a mug of coffee and changed into her work clothes. She should eat, but her stomach churned, and the thought of food made her gag.

At the store, customer traffic was light, and she

distracted herself by cleaning the back room and putting out a load of freight. Trucks unloaded several times a week for the holidays. Winter shoes were already on markdown and soon the bright colors for spring would flood the store display shelves.

Nikki was kneeling by the register hanging running shirts onto a roll bar from a cardboard box when the bell jingled.

She groaned.

Her headache hadn't abated, in fact, it had gotten worse. Her muscles were sore, probably from sleeping in a ball, and her neck was stiff, causing pain to run through her shoulder blades and into her head.

She longed for a cup of coffee to soothe her scratchy throat.

Dane's office had a coffee maker they used on a regular basis, and he started storing cream in his mini fridge for her, but she didn't want to go in there.

Nikki flinched and rose from her knees to greet her customer.

She wiped her tears and pasted a fake smile on her face. "If there's anything I can . . ." She faded when her eyes met Brett's. "Come to bitch me out?"

"No," Brett said, standing in front of the counter. "He told me what happened, and I'm asking you to forgive him. He didn't understand, and he jumped to conclusions."

Nikki snorted, making her head vibrate with pain.

"Dane's hurting."

"*He's* hurting? It's his own fault. If he would have listened to me last night . . . I tried to explain that I didn't want anything with Eric, but he didn't believe me. If he loved me, he never would have believed that I would do something like that to him. Ever. But instead, he thought the worst of me, as quickly as he could. Don't you dare put this on me."

"Dane talked to Eric after you ran off. Eric admitted to setting up the whole thing and told Dane he didn't deserve you. He believes it."

Pain and anger made her see red around the edges of her vision.

"Well, maybe he doesn't," Nikki said, pushing against the counter until her knuckles turned white, "if he believed anything Eric has to say instead what I tried to tell him. He told me we were done. So, none of this concerns me. Please go," she said, wiping her cheeks. "Unless you need a new running shirt or a pair of shoes, just go. Dane has more problems than I can help him with. Until he figures out his mind, he'll never be able to give away his heart."

Brett took a step back. "I'm sorry."

Miserable, Nikki turned away and grabbed another hot pink shirt from the box. "No more than me."

⁂

AFTER ONE OF THE longest days of her life, she finished her shift and closed the store. She possessed too much integrity to not do less than her best, and she left the store with everything in its place. Grateful she hadn't shared her shift with someone, she locked up.

After making the bank deposit, she drove home, the heater blasting, but the heat didn't keep her from shivering, and her whole body shuddered.

Nikki craved some soup or a cup of coffee, but she didn't have the energy to make either. She stripped and pulled on a pair of flannel lounging pants and a long-sleeved matching top. Freezing, she dove into bed, pulling the blankets to her chin trying to warm herself. She would have to call in sick to work tomorrow, but Margie would be there.

Dane would think she was avoiding him. He would be relieved to see her resignation letter she placed on his desk before leaving for the day.

Tears seeped into her pillow as she cried and shook with the chills.

She didn't think she had felt this bad in all her life.

CHAPTER EIGHT

D ANE PROWLED AROUND his apartment like a caged cat, thanking Christ Brett had finally left. He'd brought Dane home from Ian's bar, plopped onto the sofa and zoned in front of SportsCenter, like he was on some kind of suicide watch.

Thankfully, it hadn't come to that, and he resented Brett's presence when all he wanted to do was lick his wounds in private.

He kept replaying the words he'd shouted at Nikki in the hallway the night before, kept seeing Eric's lips on hers, his arms wrapped around her.

She was scheduled to work at the store that day, and he wondered if she'd gone in, or if the store was locked tight during business hours.

Feeling like a bastard, he'd given in and called, and when she answered, he'd hung up without saying anything, ashamed he would think that of her.

He'd never learn.

She'd sounded sad and tired.

Her car had been gone all night, but that hadn't stopped

him from stepping onto his balcony every ten minutes to see if she'd come home.

He only relaxed when he heard her apartment door open and shut after closing the store. Used to knowing her every move, it bothered him when he didn't know where she went, or what she was doing.

He tried to think of a way to talk to her about what happened.

Maybe he could talk her into a wintery run in the morning. He could apologize while they ran, and he wouldn't have to look at her, see all the hurt he inflicted.

They could end it amicably because she sure as hell wouldn't want to be with him now, and he couldn't blame her. He'd tell her he still wanted her at the store; he would stay out of her way and spend his days at marathon headquarters like he'd said he would.

This wouldn't have happened if he hadn't been selfish and pursued her.

The situation was exactly what she'd feared would happen when she'd put him off at the beginning. But he had worn her down, not caring about anything but having her. For a few blissful weeks, he thought maybe it would work between them.

Dane was sluggish and moody the next morning when he crawled out of bed. Going for a run was the last thing he wanted to do, but he started coffee and pulled on his running clothes. Even if he couldn't convince Nikki to go, he needed to get some air whether he felt like it or not.

He stood in front of her door sipping his coffee debating if he wanted to knock or use the key she'd given him.

She'd want it back now.

He knocked, and when there wasn't an answer he tried the doorknob.

Alarm slithered around his belly when it turned easily, and Princess Snowflake meowed pitifully on the other side.

He stepped into her apartment and scooped up the cat in one hand, careful not to spill his coffee on her beige carpet.

The cat's food and water dishes were empty. It explained the meowing, and to Princess Snowflake's relief, he filled both for the little scamp. The coffeemaker was cold and he started a fresh pot.

Even if Nikki didn't want to run, she would still want to drink some while getting ready for work. Scooping grounds into the liner, he paused for a moment. This wasn't his place anymore, but he continued, and after turning on the machine, he found Nikki in bed.

"Hey," he said, stepping into her bedroom. His heart slammed and a nervous sweat covered his skin. "I was hoping maybe we could run this morning before opening the store. We need to talk about what happened."

"G-G-Go away."

The mattress dipped with his weight when he sat next to her.

"Nikki?" he asked uncertainly, and he moved her hair from her face. "Oh, honey, you're burning up."

"N-no," she said, shivering. "Cold."

Dane swore. She was hot, and he tried to swallow back a knot of fear blocking his airway. The flu could be serious, and she'd been by herself all night. "Have you taken anything?"

Nikki shook her head. "Go away."

"If I leave, you need to have someone with you. You can't be alone when you're this sick. Who do you want me to call? Alyssa? Your parents?"

"No. Alyssa is f-flying to visit her parents s-soon. My

sister will be in town in a few days. I don't want to bother my parents. Everyone is b-busy."

Dane rested his hand on her feverish forehead, trying to guess how high her temperature could be. He didn't have a thermometer at his place, and he hadn't seen one in her bathroom, either. "Then who?"

"No one." Nikki pressed her face into her pillow.

"I'm not leaving you alone with your fever this high. It's not safe. If you won't let me call someone for you, you're stuck with me."

When she didn't answer, Dane smoothed Nikki's hair before pulling his hand away. "I have flu tablets in my apartment. Since you haven't taken anything, I'll give you some. We need to get your fever down, and you need sleep."

In his apartment, he changed into sweats and a sweat-shirt, and he found the liquid gel capsules he kept from the last time he was sick.

He texted Margie and he told her Nikki had come down with the flu and not to expect them for a few days. He wanted to take care of her, but he told Margie to call if she needed anything.

He may be able to leave Nikki alone sooner than that, but she wouldn't feel like going back to work until the end of the week at the soonest.

With Princess Snowflake rubbing against his ankles, he poured Nikki a cup of coffee and added a generous amount of milk. He brought the mug and pills to her, set them on the nightstand, and helped her sit up. Cradling her in his arms, he placed the pills in her hand and held the mug close to her lips. "Here, drink some coffee. The caffeine will help your headache. There's no use going through caffeine with-drawal, too."

Nikki took the mug and sipped at the coffee, swallowing the tablets.

Dane blew out a sigh when she relaxed slightly. "Stay there. I'll get you some fresh pajamas. You've soaked these all the way through." He undressed her, peeling the wet shirt and bottoms from her body.

Nikki crawled into bed wearing dry pajamas, and Princess Snowflake meowed from the doorway. Dane picked her up and plopped her onto the bed. The cat made little circles until she was comfortable and curled her white body under Nikki's chin.

Nikki's panic-filled eyes met his.

"I fed her; she's okay. I'll scoop her box later. You need to try to relax," he said, watching her shiver, standing by her bed in the dark bedroom, not knowing what else he could do for her.

He'd given her medicine, helped her change, fed her cat. He didn't want to leave her alone, but the fact was, she didn't want him there, not after the things he said and the way he treated her.

"C-can't," Nikki said, her teeth chattering.

Dane sighed and slid into bed. He took her in his arms, spooning her from behind. "Try to loosen up and go to sleep. It's the only way you'll feel better, if you can get some sleep." With his arm draped over her stomach, he pulled her closer. "Shh, shh," he whispered in her ear. "Shh."

Her shivering lessened, and she pressed her hot cheek to his arm. "That's the way. I'll take care of you, I promise. Go to sleep."

It felt like a million years since he held her this way. He'd gotten used to holding her while he slept, treating her bed as his. He felt more comfortable in her apartment than he ever had in his own.

"The store."

"I texted Margie when I changed my clothes. She knows we won't be there today. I called you out for the entire week. You need to take your time and get better; I've got it handled." Dane felt her breathe a deep sigh, and she let him pull her toward him.

If this was the last chance he would get to hold her this way, he would take it.

NIKKI WOKE AT lunchtime, stretching her sore muscles. She was far from being better; the pain had only lessened a bit in her head and she was still shaking.

Dane had is arms wrapped around her, and he opened his eyes when she turned over.

"What can I get you? Are you hungry? Do you want some soup? Some more coffee? How about some water?"

Nikki suppressed a moan in pleasure as he ran his hand over her forehead and through her curls.

"You're still pretty warm, honey. I'll make you some soup. We bought some the last time we went to the store, remember?"

She fought the tears, but they leaked from her eyelids no matter how tightly she shut her eyes.

She remembered.

She remembered all the normal things they did before their relationship went up in a puff of smoke because of his doubts and fears.

"You don't have to cry over soup, baby." Dane kissed her cheek. "I'll be back in a few minutes."

Nikki dozed while he heated up her soup, and Princess Snowflake jumped from the bed to see what he was doing.

She jolted when Dane gently placed a cold washcloth on her forehead.

"The soup is warming. I put it on the stove instead of using the microwave." He sat on the edge of the bed, holding the cool cloth to her hot skin.

"Thanks," she whispered, her tears of exhaustion trailing down her temples into her hair. She was tired, tired of everything.

"Nik, how did we get this messed up?" he asked, smoothing the tears from her skin.

"I don't know."

But she did know.

She knew the reasons why her lovely world with the man she loved imploded. If she had to give up her relationship with him then she would, because she was damned if she would sacrifice her self-worth, her dignity, to be accused of cheating over and over by a boyfriend, by a husband, who could never trust her.

Dane turned the cloth over making the cool side touch her skin and went back into the kitchen.

When he returned with a mug of soup, the scent made her stomach clench, and she didn't know if she was queasy or hungry.

Her emotions were running as high as her temperature, and the medication Dane gave her earlier barely eased the pain in her head.

"I figured this would be easier to handle than a bowl." He sat the mug on the nightstand and helped her sit, taking the washcloth from her.

The silence unnerved her, the tension thick between them, but she didn't want to talk. All she wanted to do was sip her soup and go back to sleep. Torn between wanting him with her and wanting him to leave, she opened her mouth to tell him she was feeling better, and he should go back to his apartment or go to work.

But Dane spoke first. "When did you start feeling like this? How long have you been sick?"

Nikki bristled at the concern in his voice, but she answered because she didn't want to fight. "Since yesterday at the store. I came home from my shift and went straight to bed."

"You should have called me."

Nikki pulled away. After the way he yelled at her, not giving her a chance to defend herself, there was no way in hell she would have asked for his help.

"So I could have relieved you at the store," Dane filled in quickly.

"It was a short shift. I've worked sick before."

The mug almost slipped from her hands, and Dane steadied the mug, covering her hands with his. "Careful," he whispered.

Wrapped in his arms, Nikki finished her soup.

Dane brought her more medicine and held the glass of water to her lips.

"Are you staying here?" she asked, tucking a blanket under her chin. The soup helped calm her stomach, and the medicine made her drowsy.

"Yes, I'm staying here. I'll probably go to my apartment and grab a book, but I'm staying until I know you'll be all right by yourself."

"Okay." She closed her eyes.

Dane grabbed the empty mug off her nightstand. He gave her a light kiss on her forehead, and she wondered if it was to feel if her fever was going down, or if he wanted to comfort her.

"Get some sleep. I'll be right here if you need some-thing, I promise."

Nikki slept until evening, and she rolled to her side to find Dane lying on her bed reading as he said he would be.

It felt natural for him to be there, and she wanted to ask if he'd heard from his parents. She hoped he wouldn't be angry she interfered, but she might not ever know how that all played out.

She hadn't expected to speak with him again, but it was foolish thinking on her part. They lived next door to each other, and he was her boss. She would finish out her two weeks while she found something else.

Her lease was for a full twelve months. She'd have to stick it out in the building until next summer, but she'd move into a different place as soon as she could. Until then, she'd have to toughen up and pretend bumping into him in the hallway didn't bother her.

"You've been sleeping for a while. Can I get you dinner? Something to drink?" He set the book aside and met her eyes. The room was dark but for the lamp Dane was using to read.

Nikki shook her head. She still felt horrible. Her head throbbed, her muscles ached. A bath would have been nice if it hadn't sounded like so much work. "I'm still tired and sore."

Dane put the back of his hand to her cheek. "And you're still hot. You've slept long enough for more medicine. I'll get you some."

Nikki sighed when he brought her more pills and another mug of coffee. He was taking such good care of her after the nasty things he'd thought about her.

It didn't make any sense. How he could act like he loved her when he couldn't trust her.

He kissed the top of her head.

They couldn't fix the damage. He'd broken her heart, and the cracks were irreparable.

And even if he wanted to try, she wasn't sure she wanted him to.

DANE GRITTED HIS teeth as he disconnected a call with Margie who told him about Nikki's two-week notice.

He wouldn't tell her he knew. He didn't want her to be stressed out and worried about her job. She had a place at his store for as long as she wanted one, but he couldn't make her stay, either.

He should apologize. It's what he'd gone there for in the first place, but he was tired and worried and with Nikki sick, he wasn't sure that conversation would go well. He'd stayed up all night making sure her fever was under control, keeping a cool cloth on her forehead, waking her in the middle the night for fever reducer, pain medication, and cold sips of water.

He kept an eye on her all day, feeding her soup, pushing more water on her, and lying with her while she napped.

Before bedtime, he drew a bath and let her soak while he changed the sheets on her bed. She came out of the bathroom her arms trembling as she tried to brush her hair, but she looked better, a healthy pink staining her cheeks.

Dane frowned, the feeling of déjà vu rushing him as he took the comb from her.

"Nikki—"

"I don't feel like talking about it. I appreciate you being here and helping me, but if you have something else you need to do, you should go. You've been here long enough."

Dane ran the comb through her ash blonde hair, the strands springing into their spiral curls. "I want to stay until you're feeling better. Whatever else happens, let me do that."

Nikki looked at him over her shoulder. Her bright blue eyes were clouded with pain and fatigue, and he reached to smooth the lines between her eyebrows. He wanted to kiss her, he wanted things to be back to normal.

Looking away he said, "I changed your sheets, why don't you get some more sleep?"

Surprising him, she murmured, "Stay with me."

Dane propped himself against her headboard, and she crawled between his legs and rested her head on his chest.

Pulling her to him, he took a deep breath, the scent of her hair conditioner filling his nose.

She drifted off quickly, and he pressed his lips to her forehead. Her fever had broken after the long bath, and Dane mumbled a short prayer in thanks.

She may still be sore from the shivering, she may still be tired, but she was getting better, and she wouldn't need him anymore after tonight.

Running a hand through her damp hair, he finally told her what he wanted to say.

"I came by here the other morning to tell you I'm sorry."

He cleared his throat.

"I shouldn't have blamed you. I love you so much, and when I saw you in the hallway with him . . . I didn't see you struggling, I didn't see him forcing you. All I saw was you in his arms, his lips on yours, and I let my fear take over."

He rubbed Nikki's back.

"I should have told you I loved you a long time ago, never let you doubt for a single second what was in my heart. What we had felt so right, you slipped into my life so easily, it was like a dream. I wanted a future with you; I was going to ask you to marry me. I want a future with you, but" —he swallowed— "I need to tell you this when you're awake. I'm a coward, Nik. I'm scared of what you'll say. I don't deserve you, but I'll die if you say it."

He paused to appreciate the feel of her in his arms, the smell of her hair, her hands resting on his shoulders. Her light breath whispered across his skin.

"You have every right to tell me to go to hell, that you never want to see me again, but I hope one day you can forgive me for not being what you need, what you want. And maybe one day you can see through what I'm not, to what I am. I'm a man who loves you, Nikki. I'll love you for the rest of my life. I'm sorry."

Dane eased out from under her and pulled the blankets over her shoulders.

"You'll be okay now, baby. Margie told me about your notice. I'm not taking it. I told her to rip it up and throw it in the garbage. You know I won't be at the store much after the holidays, anyway." He bent onto his haunches and smoothed her cheek. "You won't have to worry about seeing me. Call Margie when you feel well enough to go to work."

Dane pressed a kiss to her temple.

"I'm sorry about Christmas. I love you."

He touched her hair one last time before he let himself out of her apartment and out of her life.

CHAPTER NINE

"THANK YOU FOR letting me stay here while you're in Florida," Nikki said as Alyssa opened the door to Princess Snowflake's carrier.

It took a moment for the cat to venture into the new territory of Alyssa's loft, and Nikki blew out a sigh of relief when the white cat tentatively stepped out of the pink crate.

Alyssa ran her fingers over the kitten's fur. "Are you going to be okay?"

"I need some time to get my head on straight. I'll have to talk to him eventually, but the distance will help me figure out what I want to do."

"You don't work with him at the store anymore?"

Alyssa had heard the whole story, from the hallway fiasco with Eric to Dane's parting kiss goodbye when she'd been sick.

Nikki shook her head. "He comes in on my days off to do paperwork or to see how things are going. Margie always tells me he'd been in and how he looked. I never ask, but she wants me to know how heartbroken he is."

"I think you should put him out of his misery. Tell him you heard him and you accept his apology. I don't understand what staying here is going to do for you, Nik."

"I need to get through the holidays. I need to think about what I want from him. An apology isn't enough. I need to know he trusts me not to screw around behind his back, and right now, he doesn't. You didn't see his face when he was yelling at me. He attacked me when he should have been standing up for me. No, this has a lot more to do than just with me and I *will* talk to him, but I think space will benefit us both. If he truly loves me, he'll wait."

Alyssa gave her a hug, and she leaned into her friend's embrace. "Call me if you need anything. You know I'll be around to talk."

"Thanks, but don't worry about me. Have a fun time and soak up some sun."

She gave her a small smile, and they rode to the airport in silence.

Sipping a beer, Dane sat on his couch, mindlessly watching TV when his phone buzzed.

He felt as if he'd been pushed back into the lonely days and nights before Nikki, when nothing but frozen pizza and ESPN loomed on his horizon, broken up with nights with Holly when he felt like company.

Even though Christmas Eve was the next day, Dane lost the joy he shared with Nikki over the impending holiday.

He hadn't bought her anything, and it was just as well now, since he wouldn't have the chance to give her a gift, anyway. He'd be surprised as fuck if she ever wanted anything from him again.

With disinterest, he picked up his phone and scowled when his father's name flashed at the top of the screen.

Dane couldn't remember the last time his parents had voluntarily talked with him, and for a moment he thought about ignoring the call.

Whatever his dad wanted to tell him was probably the same bullshit he'd heard for the past three years, and he could leave it on voicemail. Then he could delete it without having to hear it. With Nikki gone, he wasn't in the right headspace to deal with his parents' bullshit now, but against his better judgment he pressed the green Accept button.

"Hello?" he asked, unease prickling his skin.

"Dane?" His father's voice floated through the phone and held a touch of uncertainty.

This was new.

Dane muted the TV.

"Yeah. What do you want?"

He wasn't going to make this easy.

"Your mother and I were wondering if you would come for Christmas. We, ah, want to talk to you."

His father's words hit him like a sucker punch to the stomach. If he hadn't already been sitting down, he would have fallen onto the first available surface.

"Why?"

He was wary, no doubt about it.

His Christmas was going to be shitty enough without being lured to his parents' house by the thought of a truce and then be bombarded with more of the same crap.

Silence and the cold shoulder were a lot better than their high and mighty "sleep in the bed you made" bullshit.

His father cleared his throat, and Dane smirked.

Ah-huh. Nailed it.

Dane's second shock came when his father said, "It's

been brought to our attention we were wrong. Your mother and I would like a chance to set things right."

He took a long drink of his beer to wet his parched mouth.

It couldn't be that easy.

"I can stop by tomorrow, but I"m busy Christmas Day," Dane said. He wasn't going to leave Brett hanging—not the way his parents had done to him for the past few years.

"I'll tell your mother, and she can have dinner ready. We appreciate it, and it's more than we deserve."

Can't argue there, Dane thought, throwing his phone onto his couch.

But he wasn't doing anything for Christmas Eve.

Nikki was working the short four-hour shift at the store insisting the other employees have the day off to spend with their families.

If he hadn't hired her, he would have been manning the twelve to four shift himself because Nikki was right. The store shouldn't even be open, but sometimes a few stragglers came in and spent a ton of money at the last minute. Those stragglers made it worth opening, and it was nothing to him since he never had plans.

After a sleepless night, Dane arrived at his childhood home the next day carrying a bottle of his mother's favorite wine. He didn't know why he bothered with any of it, and he mentally prepared for the conversation from hell.

He couldn't help but feel this was like before when he was going through his divorce. He braced himself for censure, disappointment, and anger, for recriminations and blame. Nothing he'd done had been right. Liz's unhappiness had been his fault; the reasons for the divorce falling on his shoulders.

It had been impossible to defend himself when he'd already been accused, tried, and sentenced by the jury.

Shifting his weight from foot to foot while he waited for someone to answer the door, he wished he would have turned down his dad's offer.

He wasn't in the mood for this.

If things hadn't been shot to shit with Nikki, he would have been with her now, having Christmas Eve dinner and exchanging gifts at her apartment. Cuddling and watching a stupid Christmas movie on Netflix. That's what he wanted to be doing.

He missed her so goddamned much.

Her car was never in the lot anymore, he never heard her come and go.

There was a small possibility they were missing each other.

She was still going to work and doing a fantastic job. A completed employee handbook had landed on his desk a couple of days ago waiting for his approval.

With flying colors, she'd come through with her promise.

Professionally written and formatted, the handbook outlined every policy they followed, and even a few he wouldn't have thought to include without her human resources insight.

He couldn't have found another person who would have done it better, and he admired her dedication to his store even though their relationship was over.

His attention jerked to the door when his dad answered.

"Merry Christmas, Dane," his father said, opening the screen door.

"Dad," Dane muttered. "Here's wine for Mom. I'm assuming she still likes it."

Darren took the bottle, glanced at the label, and smiled. "She sure does," he said and patted Dane on the back. "Let's go into the living room. I'll pour you a scotch. Your mom put a roast in the slow cooker this morning. We can eat anytime, but she's set out a tray of cheese and crackers to start."

After hanging his jacket in the foyer, Dane followed his father through the house he hadn't stepped into for years.

It smelled the same, looked the same, and his mom looked the same too, as she came into the living room, her hands held out in front of her in welcome.

He tensed and stood near the couch, feeling like an unwelcome stranger in the familiar room.

"Dane," his mother said, taking him into her arms. "I'm glad you were able to make it."

It would have been rude not to return her embrace, and he did so half-heartedly with a hand to her back.

His father poured him a drink and motioned for him to take a seat.

Reluctantly, Dane sat on the couch, perched on the edge of the cushion, prepared to bolt any moment. He didn't trust what his parents were doing, why they'd invited him for a visit.

"You probably want to know what this is about," Darren said, then took a sip of his drink.

"It would be nice. I want to know if I wasted my time."

"We were wrong," his mother said, taking a seat next to him on the leather couch and placing a small hand on his knee. She held a wine glass filled with a deep red in her other hand, and the liquid rippled in her trembling hand.

He searched for the lie on her face, but his mother gazed back intently, sincerity shining in her bright blue eyes.

"I'm going to need more than that."

"About Liz, about your divorce. Someone said she's the horrible, selfish person you told us she was all along. We didn't believe it then, but we can't argue with you now. We agree it would have been impossible for you to stay married to her."

Dane set his jaw. "Who made you see that, when I couldn't? I tried, God, how long did I try before I finally gave up?" He laughed bitterly and took a swallow of his drink.

"Nikki stopped by here a couple weeks ago," his mother said and brushed the hair from his forehead.

"Nikki?" Dane asked. "I haven't talked to her in—"

"She came by all dressed up, crying her eyes out. We thought she was at the wrong house looking for a Christmas party. I would have sent her off," Peg admitted, "but she was adamant she speak with us."

"We let her in, and she explained about your marriage, how greedy Liz was, and still is, how you tried to make your marriage work." Darren sighed.

Dane stared at the cream carpet, his eyes burning.

Clutching her wine glass, Peg stood and started to pace. "We didn't believe her, not at first. We need to be honest and tell you we thought she was defending you because she was in love with you. Then she told us you two had run into Liz and her husband downtown?"

Dane nodded.

"Nikki told us the things Liz said, how angry and cruel she was toward the both of you. We shouldn't have punished you for looking out for yourself, saving yourself. It takes two to make a marriage. What was going on between you and Liz wasn't our business, and we should have stayed out of it. We were wrong, and we're sorry." Peg wiped her eyes.

Darren looked at his hands, his fingers twisted in his lap. "We're asking you to forgive us. And let us try to mend what we've foolishly destroyed."

"What was she wearing?" Dane whispered.

"Nikki? A pink lace dress and a blue coat," Peg said, taking her place on the sofa. "She told us you two had a falling out and weren't together anymore. Can we ask what happened? You can tell us to mind our own business, and this time we'll listen."

She tried to laugh, but it came out as a watery hiccup.

"You can ask, but I don't want to tell you. It's all my fault. We . . . had a fight. I don't know why she drove here after."

"All she said was you wouldn't be together for Christmas, but she wanted to do this for you."

Darren slid the glasses from his face and wiped his eyes.

"I have to say, she is one brave little girl, and we appreciate what she did. We were stubborn, and stupid. We never liked Liz, and I guess it was our way of telling you we told you so."

"I remember."

Nikki came here after he accused her of vile things. What did that mean? Had she done it as a final way to say goodbye? They weren't together anymore, but she didn't want him to be alone anymore and tried to fix his relationship with his parents as one last token of goodwill.

He hoped it was to show him she still loved him, that after things had settled, that she would give him another chance. That this truly wasn't her way of telling hims he never wanted to see him again.

"Do you think you can forgive us?" Peg asked anxiously.

"Mom, I need to be honest. It's going to take a while," Dane said, taking her hand. "I was alone when I could have used some support. I went through my divorce without you, I opened the store without your help or congratulations. I'm going to need time. *We're* going to need time. I can't go back to the way things were before and pretend the last couple of years didn't happen."

"When you told me you were busy tomorrow, we were hoping you made plans with Nikki." Darren bit into a cracker.

"We're not together." Dane knocked back the rest of his scotch.

"I asked her for a number, a way to reach her, but she declined. She did say she manages your store," Darren said.

"Yeah. She wanted to quit after our fight, but I wouldn't let her. I have plans with Brett tomorrow, and I don't want to stand him up. We've spent the holidays together for the past few years."

"I see." Darren cleared his throat, and his eyes sparkled with humor. "Well, the invitation for dinner is still open, and we'd like it if you stayed. Plus I don't think your mother is done speaking with you yet."

He and his parents ate dinner without speaking much, but the tension had eased. By the time his mother served the pumpkin pie, Dane knew things would be all right. It would take time, as he warned his mother, but it was more than what he'd had three hours ago, and he owed it to Nikki.

His father found him standing in front of the tree, the glowing green, blue, and red bulbs wavering in his teary vision.

It'd been years since he'd been home for the holidays. A smile quirked his mouth. He was positive this was the same tree they put up every year.

"Your mother chased me in here while she cleans the kitchen. Here," Darren said, handing Dane a cup of steaming coffee.

"Thanks." Dane poked at a glittering angel he made in fourth grade.

Darren perched on the arm of a chair near the tree. "You know, Nikki also mentioned Liz accused you of being poor, and ah, I mean, is your store . . ." he trailed off, red staining his neck.

"In the black? Yeah. It has been for a long time, and I budgeted to hire Nikki. I've been pumping a lot of cash into the loan because I don't want to owe the bank longer than I need to."

"So, you don't need an investor or silent partner? Your mother was badgering me about it while we cleared the table. If you need some fast cash—"

Dane chuckled. "No, Dad, I'm fine. I'm not in the hole, not going bankrupt. I've thought a lot about my marriage to Liz, and it wasn't only money that caused our problems. She's unhappy for other reasons, and she thinks money will fill the void. She hasn't realized yet it won't. Maybe she never will."

He took a sip of coffee.

"She messed me up. She made me believe I'm not enough for anybody. After the holidays, I'm going to start seeing a therapist. I need to talk about some things, get them out of my system. I kept thinking if I found a woman who would put up with me, maybe love me a little, those feelings would go away. But what I had with Nikki was the best I'll ever find, and my insecurities were still there. I'm not going to be of any use in a relationship with anybody if I'm always going to feel like this."

Dane glanced at his father and was shocked to find respect in his father's eyes.

"It doesn't help we weren't around," Darren said.

"Yeah."

"When you reach that point, Dane, if it helps, we'll go with you."

Dane turned to his mother's voice.

"I think your father and I need to figure out why we felt the need to punish you for something that wasn't your fault. Perhaps some family counseling would do us all a little bit of good."

"Thanks, Mom. I'll let you know."

The evening nearing its end, he set his coffee mug on the fireplace mantle.

"Dane, wait."

"Mom, it's getting late, I think I should go." He didn't mean to sound so sharp, but he wanted to go home, look for Nikki's car. If she came home, he didn't want to miss her.

Peg pushed a burgundy velvet box into his hand.

Dane opened the lid. "What's this?" He studied the platinum ring, the pink stone glittering in the lights of the Christmas tree.

"My mother's engagement ring. I'm giving it to you, for Nikki, when you ask her to marry you. I never wanted Liz to wear it, but Nikki, she's exceptional. I would be proud if she accepted it. It makes her wedding band choices some-what limited, but I don't think she'll mind."

Dane closed the lid with a snap. "Mom, we're so far from that. We're not even speaking right now. I can't take this."

Peg pushed the little box back at him. "I don't know what you two fought about, or why she was crying, but she said she loves you. A fight won't change her heart. You haven't spoken with her since then?"

"She had the flu a little while ago. I took care of her." He laughed. "You probably don't know she lives next door to me."

"Dane," his mother sighed, happiness lighting her face, "you glow when you talk about her. Your eyes are brighter than the Christmas tree. You can fix this," Peg said, wrapping her small hands around his and the ring box.

"She said that? She said she loves me?"

Peg nodded. "She said it was love for you that brought her here."

"I pushed her into a relationship because I couldn't think about anything but being with her, and when I got my way, all I did was accuse her of being like Liz. I know it isn't true, but I couldn't stop it. I need to apologize for the way I acted, give her space, and let her decide what she wants. I hope after all I've put her through, it's still me. I need to go, but this was nice."

Dane said goodbye to his parents and stepped out on the porch. The stars twinkled in the sky, his breath white puffs in the air. It was a decent first step, and he needed to thank Nikki for what she did.

When he pulled into his parking space his palms were sweating and perspiration gathered under his arms. He hadn't seen Nikki since he left her bedroom the night he poured out his feelings to her in the dark.

Tonight he would tell her what he said while she was sleeping, and he'd accept what she told him, even if it broke his heart. It would be fair play, after all.

He'd broken hers.

Dane knocked on Nikki's door and waited. Her car wasn't in the parking lot, as it hadn't been since she recovered from the flu. Still, he knocked again and waited. He frowned when he didn't hear Princess Snowflake mewling on the other side of the door; usually, the cat was there to welcome him.

He pulled his keys from his jacket pocket. For the first time since she'd given it to him, he used the small silver key to open her door.

The moment he stepped into her apartment, Dane knew she wasn't there and hadn't been for a long time.

Princess Snowflake's water and food dish weren't on the linoleum floor, and her coffee pot and microwave were unplugged. The refridgerator was empty but for a half bottle of wine and a couple bottles of his beer.

Panic gripped him. She couldn't have broken her lease and moved out. He strode down the carpeted hallway. The cat's litter box was gone. After flipping on the light in her bedroom, he opened her closet doors and discovered half her clothes were missing.

All her toiletries were gone from her bathroom.

The lights on the Christmas tree they'd decorated together were unplugged, and it stood in the dark living room like a tall, black blob.

One lone gift lay under the tree, and reading his name on the card she'd pushed under the curling blue ribbon, Dane picked it up.

He sat on the coffee table and pulled the card from the envelope.

A cartoon decorated the front of the card. On a bed, two pairs of feet wearing running shoes poked out of the bottom of a comforter. Under the photo, the caption read, "You burn as many calories having sex as you do running five miles."

Inside the card, in her pretty script, Nikki had written,

"Dane, I'm looking forward to doing both with you—all year. Never forget I love you. Merry Christmas and Happy New Year. Always yours, Nikki." Under that, in smaller script, she added, "Remember, ten bucks!" and a smiley face.

Dane slit the tape holding together the shiny blue and silver gift wrap. He flipped on the end table lamp and stared at the picture. Ten bucks. For ten bucks she'd put his entire world into his hands.

Tears dripped onto the glass, and his sobs echoed in the empty apartment.

There was no one to hear.

Nikki was gone.

Nikki admired her sister's strength. Stacy and her husband were no closer to conceiving than they had been last year and were discussing giving up.

Holding a cup of hot cocoa, Nikki ventured onto her parents' back porch. She missed Dane and tried not to let her melancholy ruin Christmas with her family. Trying to find a little sliver of holiday spirit, she took in a shuddery breath of crisp air.

"Tired of me already?" Stacy said, stepping outside with a blanket wrapped around her shoulders in lieu of a jacket.

"No. Stace, I have to apologize. I never understood what you were going through until now."

Stacy blinked eyes that were exact replicates of Nikki's. "You've met someone."

Nikki nodded, staring into the yard covered in snow. "Yeah."

"Where is he? I would've liked to have met him."

"We had a fight and didn't fix things before the holidays. We're not on talking terms right now."

Stacy pulled her onto a whitewashed wooden swing, almost tipping her hot cocoa down the front of her jacket.

"If I know anything, it's that time is short. If he's the one, fix it. You're wasting time, and it's so valuable. Every day you let go by is one day less you can be with him. Don't take that lightly."

She leaned into her sister's side. "I know. I think about us getting married, starting a family. But he's got some problems, and I don't know if we can get past them."

"Hey," Stacy murmured, nudging her shoulder.

She met her sister's glittering eyes. Their parents hadn't spared the Christmas decorations, and white twinkle lights sparkled under the snow covering the rails of the porch.

"What?"

"So what if he has issues? We all do. What if Jack divorced me because I'm having problems getting pregnant? Would you blame him? Would you say, 'Oh, Stacy has *problems*. Why should he put up with her? He should find someone else.'"

"Of course not," Nikki said.

"Then fuck this guy's problems. If you love him, stand by him and work it out. If I've learned anything through this whole thing, it's that I know Jack loves me. My pain breaks his heart. Your guy, the guy you say you love, his *problems* should be breaking yours."

That was too close to the truth, and Nikki pursed her lips against the deluge of emotion that wanted to break free.

His problems *had* broken her heart, just not in the way her sister meant.

She wiped a tear from her cheek. "I've tried to help him. But he needs more than me."

Taken in by her sister's sympathetic look, Nikki let the words pour out: Liz's and Dane's marriage, the hallway scene with Eric and all Dane's accusations, visiting Dane's parents, Dane taking care of her while she was sick.

Stacy's lips parted wider with every story, but when Nikki finished, she snapped her mouth closed. "If Dane knows that Eric set you up, why don't you talk to him and end this mess? Why are you dragging this out and making him even more miserable?"

"Dane didn't trust me, and that's the bottom line. He told me he was sorry, but how he reacted still hurt. The look in his eyes, the hate. He hated me in that hallway, even if it was just for a second."

Nikki gave her mug to Stacy and stood. She leaned against the patio railing, tugging the ends of her scarf.

"I understand it, now, after thinking things over. All I did when I first started working at the store was talk about the rich guys I dated. It was my way of telling him I wasn't available because he was my boss, and I didn't want to get involved with him. So maybe it *did* seem like I was bragging about how wealthy Eric is."

"And since his ex-wife is like that, he assumed you were, too," Stacy said and took a sip of the hot chocolate.

"That's what bothers me the most. When we were together, he couldn't see I wasn't like Liz, despite the men I dated. He didn't see *me*."

"You're not the first person he's dated since his divorce, are you?" Stacy asked, dismayed. "You don't want to be his rebound girl."

"No, but that was another thing that didn't help us. He dated someone for a while. She was waiting for him to ask her to marry him, but when he met me, he dumped her. I didn't know how to feel about that. Still don't, to be honest."

"I think it's a good thing," Stacy said.

Nikki brushed some snow off a strand of lights. "Why would you say that?"

"Because it proves he loves you. He didn't commit to her, and he dumped her the second he set eyes on you. If he had any other intentions, he would've strung both of you along. Seriously, I think it's a good sign. I mean, he wasn't going around accusing this woman of cheating on him the way he did to you, right? He didn't care what she did. But he cared about what *you* did. Or what he thought you were doing. What are you going to do now?"

"We need to talk, obviously. We need to work through his relationship with Liz, and Holly, too, I guess, or we'll never have a relationship of our own. I don't know if his parents contacted him, but I hope so. He needs them to get over what Liz did to their marriage."

"That was brave of you to go talk to them. You have balls, that's for sure."

"They're nice people. A little misguided, like me, if I can believe my crazy sister." Nikki huffed a laugh. "But I wasn't thinking about what they could have said, or if I was scared to meet them. I wanted to help him because I love him. Despite everything, I love him."

"Then you'll work it out. But it sounds like it's going to take a lot of work."

"I'll do whatever it takes. I just hope it will be enough."

"You still not talking to her?" Brett puffed at Dane's side.

The trails had been cleared for the skiers, but the paths at Eagle Pass State Park were still crusted with snow.

Dane smirked. Brett's voice strained as he tried to keep up, always a step behind his steady pace. "You need to run more."

"You try finding the time," Brett said, panting. "All I do is coordinate that fucking marathon, I forget I run them, too."

"I've been helping more since I stopped seeing Nikki."

"I can't believe you're still not talking to her. What the fuck?"

"I'm a coward," Dane said. "I haven't apologized for what happened in the hallway. Fucking Eric. He played me like a game of baseball, and I let him. It's too late now anyway, she moved out of her apartment—"

"Totally moved out? She broke her lease?"

"No. She hasn't moved anything out, but I used the key she gave me to look around and she's not sleeping there. She works her shifts at the store, but that's not where I want to confront her. The last thing I need is for her to quit. She already tried to put in her notice, but I didn't accept it and she dropped it, thank God."

Except for Brett's wheezing, they ran a half mile in silence. "I saw my parents for dinner last night."

"Holy shit." Brett gasped, and Dane didn't know if it was from his news or if the last couple miles were going to finally do him in.

"Yeah. Ah, after I yelled at her, Nikki went to my parents' house, and she told them about our scene with Liz downtown. They finally believed all the things I've been trying to tell them, and they fucking apologized. I almost had a heart attack."

"The way I'm going to if we don't slow down. Nikki did

good then."

"Yeah," Dane said, slowing his pace, giving Brett a break. "It's Christmas, and I haven't tried to call her to thank her, but my parents were really" —Dane sucked in a breath— "impressed with her. They liked her a lot, if that means anything."

"Huh."

"That's what I said. It shouldn't mean that much to me, but I guess it does. We all want our parents' approval."

He fell silent in embarrassment.

Brett didn't have his parents' approval and never would.

To fill the awkwardness, Dane said, "My mom gave me my grandma's engagement ring to give to Nikki when I ask her to marry me."

Brett looked at Dane out of the corner of his eye. "Are you going to?"

"I have to apologize first. I was a dick. I didn't trust her, and I bailed at the first sign of trouble. That's not the kind of man she needs in her life. Eric was right about one thing. I don't deserve her. And he might be right about something else—I might never get her back if she can't forgive me. It's like she talked to my parents and then fell off the face of the earth."

Dane slowed to a trot then stopped, wiping sweat from his forehead with his glove.

"You don't have a game plan?" Brett asked.

"I've decided to get counseling. My truce with my mom and dad will help, but like I said, I turned on Nikki instead of listening to her. It's on me to fix that part of myself. Maybe we can turn this around if I can prove I'm working on it."

They ran another mile over the crusty snow in silence, the bare tree limbs rattling in the wintery air.

When they neared the end of the trail, they slowed.

Brett should have told him he couldn't go thirteen miles. Dane chuckled.

He'd be a shitty marathon director if he couldn't run a half marathon.

Doubled over, Brett glared, and it made Dane laugh harder.

"Shut up, dumbass." Shaking out his legs, Brett said, "I've decided to write a book. What do you think?"

Dane's laughter died. "I think that's great. What about?"

"Running, I guess. I haven't decided if I want to write, like, a beginner's manual, or how I got the Tower City Marathon together, or both."

"Sounds like you have some interesting topics."

"The problem is, I can't write. I would need help."

"Nikki wrote a damn fine handbook for the store. You should ask her to help you. She's really getting into the women's run. If you go into the history of the marathon, you could work on it together."

"That's an idea." Brett paused. "Alyssa writes."

"Alyssa? Nikki's friend, Alyssa? She writes romances. Are you going to write a running romance?"

Brett snickered. "Fuck, no. That sounds painful. Who would read that?"

"Nobody. Alyssa doesn't run anyway. She wouldn't give a shit about your manual. Nikki's your better bet. Come to the store and take a look at the handbook."

"Yeah, I will. What are you doing for New Year's Eve?"

"Going to bed early and worrying about Nikki. I don't know where she's been staying, and it's driving me crazy."

Dane's truck came into view, and he rolled his eyes when Brett blew out a, "Thank you sweet baby Jesus."

"I'll bring you home, you pansy. Are we still doing pizza?"

"Yeah. I wouldn't miss our yearly tradition. How come you're not spending Christmas with your parents since you kissed ass and made up?"

Dane slapped Brett on the back. "Because I wouldn't miss our yearly tradition."

NIKKI ATTENDED KAYLA's wedding with Alyssa who had flown back from Florida in time for the ceremony.

During the bleak winter days, all Nikki did was work at the store, take classes at the gym, and spend time alone.

On New Year's Eve, she watched a movie with Princess Snowflake and resisted calling Dane to wish him a Happy New Year. She could have spent the holiday with him, but she needed this time to herself.

Her sister frequently called, trying her best to pry information out of her, but she avoided conversations about Dane. She hid in Alyssa's apartment, and when the temperatures cooperated, ran the cement sidewalks in the park behind Alyssa's loft. S

he thought a lot about what she would tell Dane when she decided to see him. It was difficult to be away from him, and she would move home soon.

A couple more days. A couple more days and she would call him.

They needed to talk.

DANE AVOIDED THE store. He didn't want to be tempted to

talk to Nikki and make things worse. Instead, he spent time with his parents and went to counseling. He cut back on his drinking, and he felt good, his head clear.

His mother was concerned he and Nikki were still not speaking.

Despite Dane's objections, his father gave him a wooden rocking chair he'd made as part of a hobby he'd picked up now that he was close to retirement.

He could picture Nikki sitting there, holding their baby, and choked up, he could barely tell his father thank you.

He spent hours in counseling, talking about Liz, what she had done to ruin his self-worth. He spoke about Holly, how he'd used her for comfort. He explored his feelings for Nikki.

Through his sessions, he realized he loved her more than ever, and if she didn't contact him soon, he would. He didn't want to let any more time go by, and, as his therapist pointed out, she deserved an apology whether or not she wanted to take him back.

They spoke about his parents, about the role Nikki played in helping them be on speaking terms again. He told his therapist how grateful he was to Nikki, but his therapist cautioned him not to get caught in a trap thinking he needed to repay her somehow. She'd spoken with his parents voluntarily, and Dane owed her no more than a thank you.

He was through carrying a relationship on his own.

Dane spoke to his therapist for hours, and he felt purged, light, free. Feelings and emotions that had weighed him down since his divorce were gone, and he could ask Nikki to marry him without all the extra baggage she'd tolerated while they'd been together.

After a particularly heavy session, he drove back to his

apartment complex, drained. He was tired and his head throbbed, and all he could think about was a hot shower and a meal.

Pulling into the parking lot, he slammed on the breaks, and almost clipped Nikki's car.

She was home.

He wanted to run into the building, pound on her door, demand she speak with him. Instead he paused, took a deep breath, and went through some of the relaxation exercises his therapist had taught him to curb his temper.

That was something he was working on. Learning to think before jumping straight to pissed.

Dane wrapped his hand around the worn velvet ring box he carried since his mother had given it to him.

Nervous about seeing Nikki after such a long separation, he swallowed past the lump in his throat. As he shoved his key into the lock of his apartment door, he heard Princess Snowflake mewing. The little cat knew he was home.

He showered, going through the motions, and dressed in jeans and a blue cotton button-down dress shirt. He was debating on trying to eat something when his phone chimed with a text.

Dane blew out a breath when he saw Nikki's name at the top of the screen. His fingers shook as he opened the message.

Can you come over for a few minutes? We need to talk.

Breathe, he reminded himself. She wanted to talk to him. She wanted to tell him she didn't want to see him ever again.

No, that wasn't it. She told his mom and dad she loved him, and she wouldn't have lied. If she didn't love him, she wouldn't have defended him.

Breathe. You can work this out.

Sure, now? he typed.

Yes.

Gently, as the ring represented everything he wanted, he pulled it from the velvet slot and slipped it into the front pocket of his pants. He prayed he would have the chance to give it to her.

He knocked on her door, and when she opened it, the scent of lasagna met his nose. Princess Snowflake wound figure eights around his ankles, butting her head against his legs.

He met Nikki's eyes, and he lifted a hand to her face and brushed the pad of his thumb along her cheekbone. "I've been worried about you. I didn't know where you were."

Nikki pulled the door open wider, and Dane stepped inside her apartment. "I've been staying at Alyssa's. You know, to take some time. I made dinner if you would like to stay."

"I'd like that," Dane said, following her into the kitchen.

"We can sit in the living room," Nikki said, gesturing to the couch. "Would you like a beer? I have some wine or coffee?"

"Coffee would be okay. I'm trying not to drink as much as I used to," he said and smiled, running his fingers through his hair, self-conscious, both anticipating and dreading her reaction to the changes he'd made in his life to be a better man for her. For them.

She raised her eyebrows, but then returned his smile. "Okay . . . I'll make coffee then."

Dane watched her move about her kitchen and realized she was nervous, too. Her hand shook as she measured grounds for the filter, and she nearly toppled the can when she pushed the lid back onto the red plastic container.

He blew out a breath when she joined him on the couch, and he couldn't get enough of her. She wore black yoga pants with a mint green sweatshirt. The neckline was stretched out, and his eyes traveled along the curve of her exposed shoulder. Her hair was a tangle of curls, and her feet were bare. She looked lovely.

"Nikki—"

"Dane—"

They broke off at the same time, and she laughed. "You go first."

Dane cleared his throat. This was the moment he'd wished for; the moment he'd been afraid of.

His heart pounded, and he shifted uncomfortably on the couch, his skin prickling under her gaze. "I have a lot to apologize for, but first I want to thank you for going to see my parents. We've been speaking quite a bit since Christmas Eve, and I don't think we would've ever talked again if you hadn't told them about Liz. They believed you."

He reached out to trail his fingers down her curls, wanting to pull her into his arms.

Slowly, he reminded himself.

Nikki took his hand. "I'm glad."

When she didn't say anything else, he continued. "I've, ah, been seeing a therapist, Nik. I should have a long time ago. I've been working through what Liz did to me, how I treated Holly. I've been talking with him about my parents."

He closed his eyes for a moment and took a deep breath.

"And how I treated you. I owe you an apology. Please believe me when I tell you what I put us through, what I was going through when we were together, wasn't your fault. You didn't do anything wrong. When I saw Eric's arms around you, kissing you, all my darkest nightmares came true. In my mind, I was losing you to someone better than me, who deserved you, who could give you all the things I couldn't."

To avoid her gaze, he watched the coffee drip into the carafe. "He told me a few things after you ran away . . . they were all true. I didn't fight for you, when that should have been my first instinct. I let you go, and that will always be my biggest regret. I should have told you this a long time ago."

Nikki leaned into him. "You did. The last night you took care of me. I heard you. I wasn't sleeping."

Nikki fidgeted near the Christmas tree she hadn't taken down yet.

He looked wonderful. It'd been weeks since she'd seen him last, and looking at him now in his jeans and dress shirt made her want to crawl into his lap and let him wrap her in his arms.

"I understand how you felt; I do. I know when we met I was dating a lot, and please believe me it was coincidence those guys were always well off. I wasn't looking for a rich man. I never was, and I tried to make you understand that when we were together. That's not me."

His elbows digging into his knees, Dane leaned forward to interrupt her.

She shook her head to stop him. "No. I'm not going to take the blame, not even part of it. That's all yours. But I'm trying to explain I see the reasons behind your outburst. I was dating, and I was dating wealthy men. Mixing that with all the years you'd been living with Liz's accusations, well, it was bound to happen. And maybe it was better to get this all out of the way, out into the open now, before it could really hurt us."

She twisted her fingers in front of her.

"I'm glad you're seeing someone to work out your feelings. If you need me to go with you, I will."

"Nikki."

She heard the love in his voice, and she knew he wanted to hold her, but she wasn't done.

"I was dating," she said, determined that they put all their feelings into the open.

She wanted them to be able to start their new year, their new life, with a clean slate.

"I wanted to fall in love, find a man who wanted me, who wanted a future. I took time at Alyssa's to make sure it was *you* I was missing, Dane, and not just anybody. The longer I was away from you, the more I realized it *was* you. I missed the way you would nuzzle my shoulder to wake me up for group runs at the store. I missed the way we would make love when I could convince you to stay in bed."

She smiled, her eyes filling with tears.

"I missed watching TV with you, cooking dinner together. I missed coming home from working at the store knowing you would be here waiting for me. I missed hanging out with you at marathon headquarters goofing off with the volunteers. The night I was sick, you said we fit like we've always been together, and I wanted to make sure it was like that for me, too. With you."

She started crying then, and Dane held out his arms.

Nikki curled into his lap, reveling in the warmth of his embrace. She'd missed this man so much. "You know the worst part?"

"There were lots of worst parts, baby," he murmured

into her hair.

She sniffed. "The worst part was when I came back from Alyssa's, I opened the door to the apartment, and it didn't smell like you anymore. You were gone, like you were never here."

"I was here. I looked for you and found the Christmas gift you made for me."

Nikki pulled back and wiped her cheeks. "Ten bucks."

Dane reached for his pocket and pulled out the ring. "It's worth a little more than ten bucks, but, marry me, Nikki. I love you. Share my life with me. Share the store. Let me give you children. I want it all, and I want it with you. Please."

Nikki's eyes widened. The diamond was huge and set in a sparkling platinum band. "Oh, but you shouldn't have—"

Dane slipped the ring onto her finger. It was a perfect fit; that wasn't a coincidence. They were meant to be.

"I didn't. My mother gave it to me to give to you. It was my grandmother's engagement ring. She said she didn't want Liz to wear it, but when you went to see them, to explain, they fell in love with you the same way I did. She wanted you to have it. Say yes."

Nikki framed Dane's face with her hands and placed a gentle kiss to his lips. "Yes. Yes, I'll share your life, and the store, and everything else. We'll be happy. I love you so much."

Dane stood with her in his arms, and he carried her to her bedroom. "We will be happy, and I promise you one more thing."

With her heart full of his love, Nikki wrapped her arms around his neck. "What's that?"

"I will never, ever, make you run away from me again."

CHASING YOU

Chapter One

Don't allow anyone to make you do anything you don't want
to do—Alyssa

Sometimes someone other than yourself knows what's best
for you—Brett

WITH THE TOE of her black high-heeled boot, Alyssa
Barnes kicked her black suitcase across the hardwood floor
of her loft apartment.

The plastic case skidded across the shiny wood and
stopped only when it crashed into the wall painted a delicate eggshell white.

The impact rattled the pictures hanging in the hallway,
and one gold frame gave way, falling from its nail to land on
the floor, the glass shattering.

Perfect.

She finished the job, slamming her apartment door. She dropped her purse, pulled off her boots, and was about to fling her jacket when a knock on her door interrupted her tantrum.

Not now.

After such a disastrous trip home to Tower City, she needed time and space. What she desperately wanted was a glass of wine, her emergency stash of chocolate, and a hot bath.

She ignored it. No one knew she was home. Well, no one but Nikki, and she was the one who'd picked up Alyssa from the airport.

Brushing away slivers of glass, careful not to cut her fingertips with the shards. she studied the picture. In the photo, she was standing with Nikki in the corridor of the hotel where their friend Kayla had held her wedding reception. Nikki looked strained and sad, and Alyssa, well, she looked tired and . . . fat.

Alyssa was happy Nikki had gotten her own problems straightened out and was on her way to her own happily ever after.

She wasn't so lucky.

Grimacing, she pulled at the waist of her jeans, hating the feel of them cutting into her skin.

So maybe she gained a little weight on her trip. Book tours, seminars, and book signings were stressful, and the food was never in short supply. What was she going to do, turn down chocolate cake?

Yeah, right.

As she hung the picture back on the naked nail, she noted to herself to buy a new frame. She let the suitcase remain where it lay and shuffled into the kitchen to begin phase one and two of her recovery.

The knocking came back.

Whoever was at the door was *not* going to give up.

Alyssa sighed. She wasn't going to get any peace until she sent whoever it was on their way.

Just as she was about to open the door, someone pushed it open, striking her on the forehead.

"Holy shit." She slapped her hand to her temple and doubling over in pain.

"Fuck. I am so sorry."

Alyssa's gaze jerked up at the sound of his voice, and the rage mixed with disbelief made her forget the sharp throb racing through her skull. "Get the hell out of here," she said, narrowing her eyes at her visitor.

"Aw, don't be like that." He stepped into the hallway of the loft, his eyes already looking around her living space.

Her living space. The space she had not permitted a man to enter.

Ever.

"Get the hell out of here," she repeated, stepping in front of him, forcing him to stop.

"Nice place you got here." He dodged around her and wandered into the living room, taking in the gleaming wood floor and the white vaulted ceiling. "What's up there?" he asked, his eyes traveling up a wooden staircase, a white handrail attached to the wall.

"My office." She followed him as he strolled, his hands shoved into the pockets of his jacket, keys jangling.

The man's size didn't intimidate her, and she glared at him when he turned his cool hazel eyes to her.

His blond hair shone in the light streaming through her balcony doors, the late afternoon sun creating a halo around his head. He was no angel, and she wished he would leave her alone and go back to hell where he came from.

She shook him off and headed to the kitchen to proceed with her plan. It didn't matter if he was the only male she'd ever let inside her apartment. She wasn't going to do anything with him.

There would be no intimate embraces, no soft kisses.

He wouldn't sleep in her bed, leaving his scent on her pillow.

She wouldn't be forced to remember him in her kitchen drinking morning-after coffee because there wouldn't be a night before.

She was done with men. Done being hurt, being humiliated. No one wanted her, and she was perfectly fine with that. Experience had taught her she would rather be alone than abandoned.

Turning her back on her unwanted and ill-timed guest, she started her search.

She didn't cook; she didn't count microwaving meals and making sandwiches.

Nikki cooked, and Alyssa always enjoyed eating with her, but those meals were fewer and more far between now that Nikki was engaged.

Her eyes slid to the man still milling about her living room fingering her knickknacks and book collection.

Alyssa shot down a twinge of empathy and sympathy. She remembered what he'd told her, remembered how she felt when the barb had dug underneath her skin. The thorny insult may very well still be there.

She pressed her fingers against her forehead where a lump was forming.

Great.

Groaning, she grabbed an unopened bottle of wine and a wine glass. She easily broke the seal of the cheap pink champagne she favored and twisted off the cap. After pouring and draining a glass, she dug into the cabinets for her stash of truffles and hummed in happiness when she found a full package.

The man in her living room turned from the partial view of the park through her balcony doors. "How's your head? I didn't mean . . ."

Alyssa chugged more of the champagne. "This will go a long way."

She took a swipe at her aching forehead before stuffing a melting truffle into her mouth.

"What the fuck are you doing here, anyway?"

She wanted to move on to phase three of her plan: a long hot bath. Flying made her feel filthy, and she needed to wash the travel smell out of her hair, the dirt from her skin.

When an answer wasn't forthcoming, Alyssa looked up from choosing another truffle from the box.

He shuffled his feet, his running shoes making the floorboards creak. His warmup pants matched his t-shirt which matched his warmup jacket. They all bore the logo of the Tower City Marathon.

Her gaze reached his face, and she pushed down the feeling of sadness for the man standing in her loft.

"I see you've gained a little more weight," he said instead of answering her question.

The words washed over her, freezing her to the bone.

She knew what she was, goddammit.

Alyssa's throat burned, and she swallowed the acrid taste the sweet champagne had turned on her tongue.

"Get out. Get out, right now."

Her chin trembled, and she clutched her wine glass.

He took a step forward. "I'm sorry. That's not how I meant it."

This was too much. "Just go. Go, and don't come back."

Alyssa pressed the back of her hand to her lips.

His shoulders sagged.

To make sure he left, she followed him to the door. She drained her glass as he looked back at her.

"I'm sorry."

The last swallow of champagne hit her head and loosened her tongue. "Fuck off."

He let himself into the hallway, closing the door with a soft click.

Alyssa paused for a moment.

She flung her goblet at the place he'd been just moments ago and smiled grimly as the delicate stemware broke into a million pieces.

Glass everywhere.

Shattered.

Like her heart.

***

Chasing You is available in paperback, Kindle, and Kindle Unlimited. You don't have to wait to read Brett and Alyssa's story.

Read it today!

ACKNOWLEDGMENTS

A heart-felt thank you to Pat and Joshua for giving *Don't Run Away* a chance.
I learned so much from your feedback.
I'm not sure where I would be without you!

Thanks to my family and friends who believe in me;
I couldn't do this crazy writing thing without you.

Vania Rheault has lived in Minnesota all her life. In 2003, she graduated with a BA in English with a concentration in creative writing. When she's not writing, she's reading, playing with her three cats, or going to movie night with her sister.

Find Vania at www.vaniamargene.com and these other social media platforms:

www.ingramcontent.com/pod-product-compliance
Lightning Source LLC
Chambersburg PA
CBHW021003120726
47905CB00009B/2830